THE
ANTARCTIC
DECEPTION

*A Sequel to The Kuiper Belt
Deception*

Donald F. Averill

The Antarctic Deception

The Antarctic Deception

A Sequel to The Kuiper Belt Deception

ISBN 978-0-9995915-4-3 (paperback)
ISBN 978-0-9995915-5-0 (digital)
Published by Book Agency Plus
www.bookagencyplus.com

Acknowledgements

I would like to thank Robert Griswold and Barbara Schroeder for reading the manuscript, making suggestions, and assisting with the editing.

CONTENTS

Chapter 1

"What made you decide to disappear from society for several years, Mr. and Mrs. Burke? Why did you want to hide?" The diminutive, balding man adjusted his belt and tried to straighten his clothes. His pink dress shirt seemed to be trying to escape from his belly bulge. Sitting across a metal table from the couple, the uncomfortable lawyer was recording every word of the interview. Hidden cameras were focused on former astronauts Gina and Sunul Burke. Psychologists would pore over the audio and video records to analyze the couple's expressions for possible lies.

Sunul and Gina both began to laugh. Sunul leaned forward, "You *know* the answers to those questions. If you expect us to sit here and listen to your asinine questions, forget it. We voluntarily came in. We don't have to give you any answers at all." Sunul looked the International Space Agency's rep in the eyes for several seconds. Neither man blinked.

The lawyer looked down at the screen on his digital notepad/recorder. "You people violated your contract with the Agency."

Gina had had enough, "You're a lawyer, correct? If we take you to court, we will prove the Agency lied about our mission and tried to maroon eight astronauts 4.5 billion miles from Earth, and planned for the pregnancies, even though your medical staff told us they had given us preventative medication."

"I grant that you had no idea you were not going halfway to Alpha Centauri and we had no idea you would be clever enough to come back before we sent a team to relieve you, but when you returned with aliens on board, we had to isolate them for the good of the planet. We want to know where they are. I mean Licon Mason and Miranda Patel, of course. Who is taking care of the children?"

Sunul and Gina stood up, pushing their chairs away from the table. Gina said, "How would we know where they are? *We have no idea! Have you asked their parents?*"

The lawyer slammed his palm on the table and yelled, "*Liars!*"

Sunul walked slowly around the table, grabbed the lawyer by the shirt collar with both hands and jerked him out of his chair. "*You little pip-squeak!* We don't know where they are. Call us liars again and I'll stuff those glasses down your slimy throat! Come on Gina, we're out of here." The Burkes, in their early thirties, physically fit, and from four- to six-inches taller than the lawyer, helped the automatic door close as they exited the interrogation room.

The Agency lawyer straightened his shirt and tie after watching the two former astronauts walk from the room. He knew they were correct; the Agency had no power to hold the Burkes. The older generation officials that had run the "Far Ice" program the alpha group had been sent on had been forced to retire three years earlier when their deceptive practices had been uncovered. At that time, the eight astronauts were still hiding in the Colorado wilderness with their offspring.

"Let's liberate the kids from Building 402. Miles and Libby will be waiting. You know, I don't trust that place after what they put Licon and Miranda through." Gina hoped the receptionist she had put to sleep years ago was still working there. She wanted to apologize for the rough but humane treatment. Before they met with the lawyer, they had left their kids with a security agent at the juvenile center because they were running late, so they hadn't met the receptionist at the inside desk. They had to get the appointment with the lawyer out of the way before they could interview for positions as trainers of future astronauts.

Sunul was going to apply as an astronaut trouble shooter since he had been the prime force behind the alpha group's unassisted return from the Kuiper Belt. It was a relatively new position at the training center in Florida. Gina, a physician, was going to be evaluated for a job as an off-world medical clinic module designer. She had the best knowledge of medical needs for deep space vehicles and space stations of anyone alive. With the new administrators at the training center, they felt it was time to re-enter the field of space exploration. Besides that, they both needed to earn a living, they had two children to raise, a seven-year-old boy, Miles, and a three-year-old girl, Libby.

They exited the air-conditioned administration building, designated structure 500, and began walking the quarter mile distance to Building 402. Sunul was noticing the different look of the base. The old unadorned concrete of the base had changed in the last eight years. A variety of trees, bushes, and flowers had been planted between and around the various science buildings and administration complexes.

"The base looks nicer now, doesn't it, Sunul?"

"I was just thinking that same thing. Have you noticed the gardeners? They seem to all be doing the same thing at the front of the last three buildings we've passed. They all have hand clippers and they're pretending to trim the shrubs and grass around the entrances to the offices. I think we're being watched."

"Really? I haven't noticed, but I didn't even think about it. I've been looking ahead at the flags and trees. You know, those flowers look artificial."

"Let's stop for a moment. You can adjust your shoe. Look back two buildings. Is the gardener still there?"

Gina stopped and Sunul steadied her as she bent down and looked back past her legs.

"No gardener. He's gone."

"When you stand up, look ahead to the next building. Does the man with the clippers have a gold ring in his left earlobe?"

"Uh-huh. You saw him before?"

"Yep, two buildings back. It's the same guy. He's not clipping anything, he's just making noise with the clippers."

Gina grinned. "Hmm. What do they think we're going to do, steal some flowers?"

Sunul laughed and they continued toward Building 402.

They could see the entrance to Building 402 as they rounded a corner and crossed the street when they were about fifty yards from building 401, the structure adjacent to their destination. A flash of light from the front of building 401 nearly blinded the Burkes, but it was just a momentary reflection of afternoon sunlight from the front door glass. A figure from the building was striding toward them, but they couldn't identify the individual at first, he was just a silhouette, but something was familiar about his walk.

"I think that's Rob Griswalt, Gina. What's he doing here?"

"Yeah, I wonder. I talked to Leanne last week. She said Rob was looking for a job off base."

"I remember you said that. Let's talk with him for a minute."

Rob was dressed in a light-gray uniform and wearing a white baseball cap with a multicolored logo that spelled OWLS in script capital letters.

"I thought I recognized you two. How are the Burkes?"

Sunul and Rob shook hands and Rob gave Gina a hug.

Gina replied, "We're fine. We just walked out of an interview with a lawyer. He asked us where Licon and Miranda were. We told him we had no idea and he called us liars. For a second, I thought Sunul was going to make him eat his glasses." Gina smiled and Rob laughed.

"I'll bet it was the same little bastard that talked to us. We said the same thing. He didn't call us liars, though. He just sat there steaming."

"What does OWLS stand for, Rob?"

"I'm sure you've heard of One World Express, Sunul. OWLS is a part of that company. It's One World Laboratory Security. They hired me to take care of the base fire alarm and security problems. They've been having too many false alarms lately, so they sent me to check out the system. It seems the base electricians are only able to change lightbulbs."

"What's in building 401 besides the food prep area?"

"A bunch of secretaries writing grant proposals for the next congressional budget committee. Most of the girls are overweight or married, or both. Fortunately, I don't have to bother much with that building. Anyway, it checked out with flying colors." He smiled, licked his lips and said, "I grabbed a chocolate covered donut when I was in the cafeteria."

"Are you being surveilled, or have you noticed, Rob?"

"Yeah, the first week I was on the job. I haven't noticed anything since. How about you?"

"The gardeners seem to be more interested in us than they are in the shrubs and flowers. Send us your number, we might need to talk. Gina spoke with Leanne last week but she didn't mention OWLS."

"I was under evaluation for two weeks. I was just made permanent this week. She probably didn't want to jinx me. I think the agency helped me get in with OWLS. Could be they want to keep track of me, and the pay is better than an astronaut's. Less dangerous, too. Well, I've got to get across the base to another building. It was nice seeing you guys. Say hello to the kids for me."

Sunul and Rob shook hands and Sunul said, "Tell your kids hi for us. Alpha group needs to have a reunion before long. We'll be in touch."

Rob backed away, waved, and said, "Bye, Gina. Keep Sunul in line."

"Bye, Rob. I'll talk with Leanne soon."

Sunul and Gina continued toward Building 402 and Rob disappeared behind building 401 to wait for the base transport vehicle.

"It was good to see Rob again. He looks relaxed and happy with his new position. I hope Leanne finds something to do besides take care of the kids. She's homeschooling them, isn't she?"

"Uh-huh. But she *is* working at home—fixes com units for the base. I forgot to tell you."

"It's good that she's working, she's very bright. When the kids get a little older, maybe she'll find a job on the base." Sunul opened the door and they went straight to the receptionist's counter. Sunul whispered in Gina's ear, "As soon as we get home with the kids, I want to drive to the main post office to see if my sister has sent me a letter."

"Okay. We'll have a picnic at the waterpark when you get back."

Gina recognized the receptionist immediately, it was Angie, the young woman she had anesthetized when they had liberated Miranda and Licon from the children's activity center about six years earlier. When Angie looked up from her work screen, she moved her right hand under the counter to find the alarm button; she recognized the Burkes as they approached.

"Hello, Angie. I want to apologize for sticking you with that needle, but we had to remove those children from being used as laboratory rats. I think you understand. That doctor had gone way too far. What he did reminded us of the Germans subjecting the Jews to torture in the guise of medical research."

Angie began to relax, lifted her hand from the panic button and said, "I understand. You know, I wasn't aware of what Dr. Kilmer was doing to investigate the pain threshold of the children. I felt bad for you guys when I found out about him. I'm glad you took those kids away."

"That's nice to know. Could you please bring our children to us?"

"Sure, I'll ask for them." She spoke into her console, "Please bring the Burke children to the front desk, their parents are here." She smiled and said, "We've changed procedures since you were here."

While driving home, the kid's voices coming from the backseats indicated they had enjoyed their time at the children's center. They had enjoyed the experience in the activity room while Gina and Sunul were being interviewed. The Burkes exited the base and drove about two minutes to their rental, a 1,800 square-foot ranch surrounded by colorful river rock and palm trees. There was no lawn to water; little rain fell in the neighborhood of the space agency base of operations.

Sunul stayed in the driver's seat as Gina ushered the kids into the house. He backed out of the short driveway and drove five minutes to the downtown postal complex, parked in a fifteen-minute zone, and entered the first-floor lobby of the glass-walled six-story building. He made his way to the general delivery kiosk and asked the clerk for his mail.

"Name, please."

"Sam Schroeder. If there's a letter, it'll be from France."

"Name of sender?"

"Priscilla Girard."

The clerk spoke the name into his computer screen and an envelope was dispensed from a slot on the counter in front of Sunul. He pulled the personal message from the slot and stuck it in his pocket.

"Thank-you." He waved to the clerk, left the building, and returned to his car. He decided to wait and open the envelope and read it with Gina. She had never seen a letter from Sunul's sister. As he drove back home he imagined the message was another short note about living in Paris, attending art exhibits, and escorting her daughter to the Eifel Tower. When he wrote back, he wanted to tell Priscilla of his new position at the space agency and some of the antics of Miles and Libby.

He parked the car and entered the air-conditioned living room. The kids were watching a wildlife adventure program about whales in the Pacific Ocean. The eight- by ten-foot screen made the viewer feel almost as if he or she were swimming with the monster marine mammals. Miles had the sound so loud that the house seemed to vibrate with the sounds from the wall and ceiling speakers. Sunul clapped his hands to get Miles's attention. He mouthed the words, "Turn it down."

Miles smiled, nodded, said, "Okay, Dad," and reduced the sound to a normal listening level.

"Thank-you." Now Sunul would be able to think clearly.

Sunul sat down, fished the letter from his pocket, tore off the end of the envelope, and extracted two sheets of lined pink stationery. Gina was busy so he began to read. He finished the letter, got up from his favorite chair, and walked into the kitchen where Gina was filling a picnic basket with odds and ends from the refrigerator and making sandwiches.

"Priscilla has cancer." He stood there holding the letter in his hand, dropping it to his side. He felt as if someone had kicked him in the stomach, expelling all the air from his lungs. He pulled out one of the bar stools, slumped down, and leaned on the counter—holding the letter out for Gina to read. In spite of not being very close to Priscilla, cancer was about the last thing he wanted to hear about his older sister.

Gina read the two pages, folded the letter and handed it to Sunul.

"Breast cancer can be difficult, but with chemotherapy and perhaps some surgery, she'll be fine. We don't know the extent of the problem. She sounds positive—upbeat. I need to talk with her and maybe her oncologist."

"What about finding Licon and Miranda? They'd donate some blood."

"Finding those two in eight billion people would be more than a nightmare. I hope we don't have to resort to searching for them."

Sunul thought for a minute and said, "I'm going to contact the Masons and the Patels to see if they've had contact with their older children. Maybe they know where Licon and Miranda are."

"Don't forget their new names: Adam and Eve; the names they have chosen."

Chapter 2

The other two pairs of the former alpha group: Jar'l and Monel Mason, and Hugh and Triel Patel, had found jobs outside the ISA. Fortunately, they lived nearby in Eastern Shores, Florida, a suburb of the base that had sprung up when travel to the closest potentially habitable planet had become a biweekly event. Off-world excursions to Mars had been taking place twice a month since 2086 to return and replace the personnel and supply materiel to the expanding colony which now had over 200 scientists and engineers.

The oxygen production reactors and the release of bound water had begun in 2085. However, operating the production plants at thirty-five percent efficiency was keeping development of the land and atmosphere at a snail's pace. One of the biggest problems was the lack of a rich source of hydrogen. Only small quantities of subsurface water had been found. The Agency had considered mining the giant planets' satellites for water and methane, both present as ices at the great distances of the source material from the sun. Transporting huge quantities of raw materials was a major problem—the cost was outrageous and potentially dangerous.

Sunul phoned the Masons to ask whether they had been contacted recently by Licon. On the fourth ring, Jar'l answered.

"Hello, Sunul. Have you been in touch with Licon?"

Sunul hesitated. He thought to himself, "Why would Jar'l think that I would have been in contact with his son." Before he had a chance to answer, Jar'l said,

"I sure wish Adam were here, he could help me find Licon."

That last comment told Sunul that Jar'l was in trouble so Sunul went along with it.

"I haven't seen Adam or Licon since we were together in Colorado. I called to ask if you would like to have an alpha group reunion."

Jar'l replied, "We should get together, ASAP."

"I'll call Rob and we'll see you guys soon. Bye."

"Bye, Sunul."

Sunul knew something was wrong at the Masons. He called Rob and told him Jar'l needed immediate help. Rob was still at work but he would make an excuse and leave immediately.

"Okay, Rob. Meet me about two houses west of the Mason's ASAP."

"Right, boss. I'll be there in about ten."

Sunul shook his head. "He's still calling me boss." Sunul put down the phone and called to Gina, "Rob and I are going to the Mason residence. Something is wrong over there. It's an emergency; I'll be back as soon as possible."

Sunul was out the door and getting into his car before Gina figured out what Sunul had said. She ran to the door and saw Sunul driving away from the house much faster than normal. She hoped he didn't get a ticket, family credits were running low. She stood at the door and thought, "What can I do but wait?" She shut the door and made a decision. Returning to the kitchen, she grabbed the picnic basket, a blanket from the hall closet, and joined the kids in the living room. They would have a picnic on the living room floor and watch the whales and dolphins. Miles had turned the sound up again so the room vibrated when the whales sang.

Sunul arrived at the prearranged meeting place, and much to his surprise, Rob was waiting in his OWLS truck. They met behind the truck where they couldn't be seen from the Mason's home. Rob handed Sunul an OWLS baseball cap and a firearm.

Sunul frowned, "How'd you get here so damned fast?"

"Security vehicles can go twenty mph over the limit. That gun is only for stun. If you shoot it, aim for the sternum; it'll take the wind out of anyone's sails. We might have to defibrillate afterwards. I've got a defibrillator in the truck—haven't had to use it yet."

"All right. What's our story?"

"We'll go to the front door and I'll talk my way in. We need to get inside and then we'll have three against two. I hope. If Monel and little Leona are being held in another room, we'll have to make some threats." Rob smiled, waved his stun gun, and stuck it in his tool box.

They stepped out from behind the truck and walked, as typical solicitors do, toward Jar'l's house, stopped in front and pretended to check the address. The brick sidewalk snaked around two shrubs and stopped at the front porch, a forty square foot slab of decorative concrete in front of the two-story. Rob pressed the doorbell. It buzzed, and they waited five seconds. He pressed it again.

"Who is it?" Sunul heard Jar'l's voice.

Rob answered, "Owl security. We have to check your alarm system. This entire neighborhood keeps sending us false alarms. We got two signals from this address twenty minutes ago. If we don't check it out, the police will get here in thirty minutes and make you leave the premises while the system is checked. What's it going to be, Mr. Mason?"

No sounds from within the house could be heard for about ten seconds and then Jar'l's voice stated,

"Just a minute." Rob's hand was on the door. He felt a click and the door swung open.

"Mr. Mason?"

Jar'l recognized Rob and Sunul immediately, but asked for their names.

Rob shook hands and said, "I'm Roy and this is my partner, James. We'd like to check your alarm system. Can you tell us where the panel is?"

"Come in, I'll show you. This is a friend—Mr. Sandini. He's from out-of-town—just visiting for a day." Jar'l rolled his eyes.

Rob and Sunul both nodded and followed Jar'l and Sandini down the hallway toward the back of the house. Jar'l stopped before reaching the back door, turned and said, "The main panel is in here." He pointed and as Sandini glanced into the room, Rob grabbed his arm, swung him around and Sunul gave him a powerful blow to the stomach. He doubled over and Rob gave the gasping man a judo chop to the neck, which dropped him to the floor. Rob pulled a roll of wire from his pocket and tied the unconscious man's hands and feet.

Rob looked up at Jar'l, "Where are Monel and Leona?"

"They're upstairs with this fart's partner. He's armed, too."

Sunul searched the bound man and pulled a gun from a shoulder holster concealed under his sports coat. The man also had a small gun in an ankle holster, which Sunul removed, took the magazine, ejected a bullet from the chamber, and dropped the gun and holster in the garbage can beside the back door.

"Boy, am I glad you guys showed up when you did. I was afraid we were alone with two thugs. They didn't say who they worked for, but they wanted Licon and Miranda. I told them I didn't know where the kids were. This asshole was going to shoot me if Monel and I didn't give them the information they wanted. The guy upstairs was going to cut Monel to make me tell them, but you guys showed up just in time. I'm glad you figured out my message."

Rob said, "Let's tell the upstairs guy his buddy is down for the count. Let me talk to him."

The three men climbed the spiral staircase to the second floor and went to the bedroom door Jar'l indicated.

"This is Owl security service. We have to check the window alarm. Open the door or we'll have to call the police to gain access. Open the door, Mrs. Mason."

"Go away, this man has a gun."

"Only one? We have four; two stun guns, and the two guns we took from the man's partner. He's unconscious on the floor downstairs. There's no way out. Tell him to come out with his hands up. If I have to use my stunner, it will stop his heart. We might not be able to revive him. We're not going to mess around."

There was a fifteen to twenty second wait before Rob spoke again. "What's it going to be? If you try to use the lady or the child as a shield, one of us will have an opportunity to shoot you. There are three of us. If, by some slim chance, you get out of the house, we will hunt you down. The internal security cameras have recorded your picture. You might as well give up. What do you want to do?"

There was about a five second wait before the man said, "Okay. I give up."

"Crack open the door and hand out your hand gun—and the little popgun in your ankle holster."

Rob motioned for Sunul to stand at the right of the door and Jar'l to stand on the left. The doorknob turned, the door opened about four inches, and a hand holding a gun was extended into the hallway. Rob grabbed the gun and slammed the door hard against the man's wrist. There was an outcry of pain, Rob jerked the door open, and shot the man in the chest with his stunner. The guy dropped to the floor, writhing in pain, grabbing at his chest. Rob frisked him and pulled a small gun from the man's ankle holster.

Rob held up the gun and said, "See! He didn't follow directions. Sunul, get some of that wire and tie him up. I left the wire downstairs near the back door. We'll make a two package delivery to the police station. Are you all right Monel?"

Jar'l was already embracing Monel and Leona. Monel looked at Rob and said, "Thanks, Rob, you're a life saver." She smiled, "I thought I recognized your voice. Are you really working security?"

Rob nodded, "Yeah. I check building security systems on the base for OWL Security. That's the first time I ever shot anyone with a stun gun—it's very effective." He smiled and pretended to blow smoke from the barrel. "It's like being a sheriff in the old west."

When Sunul finished binding the hands and feet of the thug on the floor, Rob reached down and peeled the flattened plastic projectile from the man's shirt. The flattened bullet was about the size of a poker chip and was still warm. He stuck the disc in his pocket and checked the man's pulse.

He asked Jar'l, "Did they indicate who wanted the info on Licon and Miranda?"

Monel answered, "They asked where the seven-year-old was, Rob. They don't know Adam and Eve are adults. They expected to find a second grader living here."

Jar'l added, "They said the people they are working for don't fool around. Money was not a problem, they would pay us significantly for Licon to donate a pint of blood, but since he is a child, a quarter pint would do. They said they could draw blood right here in our house. They have phlebotomy equipment in their van."

Sunul went to the window and scanned up and down the street. "I don't see any vehicle. How did they get here?"

Jar'l answered, "They put their van in the garage after they forced their way inside."

"Let's check it out. Maybe we'll get an idea who they work for." Rob started for the back of the house to enter the garage from the utility room where the other thug was lying on the floor in front of the washer/dryer. Jar'l and Sunul followed Rob and stepped over the body and went into the garage. A gray utility van was parked beside the Mason's family car. It had Rocket Body Shop written in orange script letters on the sides.

Sunul laughed, "Great name. We'll transport the two thugs to the police station in their own vehicle."

The driver's side door was unlocked. Sunul swung the door up, reached in, and touched the rear door button on the dashboard. The back of the van opened up toward the ceiling.

Jar'l and Rob were surprised at the contents of the van. A collapsible gurney was strapped to the right-hand wall and the left side was occupied by a cabinet full of medical equipment. Rob rummaged through the drawers and said, "This place is more than a modern ambulance, Sunul. Look at this stuff! It looks more like a portable operating room than a medical supply van. I'm thinking they were going to do more than take a quarter pint of blood from Licon. Looks like blood stains on the floor."

Jar'l was reading the labels of some of the drugs in one of the cabinet drawers and commented, "Most of these vials are from Eastern States Drugs,

Incorporated; ESDI. I think we can assume ESDI sent the two goons."

Chapter 3

Jar'l and Rob transported the two thugs to the city police station in the criminal's van. Sunul followed with his car to provide a ride back to Jar'l's residence. The two thugs were escorted into the station to the booking area where a slightly overweight Sergeant Schmick stood drinking a cup of coffee. He stepped forward with his belly against the counter and asked, "What can I do for you gentlemen?"

Jar'l, Rob, and Sunul introduced themselves and the sergeant reacted, "Aren't you three of the astronauts that came back from the Kuiper Belt?"

Rob smiled and said, "Yes, Sergeant, but we didn't expect thugs to be threatening us at home. We were safer out in space."

"I wouldn't have the guts to go out there where the sun doesn't shine and it's colder than a—you know what I mean," he chuckled. "It's an honor to meet you men."

Jar'l and Rob related the story of the thug's activities. As the cop listened, he took a few notes. Sunul added that the majority of the medical equipment was from ESDI.

"I don't understand why these perps wanted your son's blood. Have they got a thing with vampires? Maybe they've seen too many movies?"

Jar'l explained, "Somehow the drug company thinks my son's blood can cure cancer. They're afraid they'll lose money selling their current cancer drugs. If they're the first ones with a cancer drug that is effective against all types of cancer, they'd make millions—maybe billions."

"Ah, now I get it." He nodded and looked at his notes. The sergeant cited the possible charges against the two thugs: "forced entry, unlawful possession of firearms, threats of bodily harm...and practicing medicine without a license. Can you think of anything else, gentlemen?"

Jar'l looked at Rob and Sunul, who shook their heads, and said, "No, that about covers it. How long will these idiots be locked up?"

"Can't say. A judge will have to set bail. If bail is paid, they'll be out in a day or two. If whoever they work for pays the bail today, they could be home for dinner tonight. I have an idea that's what's going to happen. I have a feeling these guys have connections. We still have to give them a call. They're allowed one call to the outside."

Sunul said, "Please keep them as long as possible. We have to contact one other member of our group to advise him of the situation. He might have the same problem Jar'l had.
We haven't had a call from him and his wife, so maybe they're all right."

The sergeant reached across the counter and handed Sunul three cards containing the police department number and the sergeant's personal number. "Call any time fellas. I'll get someone to help you 24/7."

"Thanks, Sergeant. You're a good man. We appreciate your service and help."

"Nice meeting you gentlemen."

The three members of alpha group climbed into Sunul's car and headed to the Patels'. Triel and Hugh Patel lived about five minutes north of the Masons, so it was going to take nearly fifteen minutes through rush-hour traffic to reach them. Sunul placed a call through his car radio/phone. A message came over the speaker phone: "The number you are trying to reach is out of service. Please use an alternate number or other system of communication."

"That doesn't sound good. Either Hugh or Triel should be home at this time of day. Their research station is in their backyard." Sunul put his foot on the accelerator and began passing slower vehicles, changing lanes, and sounding his horn, causing other cars to get out of the way. When Sunul's car was within a mile of the Patels', the silence in the car was interrupted.

"Sunul Burke, you are driving erratically and at a high rate of speed. Your license number is being sent to the central police station. You will receive a summons at your current address. This is patrol officer Sinthia Sandborne, ID number 20312."

Sunul replied, "Do you know Sergeant Schmick?"

"Ah, yes sir."

"He told us to call him at any time if we needed help. Can you call him for us? We think we have an emergency at 3124 West Harbor Road."

There was a slight pause and then, "I don't see any problems at that address, sir."

"How can you tell? Where are you?"

"I'm about 500 feet above your car to the right. Take the next right, drive four blocks north; that address is two blocks east on the corner. I'll be there before you. I'll land in the vacant lot behind that address."

"Thank-you, officer."

Sunul followed Sandborne's instructions and pulled up in front of the Patels' split-level. There was a police officer knocking on the front door as Sunul's car screeched to a halt. Rob was the first to reach the officer at the door.

"Sandborne?"

"Yes, sir. Do you know the occupants?"

"Yes. They're close friends of ours."

Sunul and Jar'l arrived and were behind Rob. Rob reached past the officer and tried the door. It was unlocked, so he barged in.

"Hugh! Triel! It's Rob Griswalt, Sunul, Jar'l, and a police officer. Are you here?"

They heard silence, except for the ticking noise from the grandfather clock in the living room.

Sunul started through the house moving quickly to the back door. "I'm checking their research building out in back." As he went out the backdoor he yelled, "Hey Jar'l, check upstairs."

Sunul entered the greenhouse and was shocked. Hugh was tied to a post and blood was dripping from his right hand. When he saw Sunul, he began to weep, but was able to choke out a few words and nodded to his right. "Help Triel, Sunul. She passed out. There's a hammer—under the bench in the back."

"Why was Hugh telling me to get a hammer?" Sunul thought. Then he saw the reason. Triel had both hands nailed to the top of the work bench. The long shiny carpenter's nails were penetrating the soft tissue between her thumbs and forefingers. Blood had pooled under her hands. She had collapsed to her knees beside the bench, unconscious.

"Son of a bitch! Jar'l! Rob! Out here!" He moved to the back bench and retrieved a claw hammer and a small block of 2x4 to assist in removing the nails. He started to pull one of the nails and then stopped. If he pulled one nail, Triel's body would sag to the floor, ripping the tissue from her other hand. He had to have help. Officer Sandborne appeared at just the right time, obviating his second call for help.

"Hold Triel while I pull these nails. Don't let her fall to the ground."

Sandborne said, "Oh, my God! What the hell has happened to these people?"

As Sunul pulled the nails, Sandborne kept Triel's body from moving. Jar'l joined Sunul, scooped Triel up, and laid her on the bench. Sandborne had seen the first-aid kit and obtained disinfectant and some thick gauze bandages. Sunul and the officer wrapped Triel's hands tightly. Meanwhile, Rob had cut the ropes and masking tape from Hugh and had him sit on a small lawn chair pulled from under the work bench. Hugh was going into shock; his right hand looked as if someone had used a meat tenderizer on a steak. What hung from his wrist was no longer a human hand. Hugh couldn't imagine any bones were intact. Fortunately, the greenhouse was hot and humid, so it wasn't necessary to keep Hugh warm with a blanket. Rob took out his security phone and called an ambulance.

"Can you men carry Mrs. Patel to my patrol vehicle? I'll fly her to the nearest hospital. It's only five minutes from here."

Sunul and Jar'l carried Triel out the back of the greenhouse, across the alley and put her in the copilot's seat. As Triel was being secured in the chair, Sandborne had the rotors revving. She motioned for the men to step away and the patrol vehicle shot straight up, tilted, and swooshed away. An ambulance was approaching, the staccato, high-pitched warbling of the siren was unmistakable.

Jar'l and Sunul returned to the green house and saw Rob standing with his good hand on Hugh's shoulder. With tears dripping from his face, Hugh kept saying, "I couldn't do anything. I couldn't help Triel." He repeated his comments several times before he explained, "They kept asking where Miranda was and I kept telling them we didn't know. Then they pounded a nail through Triel's hand. I said stop, we don't know where Miranda is. They didn't believe me and put a nail through her other hand. She passed out so they hit my hand with the hammer over and over. I don't think it can be fixed."

Sunul crouched down next to Hugh and said, "Don't worry about your hand, Hugh. We're going to wrap it in ice and take you to the hospital. There's an ambulance coming for you. Your hand can be replaced with a prosthesis. The newest ones have great dexterity and even feeling. I just read about the new prostheses in one of Gina's medical journals. After a while, you won't even realize it's not original equipment." Sunul tried to smile, but he knew Hugh was going to have a painful recovery; his alpha group partner was not going to like to take pain meds, but he was a fighter. With time he would be stronger than ever.

Hugh looked at his three alpha group buddies, "Where's Triel? Is she all right?"

Sunul replied, "Triel is probably already in the emergency ward. That lady cop flew her to the hospital. I'll bet they fix her hands so they won't even show any scars."

"I got their license number. It's FL30129—on a dark-blue Warp-3 Ford."

"That's great, Hugh. We've got a sergeant at the main police station that will help us find the scum that did this."

"You'd better let the police handle it, Sunul; both those guys are bigger than you."

The ambulance attendants arrived in the greenhouse and prepared Hugh for travel to the emergency room. He could walk, but they wouldn't let him. They strapped him to an airflow gurney to provide a smooth ride to the ambulance. They didn't want to do further damage to the veins and other tissue of his mutilated right hand.

"I've got to call Gina, guys. She might be able to help Hugh make a decision about the prosthesis for his right hand. I'll drive home and let her take the car to the hospital. Can you guys check on Triel? Hugh will want to know how she is. She should be told about Hugh's hand, also. Try to break the news so she doesn't get too upset. Tell her Gina is coming over to talk with her and Hugh. Gina might have to sign papers for Triel—both of her hands will be out of commission for a few days."

"Okay, Sunul. We'll go directly to the hospital in my truck. Come on Jar'l—I'll drive."

"That's what I'm afraid of, Rob. Remember, we're not in a hurry."

Sunul talked with Gina on his way home. When he arrived at the house, Gina was waiting at the curb. Sunul kept the engine running, got out, gave Gina a kiss, and slowly walked to the house as Gina slid in the car and started toward the hospital.

Chapter 4

In the middle of the floor, the picnic basket sat on the blanket almost empty, except for one sandwich and an unopened bottle of Walla Walla wine. Miles and Libby were barefoot, sitting on the sofa. Miles was reading aloud from an old book of witchcraft and wizardry; the main character being Harry Potter. Sunul sat on the floor, unwrapped the lone sandwich, and took a big bite.

Miles looked away from the book and said, "Hey, Dad, why did Mom go to the hospital?"

Sunul couldn't tell the kids the gruesome details about the Patels' injuries, and he hated to lie. "Mr. and Mrs. Patel had an accident in their research laboratory. They needed medical attention for their injuries." He needed to change the subject. "How was your picnic?"

Libby replied, "Oh, fine," she sighed. "We missed you."

Miles placed the book on his lap. "Yeah, Dad. I was outnumbered—two-to-one."

"I'm sorry I missed it. I won't miss the next one. We'll have it in the park or at the beach."

"I want the beach. We can make sandcastles." Libby got down from the sofa and peered into the picnic basket.

"What do you want, Libby?"

"A carrot, but they're all gone." She frowned and sat down beside Sunul. "Daddy, can we go back and live in the forest?"

"I don't think so, dear. All of the adults that we lived with have jobs here now. The kids all have to go to school in September. Your mom and I are both going to have jobs at the base if everything works out right. Miles has to go to school, too."

"When can I go to school?"

"Two years from now, Libby. Meanwhile you'll stay at the activity center on the base until your mom and I get off work. You like it there, don't you?"

"I like Miss Lindsey. She's nice—and she sings. She has us sing songs, too, and we take naps. They have soft beds for us and they play music."

"How's the food?"

"It's okay. I don't like broccoli. I had some and afterwards, I had to chew some gum."

At five-thirty, Gina hadn't returned from the hospital. Sunul asked the kids if they wanted some dinner, but they weren't hungry. He guessed their in-house picnic and lack of activity hadn't burned off many calories. He wasn't hungry either, so he decided to wait for Gina before preparing anything to eat.

At 7:10, the phone rang. It wasn't Gina, it was Officer Sandborne.

"What can I do for you, Officer?"

"I was just checking to see if you were at home. I'm at Shark Point with a tow truck. We're pulling a car from the surf."

"Why are you calling me about it?"

"I thought you might be interested. The plates are Florida 30129. That's the tag Mr. Patel reported. There are two stiffs inside. Looks like they were shot in the head—small caliber."

"Whoa! Can you forward pictures to me? I'll show them to Hugh and Triel to see those are the goons that tortured them."

"I can do that. Where have you been since I took Mrs. Patel to the hospital?"

"You think I had something to do with the homicides? I've been home with my kids. You can verify that. You want to talk to them?"

"Not this evening. I'll come over with an investigator tomorrow. You'll all be there?"

"As far as I know. Gina and I might have to go to the base—depends on our job interviews. The kids will be at the children's facility, Building 402, if we're on base."

"Okay. We'll call ahead. Bye."

"Thanks for the info. G'bye."

Sunul placed his phone in his breast pocket and sat down on the sofa. He had to think of what the meaning was of the recovery of the goon's vehicle. Someone must have been wary of the thugs, or they had insisted on more credits for their brutal work. He decided to ask Jar'l for some help. Jar'l might be able to dig up information on the goon's activities. Where were they from, and who did they work for?

He stood up and looked around the room. "Where did I put my phone? Miles, did you see my phone?"

Miles was stretched out on the floor reading from his Harry Potter book, and Libby was on her way to the bathroom. Sunul stood there thinking about his recent phone call. He had just finished a call. His phone rang. Surprise! It was in his pocket.

"Hello, Jar'l. What's going on?"

"We just received a letter from you-know-who. They're in Argentina. Buenos Aires to be exact, but the letter was postmarked weeks ago. It says they sent the same letter to the Patels."

"The goons must have gotten Patel's letter. That's why they left before we got there. I bet that's why they were killed."

"What? Those thugs are dead? When did that happen?"

"Officer Sandborne called me a little while ago. Told me the goon's car was pulled from the surf at Shark Point. Both guys in the car had an extra hole in their head."

"Good riddance. But they must have passed the letter to someone else. Did the officer mention the letter?"

"Nope. But I didn't ask her, either. I didn't know you got one. Did it give any clue about their whereabouts—other than the postmark?"

"They mentioned they were going south. They said they were fine and they hoped all the members of alpha group and their cousins were well."

"That was all?"

"Uh-huh. Short and sweet."

"Well, I don't think they'll be found by anyone from here. They've probably got a couple of week's head start, too. I wish we could tell them someone is looking for them and they're in danger."

"Yeah, me too, Sunul."

"When you called, I was just about to call you. I was going to ask if you knew where the two kids were. But, I found out without asking."

"What did you want them for?"

"My sister has breast cancer."

"You have a sister? You mean you lied on your astronaut application?"

"Yeah, but it wasn't much of a lie. I haven't seen Priscilla in years and we exchange letters about once every two years. We aren't close, but she is family, and I want to help her if chemo and radiation don't do the job."

"I understand. I'd have done the same thing."

Gina arrived back home around eight o'clock in the evening. There was a little less than an hour before the sun dropped below the horizon. Although it was getting late for dinner, the kids were hungry so Sunul and Gina prepared dinner. They talked as they made spaghetti and meatballs. Sunul told her about the two dead goons and then asked about Hugh and Triel.

"How are the Patels?"

"Triel will be fine in about a week. It will take about a month until Hugh is able to regain full use of his right hand. He'll be able to go home from the prosthesis training facility in a week, then the adaptation time will begin. Day after tomorrow, the training staff will show him how to sign his name. Then it will be practice until the brain and connections to the hand become synchronized and strengthened."

"Is he in much pain?"

"No. Pain's not a problem. He'll be on drugs for a few days before gradual withdrawal occurs. Aspirin will be all he'll need for the pain—it will be like a headache for three or four days."

"They're going to show him how to make an *X*?"

"No." Gina laughed, "There's a microchip in his hand that directs the muscles to write an actual signature. He uses muscles to access the procedure. It's remarkable, and the signature varies slightly each time he engages the subroutine. The signature looks like the real thing."

"How's Triel doing?"

"She's recovering nicely, but she won't have much of a grip for about a week. That's what I want to ask you about."

"They want to stay with us?"

"Nope. Triel wants Libby and me to stay with them until Hugh gets fully adapted to his new hand. What do you think?"

Sunul smiled, "It's all right with me. Miles and I can get along fine. What about your new job?"

"If I get hired, I can start at the first of next month. There's no hurry. I'll have to meet with a committee a few times before I know what they envision." Gina looked at the wall calendar and said, "That's fifteen days from now."

"Officer Sandborne and an investigator are going to interview us tomorrow morning—said they would call ahead. I thought we would all be here. I think she wants to talk to the kids about this afternoon to eliminate me as a suspect in the killings."

"Geez! Sometimes I wish we were still in the mountains of Colorado. All we had to worry about was food and the weather—and an occasional bear."

"That's funny, a little while ago Libby asked me if we could go back to the forest. You women think alike."

"What did you tell her?"

"We all have jobs now and the kids have to go to school. She seemed satisfied with my explanation."

"Well, call the kids. Let's eat."

In the morning, which was windy and gray, there were two early calls from the base. Sunul was hired to take the next flight to Mars, and Gina was to start work on the first of the month, just as she had expected. The Burke residence was full of excitement, Sunul and Gina were relieved that they were now employed and the kids were anticipating a day at the beach, in spite of the signs of inclement weather. Miles knew that his dad would be gone for up to a month, and he spread the news to Libby.

"Daddy, where's Mars? Is it almost to Miami?"

Sunul smiled and said, "Much farther than Miami, Libby. Do you know how far it is to the moon?"

Libby thought for a moment and answered, "Pretty far?"

"That's right. Mars is much farther than that. I have to take a rocket ship to Mars. It will take me a week to get there. I'll stay for two weeks and then come back home."

Gina rushed into the living room and grabbed and squeezed Sunul's left shoulder. "Dr. Winslow, Sunul! Shania Winslow's blood will have some type of antibodies that would have formed when Licon's and Miranda's blood was introduced into her system."

"That's right! I wonder if she's still there. Maybe she's back on Earth; it's been nearly six years since you cured her cancer. She's probably back by now."

"Would the Agency tell us where she is?" Gina was still excited about getting a blood specimen from Dr. Winslow. "Her blood would be a source of antibody-mimicry response cells. We could use them to synthesize a cancer vaccine."

"If she's on Mars, nobody will tell us. Most off-world identities are hidden from the public. That's an old established norm. In the early years of the Agency, off-world deaths were kept hidden from the public; administrators were afraid they would lose funding if people were dying in space."

"Hey, let's ask Rob to find out. His security clearance should allow him to find out about Shania—don't you think?"

"We don't want to get him in trouble. I should be able to scan the list of the personnel on Mars if I'm going there. They'll let me check to see if I'm acquainted with anyone at the colony. If the Agency wants me to solve a problem, I need to know the expertise of the colonists."

"Why do you think they need your advice on Mars?"

"I have no idea, but I'll find out soon. I'll be leaving in four days."

The chime on the front door sounded, and the door sentry announced, "Two individuals: one male, one female. Law officers."

Sunul moved toward the door saying, "Nuts! They were to call ahead. I wonder why they changed their minds." He looked at the display next to the door and said, "It's Officer Sandborne and I think—a detective."

Sunul invited them in and Sandborne introduced Lieutenant Andy Wallace to the Burkes. Sunul acquainted Officer Sandborne with his family, then Gina escorted the police into the living room. As soon as they were seated, the detective pulled a small display tablet from his sports coat pocket and pressed the recall icon.

"Are these the two that tortured the Patels?"

Sunul started to say that he hadn't seen those men, but when he focused on the display, he reacted, "Those are the two that were at the Mason residence. They were arrested and taken to the police station. They're the guys pulled from the surf?"

"Yes, sir," answered Sandborne. "They made a call from the jail and a judge set bail. Someone bailed them out and they turned up dead a few hours later."

"I guess they disappointed someone because they failed in their mission and got caught. Whoever hired them must have thought they would talk, or already had." Sunul continued, "I thought you were going to show me pictures of the goons that injured the Patels. I couldn't have identified them; I never saw them. You surprised me."

Officer Sandborne stated, "I had never seen them before, but I thought they might have been part of the crew intimidating the Patels and the Masons. Thanks for the verification."

"Where are they from? Are they US citizens?"

Detective Wallace answered, "Illegal immigrants—Middle Eastern background. Everything in their background is illegal—real nice people." Detective Wallace gave a slight grin and said, "We'll get out of here and leave you to your normal routine. Thanks for your assistance."

Chapter 5

The Burkes spent a good part of the day at the beach. Storm clouds brought high winds and lightning in the late afternoon, so they returned home for dinner and a movie. The World War II movie struck gold with both Gina and Sunul. Spies were everywhere so regular communications were impossible. The heroine devised a method to communicate with her team in England by imbedding Morse code signals in her regular periodic transmissions to the Allies from the German held continent.

"Sunul! Can we do something like that?"

"I think so. Let me talk to Rob and Jar'l. If there's a way, they'll know how to do it. I've got an idea, but I don't know if it will work."

Sunul met in a park with Rob and Jar'l during lunch the next day. Sunul had picked up some fast food and non-alcoholic beverages for the group. He remembered the likes of the other two men from the training in New Mexico and their year-long journey to and from the Kuiper Belt.

He looked directly at Rob. "How can I communicate secretly from Mars with someone on Earth? I need to be able to talk to Gina or one of you confidentially."

Rob gave an immediate answer. "I can build you a small transceiver so you can record your message and copy it so you'll have two identical messages. Having duplicate messages will allow for transmission and receiver errors. Then you will need to get near the transmission aerial, or the transmitter itself, activate your message, and get the hell away from your location so no one suspects you of anything. Your message will be transmitted at ten times the normal frequency so it will appear to be background noise."

Jar'l grasped Rob's plan and said, "One of us will have to get access to the receiver and record all the messages coming to Earth. It will require a large chunk of memory, but we can do it with a ten-terabyte memory cube. Then the fun begins. We'll isolate the messages with noise levels at ten times the normal message frequency and apply a Fourier transform to remove the lower frequencies."

"And what will remain will be my message—in duplicate," said Sunul. "That's pretty clever, guys. What about me receiving a message back from Earth?"

"Your transceiver will be able to pick up communications to Mars. Jar'l can write some software to reveal our message to you. I'll put it into a com unit. No one will ever know what's going on."

"One problem, Rob." Sunul was anticipating things being overlooked.

"You're going to ask me how I'll have the right frequency, correct?"

"Yep." Sunul grinned. He knew Rob had already anticipated his question.

Rob smiled. "I'll find out this afternoon what frequency is being used. Don't get your cerebral cortex in a tizzy."

Sunul said, "Rob, you've been studying the brain again. I told you to be careful about that."

Following the laughter, Rob and Jar'l mentioned they had to get back to work. Sunul had volunteered to police the area. He threw their waste materials in a trash can, and returned home. He had three days before the next flight to Mars left from California, time to pack necessities and make plans with Gina, Miles, and Libby for his activities with the family upon his return in a month. He was hoping that two weeks on

Mars would be enough time to accomplish the job the agency wanted carried out. He was sure he would have an opportunity to contact Dr. Shania Wilson and obtain a blood sample for Gina's research plans.

The day prior to the three-hour flight to Edwards Air Force and Space Launch Base was very busy. He met with mining engineers in the morning and nuclear power engineers in the afternoon. What he couldn't cram into his augmented brain he recorded on his new com unit Rob had presented him the previous evening at the hospital's prosthetics center.

The alpha group had gathered at the hospital to check on Hugh and Triel Patel to see if they needed anything. Triel's wounds had healed with only a trace of scars and Hugh was happy with his new hand. He appeared to enjoy showing the group how he could write his name with little effort. Hugh was eager to get home and back to work on his and Triel's research activities in the greenhouse. Triel was talking about obtaining a stun gun for their protection. Rob had plenty of advice on that subject. He could get her a model SG88 for cost. It could only be fired by the owner. Therefore, the Patels needed two.

Sunul said his goodbyes and left home for the airport at 0500. He arrived in California at 0600. The three-hour trip was without incident; he slept most of the way. He was met by a female driver that looked like a rosy-cheeked teenager. She let him out at gate Mars 04 where he was scanned and escorted to the ship designated to rendezvous with the geostationary satellite above Hawaii.

Sunul was the last passenger to board the transition vehicle that would carry him and seven other passengers to the orbiting station 22,000 miles overhead. As he sat down and fastened his seatbelt, he nodded to his fellow passengers, two women and five men. The man sitting adjacent to him smiled and extended his hand.

"I'm Arthur Corcoran, physician. I go by Art."

"Sunul Burke, troubleshooter. My wife's a doctor and a health science lab designer."

"This your first trip to Mars?"

"No, but the last time I was there, I had arrived from a different direction."

Art frowned and asked, "From beyond Mars?"

Sunul nodded.

"The space agency hasn't had a voyage beyond Mars for nearly eight years. You were part of that crew?"

Sunul nodded again and forced a grin.

"I heard two aliens came back with you, but after they escaped confinement, the government was never able to locate them."

"That's right."

"So you don't know where they are?"

Sunul thought, "This guy could be working for somebody besides the Agency."

"That's correct. I have no idea where they are."

The ship audio system announced: "Embarkation will occur in one minute. Please stow loose objects and secure your seat belt. Arrival at the station will be in about twenty minutes."

Sunul glanced at Art, "Do you get airsick?"

"Never have. You think I might?"

"Never can tell. Leaving Earth can sometimes upset one's equilibrium."

Sunul relaxed and felt the acceleration gently push his body into the seat as the ship taxied onto the mile-long runway. Without any hesitation for alignment on the runway, the g-forces increased dramatically, the engines burning fuel at a tremendous rate. When the aircraft left the runway and nosed up at a steep angle, Sunul looked over at Art. He was crossing himself, obviously somewhat frightened at the steep angle of departure from the airport. Sunul smiled and decided in an instant that Dr. Corcoran was someone he needed to befriend. The doctor just might come in handy on Mars.

Just as the voice had stated, twenty-two minutes later the ship was maneuvering to dock with the geostationary terminal. Sunul observed another ship docked on the other side of the interplanetary flight station. He wondered if that was the ship he would be on traveling to Mars, or was it heading back to Earth. He would know in a few minutes.

The eight passengers attached magnetic soles to their vinyl shoes, found their luggage beside the exit door and moved into the flight terminal.

"Have you eaten anything today?" Doctor Corcoran asked Sunul.

"Not yet. I left the house early today. Didn't have time for breakfast."

"Where's home?"

"Florida—Atlantic coast."

"I'm from Oregon—flew in this morning, but didn't eat on the plane." He smiled, "I was warned not to snack before leaving Earth. I think nurses at my office were pulling my leg."

"Well, we've got about an hour before we leave for the moon."

Art frowned, "The moon?"

"Yeah, we leave from the moon to travel to Mars."

"I don't think so, Sunul. We're taking a direct flight."

"Hmm, I guess they've changed the routine since I was last in space. That's good to know. I'll have to pal around with you and learn the new procedures. In that case, let's get something to eat."

They sat down at a games table and as they ate breakfast, they played a game of chess. The doctor opened with P—Q4 and Sunul knew he was in trouble. He had never done well in games starting with a queen's pawn opening move. Ten moves into the game and it was getting worse for Sunul, the doctor was a superior player. Sunul sat studying the board for a minute before making his move.

Corcoran asked, "Do you know that gentleman behind you? The one with the short blond hair—about your size."

"Why?"

"He's been watching you ever since we sat down. I've never seen him before. I don't recall him being on the ship with us."

Sunul stood up, gathered the two trays of waste paper and plastic, and carried them to the refuse container. He took a long look at the stranger Art had mentioned. Sunul had never seen him before, either, so introductions were in order.

Sunul walked up to the individual and extended his right hand. "I'm Sunul Burke. I assume we'll both be going to Mars. I like to know my fellow passengers."

"Glad to meet you. I'm James Frieland, heating and air conditioning. I monitor the atmosphere in the Martian bubble."

"Do you play chess?"

"Occasionally. You and your friend are much better than I am. I'm a novice."

"Oh. We wondered why you were observing us so closely. We thought you might have recognized us from another location, maybe a training center."

"No. This will be my first trip to Mars. I'm sure we'll get to know each other better in the next week."

"Nice meeting you. I'd better get back to the game." Sunul turned away and on his way back to the games table, he was trying to recall where he had heard that name before, James Frieland. He couldn't recollect who had mentioned the name, but it wasn't from a recent conversation, that was for sure. Five more moves and Sunul resigned. His mind wasn't on chess after he began thinking about that name. He began retracing through the years until he thought, "Could it have been when alpha group and their children arrived on Mars on their return trip to Earth?"

Art asked, "What's that guy's name, Sunul?"

"James Frieland. Monitors dome atmospheric conditions."

"I don't believe I've ever met a Jim Frieland."

When Art said, "Jim Frieland," Sunul remembered.

"That's it!"

"What?"

"I just recalled where I had heard that name. It was on Mars on our return trip from the Kuiper Belt. He's a security agent of some sort. He just lied to me about not being on Mars before. He wore glasses back then—probably didn't need them."

"He could have had surgery. You're sure he's the same guy?"

"Almost positive. My wife would know for sure. I'll send her a photo; she'll remember if she's seen him before. She has an almost photographic memory for faces. I wish I had that ability. I remember sequences of events, but not exact details—like faces."

"You mentioned your wife is a doctor. Does she know Shania Winslow? I'm replacing Dr. Winslow."

"Yes. My wife helped cure Dr. Winslow's lung cancer about eight years ago. Is she having problems again?"

"Not that I'm aware of. She's completing another tour on Mars and wants to develop a practice back on Earth. Everyone in the colony is so healthy, she feels like she's wasting her talents. Now that the lure and excitement of life in a space colony has worn off, she's ready for a change."

Dr. Corcoran, Sunul, and several others heard the announcement for passengers on the direct flight to Mars to gather on the opposite side of the circular terminal.

Chapter 6

A female escort of slight build and medium height, dressed in a purple jumpsuit, guided the group of Martian travelers through the corridors and hatches to the opposite side of the approximately octagonal station. Sunul was the second person behind her as they moved single file. Her graceful movements hinted she had been trained as a dancer. Without assistance it would have been easy to get lost moving across the irregular structure, about three-hundred-feet in diameter, and three stories high. Each passenger was presented with an EVA suit that had been tailored from body scans on Earth. Their preflight questionnaire had been followed closely.

Not much was said amongst the group as they boarded the ship to Mars. Five minutes after taking their places in launch positions, a female voice calmly welcomed the voyagers, "My name is Judith Thorp, Captain. I will be guiding this ship to Mars. Estimated travel time is slightly over six and one-half days. Take the time to acquaint yourselves with the other travelers and enjoy the trip."

A gong sounded three times followed by a low frequency buzzer. Then the captain's voice announced, "Three, two, one, and we are on our way."

Sunul felt the ship drift away from the terminal and then he experienced a sudden force of acceleration as the engines propelled the spacecraft away from the satellite and Earth. An overhead observation screen showed the colorful Earth receding. Sunul was impressed with the obvious advancement in technology that had occurred during the past seven years. In less than two hours, the Earth-moon system could be seen filling the screen, and the ship was still accelerating.

At five hours into the flight, Captain Thorp announced, "We are no longer accelerating. You may move about the lounge area at will. Mr. Simonson will show you your sleeping quarters. Buzz for him when you need anything."

A young man, maybe in his late twenties, stood from a seat adjacent to the wall at the front of the passenger cabin and waved. He was dressed in a light-blue jumpsuit, had jet-black wavy hair, and was about five-six in height. He looked very alert, possessed prominent features; his smile looked as if it was painted on his face, and he was scanning the eight passengers with a beam of polychromatic light. Sunul wondered if Simonson was an android and noted the attendant seemed to pay slightly more attention to Mr. Frieland than any of the others.

There were two couples present and another, older man Sunul hadn't met. Although Sunul had never been very sociable, he decided to introduce himself to the unfamiliar travelers. He felt it would be an advantage to know the strengths of the others if an emergency arose. Sunul wasn't 100% confident in the abilities of the ship's crew, although he had only seen one and heard one other member, the ship's captain.

"Hey, Art, let's meet the folks."

Art put his magazine in his console and joined Sunul.

The first couple, Janis and Roy Noble, were botanists, specializing in raising nutritional plants in unfavorable conditions. They reminded Sunul of Hugh and Triel Patel, the parents of Miranda, now going by the assumed name, Eve. Sunul couldn't help thinking about the Patels, hoping they were recovering nicely, and wondering where Miranda was.

Janis and Roy mentioned that they had some ideas for Sunul to consider. They might need his help.

They had heard of his exploits on the Kuiper Belt expedition, and they had some ideas that were outside the box. Sunul was intrigued by this bright young couple. Roy was almost always smiling and was about two inches shorter than his wife. They were very enthusiastic about travelling to Mars.

The other couple, Adele and Toby Scott, were geologists/mineralogists and were eager to search for and explore caves on Mars. They were both fit and looked more like mountain climbers than spelunkers. The Scotts had been exploring caves in the vicinity of the Grand Canyon, but they had never explored while wearing space suits. Sunul and Art wished them well.

The eighth traveler was the only one that could be considered odd, in both Art's and Sunul's opinion. They wondered what the space agency was thinking. Mr. Evan Shiner was a water witch, barely over five feet tall, tanned leathery skin, and sunken black eyes. He looked to be too old for space travel, but for some unknown reason, he was on his way to the red planet. Sunul wondered if the gentleman had much success finding water with a divining rod. As far as Sunul was concerned, dowsers were objects from the ancient past and had little, if any, scientific value.

When Sunul had looked across the terminal while waiting for the ship to Mars to be prepared, he had misjudged the size of the interplanetary vehicle. He now realized the transit ship to Mars was nearly twice as large as the escape from Earth ship, although they had very similar configurations. This journey was going to be much more comfortable than the last one he was on when the alpha team travelled to the outskirts of the solar system.

The next six days were never boring; there was always someone to talk with, even though many of the conversations were about trivial matters. One discussion, however, piqued Sunul's interest. The Nobles had been thinking of cultivating soil below ground where the water and necessary minerals were in prominent supply.

"Wait a minute, folks. There is precious little water on Mars. Where are you going to get the water you need to grow crops? And also, you'll need artificial sunlight." Sunul didn't want to be pessimistic, but they had to face reality.

Toby Scott had been listening and joined the group. "Adele and I have been thinking about the lack of water, Sunul. We think there's a solution to the problem."

Janis said, "If you have an answer to the water, what do we do about supplying carbon dioxide from the atmosphere? The pressure is so low."

"What is being done with the carbon dioxide generated by the people living under the dome? Can't that be used for plant growth?" Sunul knew that answer, but he had another source of carbon in mind, exceeding the amount generated from respiration. With the speed and size of new cargo ships, solid methane could be mined from the outer planets and transported to Mars. Fuel cells running on methane had been developed in the last century and optimized during the third decade of the twenty-first century.

Unfortunately, Mar's gravity was not great enough to prevent the original water, methane, and ammonia from escaping the planet. So, the environment and time for early life to develop, in the form of animals and plants, were not present. Therefore, there was no supply of fossil fuels or hydrocarbons on Mars, and no significant source of hydrogen or oxygen to make more water. The only water present on Mars was that which was chemically bonded to metal ions or trapped in clathrates present in the dust, gas, and asteroids that originally condensed to form the planet. That was the extent of Sunul's knowledge of the formation of Mars. He looked forward to learning more from his fellow travelers and the areologist at the Mar's colony.

Toby answered Sunul's question. "Currently, the carbon dioxide is released to the atmosphere, but the Nobles think it should be trapped underground in caves at a high enough pressure so plants could use it to grow and form oxygen gas to be vented to the atmosphere."

"And you think the water needed can be removed from the compounds in the caves?" Sunul was anticipating the botanists' project.

"Uh-huh. Toby says copper sulfate pentahydrate is thirty-six percent water—and we hope there are many other compounds of that type available beneath the Martian surface." Adele sounded quite confident.

Sunul asked, "What will you do with the dehydrated minerals? Won't they reabsorb the water they have given up?"

Roy spoke up, "We need you to help us reduce the metal ions to metal which can be shipped back to Earth and sold."

"Don't you think a chemist should help you?" Sunul felt a bit uneasy to be operating outside his area of expertise. "We'd be starting a new industry."

Roy answered, "We thought of that, but if we had a chemist, we would then need another individual to install reactors in the caves, and another person for communications, and so forth. You are the one that can deal with all the difficulties."

"Well, I hope I can do what you want accomplished."

Janis and Roy smiled and responded in unison, "We know you can do it."

Sunul grinned, "I'll do my best." He thought to himself, "But my highest priority is to get a blood sample from Shania."

The rest of the trip provided plenty of time for discussion of the botanists' plans and the mineralogists' ideas for recovering water from the inorganic chemicals below ground. The dowser, Mr. Shiner, offered his talents to find underground water, but when the scientists explained they were not seeking liquid water, but chemically bound water, he lost interest in the conversation.

"Where is the most probable place to find water?" Sunul was thinking it would be a valley where water would have run between mountains, but he hadn't thought very thoroughly.

Adele looked at Toby to see if he was going to answer, but he just nodded his go-ahead.

"On the plains where lakes might have formed many years ago. As the water evaporated, it would have left hydrated minerals behind, maybe even subsurface lakes. We need to talk with the areologist to find what history of the surface is known. He'll point out the best places to look." From the way she talked, the Scotts exhibited great confidence in their knowledge and what they hoped to discover on Mars.

Toby added, "Hopefully, he'll have some core samples we can study, or we'll have to do some drilling of our own."

As the ship approached Mars, Captain Thorp announced, "We will be decelerating for about an hour before we enter the Martian atmosphere. I will warn you a few minutes before our approach. At that time, please take your seats and secure your seatbelts. Contact with the atmosphere can sometimes be a little rough."

Ten seconds elapsed before Simonson reported, "We will be landing in the dark. The ship will be moved underground, so expect some noise. When the interior green lights illuminate the cabin, you may leave the ship for the subway. Make sure you have all your luggage. The ride to the dome will take about five minutes."

Sunul was impressed with the development of the infrastructure on the small planet since the alpha group had last been on Mars seven years earlier in 2081. At that time, travel by crawler from the dome to the spaceport terminal took fifteen minutes. Sunul began to wonder how the tunnel for the subway had been dug, or had the engineers found an underground tunnel formed by subsurface water. He had started accumulating questions for the local areologists. The Scotts were probably thinking some of the same things.

Art sat down next to Sunul and said, "A subway? That surprises me. How do you think it's propelled?"

Sunul hadn't expected Art's question. He thought for a moment and spoke, "I'm guessing they use compressed carbon dioxide. Most of the atmosphere is CO_2—no contaminants would be added."

Art responded, "The Nobles won't need a source of carbon dioxide to grow their plants, will they?"

"No, but the atmospheric pressure on the planet is only about one percent of the Earth's. They'll have to compress the gas and introduce it into a closed compartment. We've got several problems to solve to make this work."

Captain Thorp's voice came over the intercom, "Please secure items in your consoles and buckle your seatbelts. We'll come in contact with the atmosphere in a couple of minutes. We will be landing in the dark. Don't be alarmed at the light from outside the ship, that's our glow from friction with the gaseous envelope around Mars."

Sunul was prepared for the deceleration of the ship when it entered the Martian atmosphere. Even though the gas was tenuous, the outer surface of the ship would begin to rise in temperature until the wings created enough lift so the ship could slow and glide to the surface of the planet. Landing in the dark would be a new experience for him. In these last few minutes, he was hoping Captain Thorp guided the ship into the atmosphere at the correct angle so they didn't ricochet off into space. Just like landing an airplane on earth, the landing of a spaceship on the surface of a planet was much more difficult than taking off.

Chapter 7

Sunul noticed three other individuals had exited the ship with the travelers: two women and a man. He recognized Mr. Simonson, so the two women must have been the captain, Ms. Thorp, and the co-pilot. The short ride to the domed colony was uneventful. The eight passengers were on their own, the subway car was completely automatic.

When they reached the dome, the vehicle slowed to a stop. A recorded voice said, "Please do not stand until you have arrived on the surface." The entire subway car was elevated to the surface. There was a loud hissing, and after ten seconds, the doors slid open, allowing the passengers to exit into a small lobby area where several people were waiting. Sunul swung his belongings over his shoulder and stood beside Dr. Corcoran.

"Know any of these people, doc?"

"Nope, but I think I see Dr. Winslow, although she's a little older than when they took her picture for the agency." Art pointed at the young woman. She smiled and walked toward him and Sunul.

The pretty doctor extended her hand, not knowing whether Art or Sunul was Dr. Corcoran. Art moved forward and said, "I'm Dr. Arthur Corcoran, your replacement. It's nice to meet you, Dr. Winslow."

"Likewise, Dr. Corcoran." They shook hands and Winslow glanced at Sunul with a questioning look. "Should I know you?"

"You know my wife, Dr. Gina Burke. We've never met, but I've heard a lot about you from Gina."

"Well," she smiled, "I hope she kept some of the information confidential."

Sunul understood what she meant and laughed. "She didn't divulge any intimate details. Don't worry."

"I'll show you gentlemen where you can bunk temporarily. After you get to know our little city, you might find different locations you might like, but we don't have many unoccupied places. Most of our neighborhoods are filled to capacity, unless you need to stay off base for any length of time. Other arrangements will be made in that case."

Shania yawned as they began walking through the complex divided into blocks, each containing six Quonset-like buildings made from the hulls of used rocket ships. Sunul thought he recognized a section recovered from the ship alpha group had crash landed on Mars seven years earlier. As soon as he was alone with Dr. Winslow, he would inform her of his sister's cancer. He wanted to ask her to contact Gina when she arrived on Earth so Gina could work on a cancer cure using samples of Shania's blood to develop a universal remedy for the dreaded disease. Gina had mentioned that perhaps Shania could work with her on the project.

When Art, Sunul, and Shania arrived at the building assigned to the two men, Shania excused herself and turned to go to her residence to get some sleep.

"Before you go, Dr. Winslow, what time is it?"

"It's four-thirty-one. Good night."

Art said, "Thank-you. Good night."

Shania waved and continued walking. Sunul waved as she walked away, oblivious of his gesture. He thought, "Oh well, I'll thank her later today."

Thirty minutes later, Art and Sunul were sound asleep in their bachelor quarters. Sunul wasn't physically tired, but needed to relax after the week in space. During the entire journey, he had wished he had been piloting the ship. When Sunul stretched out on his less-than-comfortable bed, he thought of Gina and the kids and how they were managing with the Patels.

The alarm went off at 7:00 a.m. Sunul had dreamed and remembered his revulsion at the sight of Hugh's mutilated hand.

"You were talking in your sleep," Art informed Sunul.

"What'd I say?"

"What I heard was 'Oh no! Hugh.' —a friend of yours?"

Sunul nodded as he slipped into some clean clothes. "Hugh had gotten a prosthetic hand a few days before I left for Mars."

"Well, Sunul, I'm hungry. You know of a place to eat, or do we make something here?"

Sunul smiled, "Let's try going out. I'm not much of a cook and I don't think I should trust you yet."

"I was pondering the same thing." Art grinned as he headed out the door. The two men had no idea where to find something to eat, although, had they looked, there was a map of the dome in their bathroom. Art stopped the first person they encountered.

"Is there a place to eat?"

"Sure, Rose's diner. Two huts to the right and three to the north. I'm Ned Turcel, APAQC. You new arrivals?"

Sunul and Art shook hands with Ned. Sunul quizzed, "What's APAQC?"

"That's atmospheric pressure and air quality control."

"Oh, you must know Jim Frieland."

"Jim? Oh, he tells all newcomers something different. He's full of excrement from the nearest black hole. He's CIA. He probably came along with you guys to keep an eye on you. That's about all he does. Nobody likes him—he's a loner."

"Thanks for the info, Ned. We'll see you around."

"Yeah, later." Ned turned and proceeded walking briskly as if he were late for an important meeting.

A minute later, Sunul and Art were entering the diner. A woman and a man were sitting at the counter drinking coffee and conversing. They looked up at the newcomers and nodded. Art and Sunul joined them at two of the three vacant bar stools. The diner looked as if it had come from an old movie circa the 1950s. There were menus between salt, pepper, and sugar containers.

"What can I do for you?" A female voice was coming from the menu as if by magic, but Sunul had noticed the menu was thicker than a normal menu on Earth. It had a built in com system.

Art laughed and said, "I'd like a scrambled egg, two slices of toast, and black coffee. Oh, and some orange juice."

Sunul leaned toward the menu, still standing between the sugar and salt containers, and said, "Same for me, but make it two eggs, please."

The menu answered back, "Thank-you gentlemen, it will be three to four minutes."

Art had to laugh. He was thinking about surgical equipment able to talk to the doctor during an operation and clamps arguing with scalpels about which was more important.

Sunul was amused by Art's laugh, but lack of comment. "I'm thinking our breakfast will be served by an android."

"Uh-huh. Maybe wearing a nurse's uniform." Art continued to smile until the woman sitting beside him turned and said, "Oh, Rose is a real person. She's a botanist and just cooks to try out some of her Martian vegetables on us. She'll probably put something on your plate that you won't recognize, like blue asparagus, or white carrots. By the way, I'm Dr. Amy Adahl, and this is my husband Dr. Frank Adahl. We're geologists. On Mars, we're called areologists. We're on our way back to Earth on the next ship."

Art introduced himself and Sunul and mentioned, "I'm replacing Dr. Winslow. She's been here on three tours with only two years on Earth between her first and second tours. I think she's had enough of Mars for one lifetime."

Amy was nodding her head and said, "I've stood by the outer dome wall and looked across the Martian landscape. It sure makes one feel trapped when you know imminent death awaits you in the other side of that polycarbonate wall unless you're wearing an EVA suit. I'll be glad to get back on Earth where I can hike without one of those suits or worry about the air I'm breathing."

"That's right, and we've only been here for two years," observed her husband. "It was kind of suspenseful the first couple of months, and then the excitement of the new environment wore off. I hope you gentlemen enjoy your time on Mars. Good luck."

The Adahls left the diner without further comments. Art and Sunul watched the couple stop and talk with a woman, but they couldn't see who it was. However, they would know in a moment; she appeared to be coming toward Rose's.

"Here you are, gentlemen—food from the best diner on Mars." She laughed as she slid the plates in front of the two men. Art and Sunul joined in the levity, realizing Rose's was the only diner on Mars. Rose was pushing forty, according to Sunul; her thin frame, lined face, and dark complexion seemed to indicate she had been exposed to too much sun. She couldn't weigh more than 110 pounds on Earth. He decided to ask where she was from.

"Where did you grow up, Rose?" He took a bite of toast and loaded a fork with eggs. There was a pause before Rose answered; she was watching the door open.

"Hi, Doc." Rose looked back at Sunul and said, "Argentina—on a farm outside of La Rioja. I'm twenty-five percent Andes Indian. My grandfather was a 100% Native Indian mountain climber from Chile."

Dr. Winslow waved and sat at the counter. "Coffee please, Rose." Shania smiled and said, "I hope I'm not interrupting anything, but I need you, Sunul, to accompany me on an adventure with the new geologists. They've already discovered a cave they want to explore as a potential source of water. They don't need a physician, but I'm curious about what they might find." She looked at Art and said, "I'd ask you to go too, Dr. Corcoran, but I think one of us should stay in the dome—just in case someone needs a doctor while I'm gone."

Art swallowed a sip of hot coffee, almost coughed, and replied, "That's all right. I need to investigate the dome and start getting acquainted with prospective patients. How long will you be gone?"

Shania glanced at Sunul, paused a couple of seconds, and answered, "I don't think it will take more than a few hours." She grinned, "Don't worry, we won't miss a meal."

"Great! That had me worried. When do we go?" Sunul was anxious to go exploring.

"As soon as you finish eating and I finish my coffee. My husband is cooking tonight and we want you both to come over. We'll eat around six-thirty."

"Sounds good to me." Art and Shania glanced at Sunul, waiting to see if Sunul was going to acknowledge the invitation. Sunul was thinking of something else; he realized that if he was going to be on an expedition with Dr. Winslow, he would have the opportunity to tell Shania about his sister's cancer and be able to mention what Gina had said about getting a sample of Shania's blood.

Art broke the silence. "What do you think, Sunul?"

"Oh! Sorry. I was thinking about something my wife said." He smiled and whispered, so Rose wouldn't hear, "I'm ready for some home cooking."

An hour later, Adele and Toby Scott, Sunul, and Shania were on the subway car, loaded with equipment and moving toward the spaceport. Each of the members of the expedition had on an EVA suit but without the helmet. They were conserving the air for the suits until they left the subway car; they had to wear their helmets when outside the car.

Toby explained, "We believe there is a secondary passage or old tributary shaft that connects to the subway shaft. According to the diagrams made for the subway, the side-shaft was sealed with concrete. We want to see what's in that shaft."

Sunul was thinking about getting access to the side-shaft when the car slowed and a buzzer sounded. It had only taken six minutes to reach the concrete patch.

A robotic sounding voice said, "EVA suits must be functioning. Please press the exit panel when everyone is ready to leave the vehicle."

Adele surveyed the crew and everyone reported they were ready to exit. She pressed the green panel and it immediately turned red. The information screen flashed, "WARNING: Outside pressure is six millimeters of mercury, 95.4 % carbon dioxide." The side door slid open and Toby dropped to the subway tracks two feet below. When he left the car, the outside vehicle LEDs came on and the concrete seal at the cavern wall was obvious.

"Sunul, please hand me the small laser cutter." Toby waited, looking into the car.

Sunul stepped over a large bag of unknown contents and retrieved the tool laying on the back row of seats. He lifted the battery pack and cable, laser gun, and scanned the other bags.

"That's all we need for now, Sunul." Toby was anxious to get started, Sunul could hear it in his voice.

With the equipment on the floor next to the door, Sunul dropped to the ground, and began to inspect the concrete plug in the old wall opening.

"Hand me the cutter, Sunul. We need to remove a portion of the concrete so we can look behind the cement."

"You're going to cut the cement?" Sunul knew the cement was going to be much more difficult to cut through than the rock wall. Toby's comment led Sunul to believe the geologist's knowledge of laser cutting was much less than his. Sunul decided to let the geologist find out for himself. Toby accepted the cutting tool and turned toward the cement wall. Sunul attached the cable to the battery pack and stepped behind Toby. Sunul tapped Toby on the shoulder and said, "You've got power. Proceed."

After ten minutes of frustration, Toby shut down the beam and said, "That's really tough going. Maybe I should cut the rock instead."

"Good idea, Toby, but cut on the other side of the concrete."

Toby didn't take Sunul's advice and began to slice into the rock near where he had tried to cut the cement. There was a sudden explosion which knocked both men to the ground. A portion of the concrete wall had blown out, releasing rock fragments and fist-sized chunks of cement toward the subway car.

Adele screamed, "The doctor is hurt, Toby! Her helmet is cracked open. She's on the floor gasping."

Sunul was the first to react. He rolled over, got to his feet and jumped into the car and wiped off the faceplate of his helmet. When he saw Shania's cracked headgear, he knew what to do immediately.

He yelled, "Where's the doctor's emergency kit?"

Adele pointed to one of the bags on the floor and said, "What can I do?"

"Get me the roll of sealing tape—quickly!" Sunul had placed his left glove over the major crack in Shania's helmet and reached toward the roll of tape Adele held out, but decided to have Adele manipulate the roll of tape. His left hand was still pressing against Shania's helmet. "Tear off several ten-inch strips—hurry! Half a dozen at least."

As Adele handed Sunul the strips of tape, he began to seal the major opening in the helmet. Four strips of tape sealed the major break. Three more strips sealed the minor cracks. Shania was now breathing normally, but was unconscious. Sunul inspected the fabric of her EVA suit, but couldn't find any other breaches. He watched her face and she began to squint and blink her eyes.

"What happened?" she asked. "Who is in front of me? Something is blocking my view."

Sunul answered, "It's me—Sunul. Your helmet was broken open by a projectile of rock or cement when Toby cut open the side chamber. The sealed chamber must have been pressurized with carbon dioxide. Adele and I sealed your helmet with tape from your medical kit."

Shania was trying to get up as she said, "Thank-you." She paused for a moment and then followed with, "My air level is running low; I need a new cartridge."

Sunul and Adele helped the doctor get to her feet, although when she stood, she was a little woozy. Sunul helped her sit by the wall of the vehicle and he sat down beside her to prevent her from tipping over.

"I feel a little nauseous."

"Don't throw up in your suit, doc. You'll regret it—big time!"

Chapter 8

"Adele! Is the doctor all right?" Toby was looking into the subway car, wiping the dust from his face plate.

"Yes. Sunul has patched her helmet, but she's low on air. The suit tried to keep the pressure up, but the fissures were too large. Most of her air escaped. We're going to have to cut short our investigation."

"Okay. At least we have a start. I'll get the laser equipment back in the car and we can return to the dome."

Adele screeched, "Toby, just leave the damned torch there. We're coming back later. No one will bother it. Get in the car! Please!"

Toby hesitated for a moment before reacting, but stepped into the subway car and touched the door seal panel. The rise in internal pressure could be seen on the digital wall display, but when it reached thirty percent an announcement could be heard. "Pressure leak! Hull integrity has been compromised. Use emergency speed to return to base. Do not remove headgear!"

Toby punched the red emergency panel which began to flash. The voice announced: "Be seated. Sudden acceleration will be initiated."

The subway car abruptly moved in reverse, almost knocking Toby down, but he held onto the back of a seat and sat down awkwardly. Two minutes later they were in the elevator, ascending to the surface. When the subway door opened, the air pressure indicator shot up to 100%.

The four riders had exited the car when they heard, "You may now remove your headgear." Sunul laughed, everyone had already taken off their helmet.

Shania commented, "We need to file a report immediately. The car needs to be repaired before anyone can use it."

"Where do I report it, Shania? You need to see Dr. Corcoran for a quick checkup. You might have had a concussion." Sunul was obviously concerned about her health. He also wanted to talk to Shania alone, hopefully in her office.

"You can file a report from my office; all offices are connected by computers."

That was going to be perfect. Sunul could finally get the most important request of his life finally out of his thoughts after two weeks of waiting for the opportunity to talk with Dr. Shania Winslow one-on-one.

Sunul put his arm around Shania's waist. "I think I'd better walk with you to your office. Your equilibrium might be off a little."

"We don't need to walk. We can take the hovercraft; it's on the roof. Follow me."

Sunul kept a close eye on Shania as they climbed the steps to the top of the subway elevator structure. A small hovercraft-taxi was warming up. Shania must have thrown a switch, or the craft motors came on automatically when they stepped on the roof. Sunul sat in the operator's seat next to Shania and said, "Which direction?"

"Up about twenty feet, then go to H-4; that's my office." She smiled knowing Sunul was wondering what she meant.

Following the doctor's instructions, Sunul took the craft straight up. When he looked around he saw each of the huts had markings on the roof. It reminded him of a chess board. The labels went from A-1 to A-3 on the eastern edge of the dome to N-1 to N-3 on the west. The center column hut labels went from H-1 to H-

14. Sunul piloted the craft from G-8 to H-4 and guided the taxi to the surface at the side of the hut. When the craft touched the surface, it automatically shut down the fans. Shania and Sunul entered the medical hut door and found Dr. Corcoran talking with James Frieland.

Frieland said hello and then left the office. Shania sat down and explained what had occurred in the subway tunnel.

"Thanks to the quick action of Sunul, I was only out for a minute or so. He patched my headgear with some tape and we returned to the dome at emergency speed."

"I'll give you a quick check up to see if you have any worrisome cerebral difficulties. From the way you just explained your experience, I don't believe you have anything to worry about, but you should remain quiet for the remainder of the day. I'll keep an eye on you. Have you talked with your husband?"

"No. He's on an expedition 200 miles out. He'll be back tomorrow. We'll have to postpone dinner."

Art suggested, "You can radio him."

"I don't want to bother him. He's got enough to think about that far away from the dome."

Sunul was interested and asked, "What's he doing so far out?"

Shania turned toward Sunul and said, "He and two other scientists are investigating Mar's core. They're setting off explosions and recording reflections. He didn't tell me any details—and I didn't ask." She moved her head slightly back toward Art and said, "I think I'll lie down now."

Sunul stepped closer, took Shania's arm and guided her into the adjacent room where three cots were used for temporary resting and patient evaluation procedures. When Shania was stretched out on the closest cot, Sunul glanced back and saw Dr. Corcoran talking on his com unit. It looked like he was involved in a discussion.

Sunul asked, "I need to talk to you alone, Dr. Winslow. Do you feel up to it now?"

Shania exhaled and took in a deep breath. She focused all her attention on Sunul and answered, "Sure, I'm feeling better already. What do you want to talk about?"

"Your blood." Sunul looked again at Corcoran. He was still talking. "My sister has cancer. She lives in France and is on chemotherapy, but hasn't seen much progress. Gina said she might develop an anticancer drug from your blood—using antibody-mimicry response cells—it's something relatively new."

Shania frowned. "I've never heard of it; it must be very new. I don't know of any literature about it. I suppose it's called AMR."

"I think so. Anyway, Gina wants you to work on it with her when you return to Earth. I hope you are interested, my sister might need a revolutionary treatment. Gina said I should ask you for a blood specimen—in case I should get back before you. Would that be possible?"

"But you'll be searched, Sunul. Off world specimens are not allowed on Earth-going ships since two of the alpha group children can't be located for study. You know that."

"You're right, but I can smuggle a sample back to Earth. Rob Griswalt, from the alpha group, developed a compartment inside my com unit where a specimen can be concealed. I only need 100 microliters of blood."

Shania smiled, "That's one drop I will gladly spare. Show me the device and I'll donate a sample."

Sunul extracted his com unit from his pocket and entered the code Rob had given him. A segment of the unit's side popped open and a rectangular solid was ejected. The plastic-looking solid resembled a one-inch-square memory module, but its function was completely different.

Sunul gave the tiny unit to Shania and said, "You must use a syringe and remove the desired volume of gas from the container and then inject the blood sample. The sample can be kept for two weeks, maybe longer. Sodium fluoride and a tiny refrigeration segment are inside the unit."

Shania turned the little rectangular solid over and inspected it. "If it can do what you say, it is fantastic. Nano-technology has really progressed. What powers it?"

"Rob told me it's powered by a quartz crystal that oscillates at sixteen megahertz. I don't really know how it works. When you have it loaded, I'll hide it in my com unit."

"How are you doing, Shania?" Dr. Corcoran was standing in the doorway. Shania palmed the storage device.

"I'm feeling much better, Art. Lying down seems to have done the trick."

Sunul took a step toward the door, turned and said, "I guess I'll be leaving to talk with the areologists. We'll check on the tunnel where the accident occurred." Sunul continued toward the door where Art was standing. They shook hands as they passed each other.

Art said, "Thanks."

Shania called out, "Thanks for your help, Sunul. You and your wife have come to my aid twice now."

"You're welcome. I'll talk with you again before you leave for Earth."

Sunul had dinner with the Scotts and the Nobles. He didn't have much to contribute to the areologists' and botanists' scientific discussions. He asked a few intelligent questions just to show the scientists that he was paying attention.

The next morning, Sunul walked by the medical office, hoping to see Shania and retrieve the blood storage module, but he was very disappointed, Shania was gone. There was a note from Dr. Corcoran saying he would be out of the office until early afternoon. Sunul returned to his hut where he received a call from the botanist, Roy Noble.

"We'd like you to accompany us to the site you visited yesterday. The Scotts, Janis, and I are going out there on the repaired subway car. Dr. Winslow and her husband took the other subway car to the spaceport. They left for Earth earlier today; the flight was rescheduled all of a sudden. If they hadn't taken it, they would have had to wait another week, maybe two."

"Just a moment, Roy." Sunul took a moment to consider his options. Shania wouldn't have left without leaving the module, so she must have given Dr. Corcoran a message for Sunul.

Corcoran was gone for probably six hours, so Sunul could go with the scientists to the side tunnel. "Okay, I'll be ready in a few minutes. I have to eat something first."

"Right. We'll be leaving in forty-five minutes. Will that give you enough time?"

Sunul checked his watch. "Sure. I'll meet you at the subway station at 8:30."

"Thanks, Sunul. We'll leave then."

Sunul ate quickly, showered, and donned his EVA suit. He left his com unit with his city clothes, grabbed his helmet, and set out for the subway terminal. As he walked, his thoughts kept returning to Shania's unexpected departure. "Why hadn't she called him? She must have been in a rush and it was too early to call." Those were the only excuses he could think of. Then he thought of another. She was with her husband and didn't want him to know what was going on. She didn't want to get him involved in any clandestine activities. That was the most probable reason she didn't call. Dr. Corcoran probably held the key to the location of the specimen module. But maybe the specimen wouldn't be necessary; Shania was returning to Earth before Sunul, so she could contact Gina without the secret sample stored in Sunul's com unit.

As planned, the investigation team set out at 8:30. Ten minutes later, they were peering into the formerly sealed side chamber. Toby and Adele were the first humans to see behind the concrete since it was put in place nearly ten years previously.

Two feet over their heads, small stalactites dotted the roof of the cavern. The projections extended beyond eyesight and indicated mineral-rich water had once been present. Some stalagmites could be seen starting ten feet back from the concrete wall. Closer stalagmites had been destroyed, probably eroded by the workers that had put the concrete in place.

The botanists, Janis and Roy Noble, remarked about the blue and green crystals evident on the walls of the cavity. They wanted to identify the crystals, but they suspected they were hydrates of copper and nickel ions. After their brief inspection with laser lights, Janis asked Sunul, "Is there any way we can get a door placed in this wall to keep the subway tunnel isolated from the cavern, but still allow us access?"

Sunul thought for a few seconds and replied, "I know of a way to do it, but I'll have to talk with one of the engineers in the dome. If you want to go into the cavern today, I'll cut a larger opening for you. I can use the equipment we left yesterday. Should take about ten minutes."

Before Toby could react, Sunul had the laser cutter in his hands and had begun to slice into the rock about three feet to the side of the concrete plug where it had blown out the day before. Toby stepped back to avoid the shower of sparks and gleaming embers, giving a wide berth to the rivulets of glowing red and orange molten rock collecting in puddles on the floor of the subway tunnel. Sunul straddled the puddles and guided the laser beam, cutting one-foot cubes of material from the wall, until he had an opening large enough for a person in an EVA suit to pass through unencumbered. When he had finished melting off the jagged edges, he stepped back and said, "I'll try to get a hatch installed tomorrow. Go ahead and investigate the interior while I put this equipment away. Be careful about the hot material on the floor."

An hour later at Rose's diner in the dome, the group had gathered for lunch and were discussing what they had seen behind the concrete. Rose had approached the group to take their orders. "Did you hear?"

"What's that, Rose?" Adele looked up from the menu.

"The morning flight to Earth never made it into orbit and crashed 800 miles out. Nobody was injured, but they only have enough supplies for five days. We don't have any way to reach them; they're stranded."

Sunul was shocked. Shania would never make it back to work with Gina on a cancer cure for his sister.

He had to find out if Shania had left a blood sample, but Dr. Corcoran wouldn't be back for a couple more hours. What if Shania hadn't loaded a sample into the module? He might have to return to Earth empty-handed.

Chapter 9

Adele was the first of the group to react audibly. "Can't we rescue them? Surely there's a way we can get to the crash site and bring the crew and passengers back to the dome."

Sunul knew that the crawlers could only move for an extended time at a top speed of twelve miles per hour and their batteries had to be recharged every six hours. Carrying extra batteries was a problem; the crawler batteries were sealed in a compartment that could only be accessed using equipment located in the dome. No portable tools were available and no charger would be accessible on the Martian landscape.

"Where's the boneyard?" Sunul was thinking he could convert a discarded crawler to a rocket-propelled sled that could cross the Martian surface up to fifty miles per hour. He hoped the motors from the old 5K23m ship were not destroyed. He expected the three motors would be stored in their quiescent state, but he imagined they would only need one engine for the thrust necessary to propel the sled.

He surveyed the faces around him, but there was no response. He raised his voice, "Rose! Where's the boneyard?"

Rose stepped up to the counter with half the orders. She passed out the plates and said, "I assume you mean the junkyard? We cremate human remains."

"Yes, junkyard."

"About eight years ago a ship from the Kuiper Belt skidded across the sand not far from here. All our debris is taken there."

"Great, I know where that is."

"You do?"

"Uh-huh. I was the pilot." He grinned and Rose extended her hand.

"Your landing on Mars is a legend, Mr. Burke. Do these people realize what you did?"

"That's not important, Rose. Who is the mechanical engineer for the dome?"

"There are two of them. They have twelve hour shifts." She rolled her eyes up and squinted, "Ah, Mike Haricot is on call right now. Want me to give him a buzz?"

"Please do. Have him meet me at the western gate in fifteen minutes. Tell him to bring a sketch pad."

"Will do, Mr. Burke." She turned and went behind a partition to the kitchen.

"Thanks, Rose."

Sunul practically inhaled his lunch, drank some juice and coffee, stood, and said, "I'll probably see you tomorrow. Hopefully, I'll have a hatch to place in the opening I cut in the rock."

Roy slid off his bar stool and said, "Can we help you with anything?"

"No, but thanks for the offer." Sunul left the diner and hurried toward the west gate.

A man in an EVA suit was standing at the inner door of the exit chamber when Sunul arrived. The men introduced themselves and Sunul explained what he had in mind.

Haricot said, "You need an EVA suit, Mr. Burke."

"Call me Sunul, Mike."

Sunul had forgotten about his own EVA equipment, but inside the door of the chamber, extra EVA suits were stored in a closet-like structure. He donned the large size and Mike assisted him with his headgear. Sunul did likewise and they verified the doors at both ends of the chamber were sealed. Mike pressed the exit panel and they watched the display on the side wall as the pressure dropped to 0.01 atmosphere.

The chamber door swung open and the two men walked to the crawler that was parked about ten meters away. Mike took the driver's chair. Sunul moved the sketch pad from the bench seat and sat beside Mike. As mike drove the crawler, Sunul sketched what he was thinking for the rescue vehicle.

"We're approaching the ship you brought to Mars. Except for some sand drifts, nothing has changed. The engines are dormant inside the hull."

"That's good news. Where's the junked crawler?"

"We put it in the cargo hold and removed the treads. The navigation system is still intact. We can jury-rig a power connection from the engine you want to use."

Mike drove the crawler up a sand drift and slowed when the treads began to slip. The crawler nearly stalled when on the hull, but surged forward with a little coaxing. Descending the steep sand incline made Sunul grab the dash and the seat to keep from being thrown around the cabin.

"Sorry about that. I thought it would be easier to go up and over than to circle around the end of the old ship. I was wrong."

Sunul's eyes were scanning the gleaming metal surface of his old ship, amazed at its great condition. Mike noticed Sunul's interest.

"A little sand erosion is all you might see, Sunul. Nearly zero water in the atmosphere makes rusting almost nonexistent." Mike shut down the engine and popped the doors on both sides of the crawler as well as the rear cargo door. "Show me your sketch so I can locate what we need to salvage. We'll have to assemble the vehicle right here."

Sunul showed Mike his drawings and commented, "If you can locate the metal for the struts and pads, I'll get one of the engines ready to transport. I envision the engine beneath the crawler cabin to maintain a low center of gravity and make the flow of fuel from the surface to the engine intake port automatic. A scoop will feed Martian soil into the motor.

"Sounds good to me. You want to use one of the exhaust nozzles from an engine for the foot pads?"

"Yeah. They'll withstand the frictional heating as we cruise across the surface. Cut the cone into 120 degree sections and mount each one on a strut. You'll have to solve the cushioning problem so the struts won't get torn away from the crawler cabin."

"Will do. I've got an idea how to solve that difficulty."

Sunul climbed into the cargo hold and wiped Martian sand off one of the nuclear engines. The weight of an engine on Earth would be about a metric ton, 2,200 pounds, but on Mars it was about 840 pounds, still too heavy for manual lifting. He attached a cable to the sleeping engine, and hooked it to the rear of the active crawler. Sunul swung into the driver's seat, dragged the engine from the cargo bay and oriented it into position for attachment to the junked crawler. After attaching tow lines to the bottom of the old crawler, he pulled it from the cargo hold and lined it up beside the engine. Then he joined Mike, who was inside the old survival ship's main cabin cutting metal for struts from walls.

Mike stopped cutting for a moment and said, "Take that pile out to the crawler and come back for more."

Sunul carried half-a-dozen I-beams outside and then stopped to watch as more stripping of the old ship occurred. It had been Sunul's opinion that Rob Griswalt had been the best he had ever seen with a laser torch, but he was reevaluating that notion. The torch, guided by Mike's hands, was making surgical cuts through the ship as if it were a beast possessing an overpowering hunger for metal beams.

The two men took a brake to replace their dwindling supply of air for their EVA suits and to get a drink. Mike explained to Sunul what he had in mind for the strut system and Sunul said he could fashion the circular springs from strips of the ship's hull. An hour later, all the pieces were cut and ready to assemble.

Welding and bolting the pieces together took a little more than two hours before they called it quits. Sunul was anxious to get back to the dome to talk with Dr. Corcoran to see if Shania had left a sample with him or a clue to where she might have hidden it. As the crawler moved across the sandy surface, Mike and Sunul formulated a scheme for raising the motor into position and attaching it to the bottom of the altered crawler. They decided to finish the construction of the vehicle in the morning when adequate daylight was present.

Sunul entered Corcoran's office within fifteen minutes of returning to the dome. The doctor was visiting with a patient, so Sunul waited until the woman left. Art saw Sunul waiting and asked, "What can I help you with, Sunul. I hope you're not injured."

"Nothing like that, doc. Any chance that Shania left a note for me?"

"Oh! I almost forgot about that." He fished a folded piece of paper from his breast pocket and handed it to Sunul. "Shania asked that I not look at it. I didn't."

"Thanks, Art. There's no big mystery about it. It has to do with my sister. She asked for Shania's medical opinion." Sunul hadn't lied, he just didn't want to explain. The fewer people involved, the better.

As Sunul was leaving the office, he turned and asked, "Can we have dinner this evening? About 6:45? I've got some questions for you."

Art didn't hesitate, "Sure, see you at Rose's at a quarter to seven."

On the way to his quarters, Sunul unfolded the stationery and read the note: "When you were on 5K23m, I'll bet you didn't have to worry about keeping things cold." Sunul sat down and read the note again. He was a little puzzled at first, but after a shower and donning clean clothes, he was thinking clearly. Shania's note made perfect sense. She had stored the blood sample in the medical office refrigerator. Now, Sunul had to sneak into Art's office and find the item hidden in the fridge. He knew the tiny container's location wouldn't be obvious.

It had been ten days since Sunul had communicated with Gina. When he met with Art, he would try to find the location of the communication center; the colony doctor would certainly know that bit of information, even though he was a newcomer. The com center wasn't marked on the map at the dome's western entrance.

So, Sunul now had three items to address with Dr. Corcoran. The most immediate was what supplies were necessary to carry on the rescue vehicle. The second was to get to the com center to transmit a message to Earth, and the last was to recover the blood sample from the medical facility refrigerator. He envisioned the third matter was going to be the most difficult.

Twenty minutes before Sunul met Art for dinner, he called Mike to schedule the time for the morning trek to the boneyard. They agreed to meet at the western dome gate at 8:00 a.m. Then Sunul walked to Rose's and arrived a few minutes early. Dr. Corcoran was already there sipping a glass of ice water.

Sunul sat on a stool next to the doctor. "You're early, doc."

"Yeah. I wanted to relax a bit before your high-powered brain started its frontal attack on my cerebral matter."

"You had a tough day?"

Art almost laughed, "Five patients, all who would recover without my help. I gave four of them Martian sugar pills and one some aspirin."

"Martian sugar?"

"Uh-huh. I added a drop of red food coloring to the sugar pills." Art grinned and Sunul laughed.

"Did Shania warn you about the ills of the Martian colonists?"

"Nah, they told me about it at the medical training facility for astronauts. If they come back with real symptoms, I'll prescribe something a little stronger. Most people here haven't gone through astronaut training and they aren't used to confinement in the dome or EVA suits. They usually adjust before they go crazy. I just have to watch them for signs."

They spoke into the menu and ordered dinner. While they were waiting, Art gave Sunul a list of emergency equipment to take to the survivors of the crash. Food, water, and extra EVA equipment were the major items Art had recorded. A few minutes later, Rose brought them their meals. Sunul asked Art if he was married. Art answered with a grunt and shook his head. Sunul didn't pursue the matter.

Art told Sunul the communications center was at location A-2 inside the eastern edge of the dome. The parabolic antennae were located about 100 meters farther east of the dome. The cables were underground and a remote computer kept the ten-foot dishes aligned with the earth. After dinner, Sunul was going to record a message and take a walk to A-2.

An opportunity to work refrigeration into their conversation had not occurred, so Sunul would have to find a way to search the medical office fridge at some other time. He might have to pay the office a visit when the doctor was out on a call.

As the men were having desert, Art volunteered, "I was engaged once, Sunul."

"What happened?"

"We took a trip to the Colorado Rockies for some outdoor activities. She had told me she had been looking forward to it for some time, but when she found out we weren't going to be staying in a luxury hotel, she lost interest and we returned home after camping one day. I hadn't expected to see a completely different side of her—she was a spoiled brat, so I made a decision to change my environment and move to Mars."

Sunul started laughing and said, "Pardon me for laughing, but couldn't you find a spot that was farther away?"

Art smiled and replied, "It was either this or Antarctica."

"Well, you made a good choice, although Mars is probably a little more dangerous."

Chapter 10

After recording his message and a copy on his com device, Sunul set out for the transmitter. The Quonset building at A-2 had a replica of an antique radio microphone over the door. Someone must have smuggled it aboard a craft and brought it to Mars or a very clever person with carving tools had made it locally. Sunul entered the building and saw two racks of electronics standing in the middle of the floor. Around the apparatus were four desks, two of them occupied, by a female and a male, the others strewn with small piles of paper of different sizes and colors. Apparently organization was not of fundamental importance.

The young man looked up and asked, "What can we do for you, Mr. Burke?"

Startled that he was addressed by name, Sunul asked, "Have we met before?"

"No, sir. I recognized you from an old wanted poster. I collect 'em. I have all eight of the members of alpha group. I'm glad the charges were dropped."

"Thanks. I'd like to send a short message to my wife, and I'd like you to show me how things work—not the details, just what you do to send and receive messages to and from Earth and satellites."

"I guess I should introduce myself and my wife. I'm Will Telman and my coworker is my wife, Dawn." Will stood beside his wife. He was thin, head shaved, and sported a full black beard. Sunul wondered how they had met.

"Glad to meet you—William Tell, and you, Dawn." Sunul grinned, "I suppose you've heard that before." Sunul shook hands with the couple.

Dawn laughed and said, "Many times, and also Dawn Tell dark. We thought those jokes wouldn't follow us to Mars, but that was wishful thinking."

"I won't push my luck. Will and Dawn will do fine, or do you like Mrs. and Mr. Telman?"

"The Mr. and Mrs. sound too old for us. Maybe after we have some little Martians," she laughed.

"So how do I send a message to Earth?"

Dawn, a good-looking willowy blonde, smiled and held out a sheet of yellow paper. "Just fill out this form and I'll send the message while Will shows you around." She motioned for Sunul to sit at one of the other desks. She rushed to clear room for him to write by pushing three piles of paper to the side. She laid a pencil on the writing surface, stepped away, and returned to her desk.

Sunul wrote a short paragraph telling Gina and the kids about the upcoming rescue, signed, "Love you all," and gave the yellow form to Dawn. While Dawn was processing Sunul's message, Will began pointing out the various electronic units and their functions. Sunul was holding his com unit and when Will pointed to the transmitter, Sunul stepped closer to it, feigned special interest, pressed the send pad on his com unit, and as they moved to the other side of the rack, he laid his device next to the radio broadcast equipment. His secret message would be transmitted continuously, hitching a ride on all out-going messages until he left the communications center.

Sunul made himself breakfast at seven the next morning, showered, and donned his EVA equipment. Art was still asleep when Sunul departed for the western gate. When he arrived to meet with Mike, there was a stack of medical equipment, food, and some tools piled next to the inside door of the gate. Art must have gotten most of the material placed at the gate before he retired, however, the tools must have been rounded up by Mike, probably while Sunul was getting up. Sunul was encouraged to see that Mike realized the importance of their undertaking.

Sunul heard the hissing of gases flowing into the gate chamber and stepped back when the indicator light turned green. Mike stepped into the dome, removed his helmet, and greeted Sunul, "Morning. Help me get the rest of this stuff into the crawler and we'll be on our way to the boneyard."

"You sound rested, Mike. When did you get here?"

"Fifteen minutes ago. I didn't want to waste time so I started moving things into the crawler. We might have to leave some items out there when we go for the downed vehicle. There will be at least eight of us returning to the dome and we might lack space in the rescue sled. Do you know if anyone was injured?"

"Rose said no one was injured, but they only have food for four more days. We need to get this project finished so we can pick them up."

It took ten minutes to get everything loaded. Sunul noticed a snowplow-like blade was attached to the crawler. Sunul guessed Mike was going to be moving sand in order to attach the struts and nuclear engine to the underside of the reconfigured crawler. When they arrived at the junkyard, they unloaded the rescue supplies and assembly equipment and set to work.

Mike moved sand to create a plateau about six feet high and then pulled the old crawler on top. Now they had room to weld the struts to the base of the old vehicle. Sunul had guessed right. After the struts and skids were attached, the rebuilt crawler was positioned over the nuclear engine. Levers and muscle power were used to raise the engine enough to secure it to the bottom of the rebuilt crawler. Once the engine was attached, Mike fashioned an adjustable scoop to the front of the engine to feed new fuel into the reaction chamber.

Sunul had promised the geologists he would supply them with a hatch that could be tightly sealed separating the subway tunnel from the cave behind the concrete plug. Mike and Sunul cut the last exterior hatchway and door from the old space ship and attached a towline from it to the crawler. Mike took the hatch back to the dome and Sunul followed in the rescue vehicle. The maiden voyage of the reconfigured crawler worked better than expected. Although only a few miles had been logged, Sunul was satisfied the sand sled was going to work when Mike and he took the 1,600 mile roundtrip rescue voyage.

It was two in the afternoon when the two men set out for the stranded flight crew and passengers. Besides the food and extra EVA suits present, Sunul doubled the amount of oxygen in case the return trip met with problems such as unforeseen breakdowns. Mike had lashed extra metal beams and battery packs to the roof, but hoped he wouldn't need them for repairs.

Sunul wanted to drive the vehicle nonstop to the crash site, load the passengers and crew, and return to the dome as quickly as possible. Sunul took the first two-hour driving stint and gradually increased the speed in 5 mph increments, settled on 40 mph, feeling comfortable at that speed. After half an hour, nothing had fallen off the three legged sled, so he increased the speed another 10 mph.

At 40 mph, Mike had gotten used to the vibrations and had nearly fallen asleep, but when he felt the increase to 50 mph, Mike joined Sunul on the driver's bench and began watching for rough spots ahead. He had begun to feel that some of the welds might be in danger of failing. He listened intently hoping he wouldn't hear any breaking or tearing of metal.

A tense fifteen minutes passed with only an occasional sound that he was unable to identify. He moved to the back of the cabin and looked out the windows. The marks from the three skids were obvious, as was the small rooster tail of sand and dust trailing behind the vehicle almost like a mist. He heard the sound again and watched the tracks. Then he realized the source of the bumping noise. The scoop occasionally touched ground to feed more sand into the engine. Now he could sit back and relax for almost an hour before he took over maneuvering around craters and rocky debris while Sunul spent time worrying about failing mechanical structures. Mike realized, when he was driving, his attention would have to be on steering, not on listening for failures.

Six hours into the rescue mission, Mike was back at the controls with the sun going down behind them. If they were to continue at 50 mph, they would run a risk of wrecking, so he slowed to 25 mph, the crawler lights illuminating the forward terrain for about 100 yards, leaving plenty of space to avoid obstacles or make an emergency stop.

When Mike took his place, Sunul had gotten something to eat to quell his stomach's growling, and fifteen minutes later he was sound asleep. He was back on 5K23m and Gina was outside the complex banging on the hatch yelling, "Come get me, Sunul!" Sunul was trying to move his legs, but they were stuck in a viscous mass. He would get one foot free and then he couldn't lift the other. He realized getting to the door was going to take hours, if he could overcome the sticky material covering the floor. Gina wouldn't make it; she would run out of air.

"Sunul! Wake up!" Mike reached over and shook Sunul. Mike had stopped the rescue sled, irregular rock boulders loomed at the edge of the lights about thirty meters in front of the vehicle.

Sunul was struggling to sit up, he was lifting his feet and his hands were over his head.

"Wha—what?" Sunul suddenly realized he had been dreaming. He wiped his face with his hand and sat up, frowning and blinking his eyes. "What's the problem, Mike? Did something break?"

"Nothing's wrong with the vehicle, look at what's in front of us."

Sunul moved forward and scanned the area illuminated by the headlamps. Boulders from one to three feet in diameter extended across the field of vision.

"Damn! Why didn't this show up on the satellite scan?" He answered his own question. The satellite images were taken when the sun was overhead; no shadows were cast by the rocky area and the GPS system didn't show the irregular surface either; its resolution wasn't fine enough.

"So what are we going to do, Sunul? Go around this crap?"

"How high is the engine above the ground?"

"Around four feet, the straps a little less. You want to go through the debris? We might clear all but the biggest barriers." Mike glanced at Sunul for any other possibilities.

"Well, we could skirt to the left or the right and maybe find a better place to avoid this stuff, but we'd lose time. I'm ready to go over it or shove it out of our path if we have to. What do you think?"

"I'm with you. Let's barge through. Hopefully, it will save some time. If we get stuck, we'll use the lasers and cut out a path."

"Okay. Let's forge ahead and see how far this debris field extends. We might be able to get clear and not waste too much time."

Mike added mass to the engine and increased thrust. The sled slowly moved forward toward the scattered rocks. When they were closer to the barriers, it appeared they had seen the worst of the ejecta. Mike checked the GPS screen and could see a large crater, two miles to the south, which seemed to be the source of the debris material. Steering between the large chunks of rock required tilting the gimbal from side to side repeatedly, but travelling between 10 and 12 mph for about seven minutes got them clear of the boulders with no damage to the struts.

When the rescue ship had completely cleared the scattered rocks, Mike slid his finger up the acceleration pressure panel to attain a speed of 40 mph. Sunul leaned back, relaxed, and in a couple of minutes was back asleep.

For six hours the two men forged through the Marian desert without any minor or major problems, but fifteen minutes into Sunul's next turn at driving, both men recognized a looming physical barrier. Sunul slowed the craft and stopped approximately thirty yards from the edge of a cliff. There was no reverse gear on the engine, so plenty of space was still available for turning north or south.

"Damn! I thought it was going to be clear sailing to the crash site. We'd better take a look, the sun's coming up. We don't want to waste daylight by turning and looking for another route."

Sunul responded, "I agree. Let's suit up and take a walk. It'll be good for our legs."

It was a channel about three or four yards deep and several hundred yards wide. The abrupt edge prevented passage without major damage to the vehicle. Sunul used his headgear camera to magnify the opposing edge of the channel. There was an opening they could negotiate to ascend to the top of the gorge and continue their trek to the downed transition ship.

Mike said, "This could have been one of the canals the early astronomers thought were made by intelligent beings. Too bad all those hours of peering through a telescope were wasted."

"Yeah. Those so-called canals were proven to be optical illusions long ago. Earth telescopes of that era wouldn't have been able to detect this structure. Probes sent to Mars showed canals didn't exist and the great telescopes weren't able to detect them either."

"Are we going to cut a passageway to the floor of the channel?"

"Let's do it. We'll trim off the edge and push the debris down slope to give us an incline the sled can follow. It's going to take an hour or so using the laser cutters and a shovel."

Sunul's estimate had been a little long. They were back in the sled and moving across the depressed surface in about forty minutes. Reshaping the abrupt channel edge had been easier than expected. The sled climbed the other side easily; the edge of the channel had crumbled in several places forming natural rock inclines. Sunul drove another hour and Mike took over.

Mike had eaten and was going to be driving into the morning sun, but he was prepared.

Sunul was squinting as he looked forward into the brilliant light. He thought the builders of the crawler should have include pulldown visors at the front windows. He glanced over at Mike and asked, "Did you bring sunglasses, Mike? Why didn't the manufacturers install visors?"

"No glasses, Sunul. We've got something much better." Mike reached forward and pressed twice on the touchscreen. All the windows in the cabin darkened; those facing the sun became a shade darker than all the others.

Sunul laughed, "Aha! Black magic!" He glanced at Mike. Mike was grinning.

"Martian ingenuity, Sunul—special technology imported; made in the USA."

Another half hour passed with the sun rising in front of them. Sunul watched the GPS position advance on the dash display screen. He wondered when the system would announce the closing distance to the crash site. Mike said, "I think I see the downed ship. I'm slowing down."

The female voice on the GPS system announced, "Target is four hundred meters directly east. Slow to fifteen meters per second. Twenty-six seconds to arrival."

Chapter 11

When Sunul heard the position system voice, he began climbing into his EVA suit. He knew the sled's Jetway had been removed. The only way for the travelers to transfer to the remodeled crawler was by EVA suits, but he wasn't sure the transition ship had enough units. Fortunately, Dr. Corcoran had provided for that possibility. The rescue vehicle had brought three extra medium size suits.

Mike tuned his radio to the transition ship's frequency and said, "This is Mike Haricot. I'm with Sunul Burke. How are you doing in there? Do you need any medical assistance? We brought some medical equipment courtesy of Dr. Corcoran."

"Thank God you've arrived. This is Emit Rudd, Captain of the ill-fated vessel. There are eight of us ready to transfer to your strange looking vehicle. You'll have to tell us how you got here. You want us to transfer wearing EVA units? I don't see a Jetway."

Sunul leaned forward to speak to the captain. "Has everyone got an EVA suit?"

Rudd answered, "No problem. We're all equipped and have extra compressed air. We'll bring it along. How long will it take to get back to the spaceport?"

"It took us about eighteen hours to get here, so it will take about the same time going back—unless we have a breakdown."

"You're worried about a breakdown?"

"This vehicle was assembled as quickly as we could fuse things together. We experienced a lot of vibrations as we crossed the surface; there is a distinct possibility of failure of the struts. I'm not worried about the cabin or the engine."

"In other words, we might have to do some walking?"

"Look, we're 800 miles from the dome. We'd never walk that far. I'm just warning that we might have to stop for repairs—we'll be carrying five times more weight on the way back compared to the way out—and even more weight because of luggage. We averaged about 45 mph coming out, but we'll have to be more careful returning. That will add time to our trip. Bring all the food from your ship. We might need it."

"All right, I understand. You want us all in EVA suits?"

"Yes. Then you can depressurize your craft. We'll drop our pressure so you can board the sled. When we're all inside, we'll pressurize the vehicle. Make sure you seal your hatches when you are all out. We want the recovery team to return with something that can be repaired."

It took nearly thirty minutes to get everyone on board and another ten minutes to load their luggage. The rescue vehicle was packed full and some luggage had to be stored on the roof. Mike had decided to drive for another half-hour. When the cabin was pressurized, all but two individuals removed their EVA suits and stored them under their seats. Mike and Sunul removed their headgear, but kept their suits on, even though they would be experiencing some discomfort in the somewhat restricted movement apparel. Until they knew how the sled performed with all the added weight, they wanted to be prepared for any emergencies.

Sunul moved from the front bench so he could sit beside Shania and her husband, Ed.

Ed sat next to a window in the rear of the cabin with Shania beside him on the wall-to-wall bench seat.

Sunul sat beside Shania and asked, "Did you have any problems on the ship when it went down?"

"Before I answer your question, we want to thank you for coming after us." Shania patted Sunul on the shoulder and continued, "I'd like you to meet my husband, Ed. He's a seismologist."

Ed shook hands with Sunul and smiled. "When I first saw your invention, Sunul, it made me think of a water skipper trying to make love to a plastic straw." They all laughed, as did the rest of the survivors.

"Mike and I designed this thing with a little imagination, combined with physics and remnants of the ship I landed on Mars years ago. It would have been handy to have some wheels. I think your transition ship will have to be moved on wheels so it can be studied at the spaceport. I'd like to know why it didn't reach orbit. It's amazing that no one was hurt."

Ed motioned to the forward part of the cabin to a man in uniform. He stood and started back, but suddenly sat down when the sled lurched forward.

Mike yelled, "Sorry about that. I had to goose it to get us moving. I'm afraid we're going to have a rough trip." The sled began to move, lurching forward a few times as it picked up speed. "Sunul, I'm using fifty percent more power than before."

"Yeah, the extra weight is forcing the runners farther into the sand and there's a lot more friction. I think we'd better travel at 35 or 40 mph so we don't put too much stress on the struts. I hope the springs don't fail or we'll really have a rough ride. Try to follow our tracks as closely as possible."

"You got it." Mike waved the back of his hand to Sunul.

The uniformed gentleman moved down the center aisle until he could sit beside Sunul. He introduced himself. "I'm Nate Page, pilot."

"Sunul Burke. How you doing?" They shook hands and Sunul said, "Tell me what happened."

"Normal takeoff. When I went to 100% throttle, there was a flameout—just cut out completely. That's never happened before. That was the 187th liftoff—first failure. Very unusual."

"What'd you think?"

"I thought if we went down, we were screwed. I didn't think there was a rescue ship on Mars. Fortunately you and Mike were able to save our asses."

Sunul smiled, "We're not in the colony yet, my friend."

"We are very lucky you are on Mars. I have the utmost confidence in your ability, Mr. Burke. I know about your previous visit to Mars. That landing was miraculous."

"Thanks. Most of that landing came about from having no other choice and the cooperation of my crewmen. None of us wanted to sacrifice any of the four children on board. We were able to obtain good fortune from a bad situation—we were out of fuel and had no choice but to crash land. Say, could you takeover from Mike? He needs some rest and I have to talk with Dr. Winslow for a few minutes."

"Sure. I'll watch him for a few minutes and then assume control."

"You won't have any problems. This thing drives more like a car than a plane or rocket. All you have to do is follow the tracks."

Captain Page worked his way back to the front of the rescue vehicle and sat beside Mike. Mike had heard what Sunul had said and expected to be joined by a replacement driver.

Shania whispered to Sunul, "Did you find your package?"

Sunul shook his head. "Haven't had time. Mike and I spent two days building this pile of junk as a rescue vehicle. I'm a little surprised it's operating so well." He laughed and said, "Sorry it's not more comfortable."

"Well, your sample's in the refrigerator in the medical lab—in the bottom ice tray." She smiled.

"Thanks for the note. I knew where to look, but not in a specific location." He whispered, "Does Ed know about this?"

"Uh-huh. We have no secrets. He wants me to help, anyway I can."

Ed had his eyes closed and was listening to a seismic report from Earth about the Pacific Rim. It had been recorded at the communications center and downloaded to his com unit. He wasn't paying any attention to his wife's conversation.

The sled slowed somewhat when Captain Page took over from Mike, but the decrease in speed only lasted for about ten minutes. As the captain became used to the controls, the rescue ship regained its previous rate across the sandy surface. Two hours later, Sunul spelled the captain. Now that there were three drivers, lack of sleep was not going to be a problem. Two hours on and four hours off gave each driver time to eat and rest.

Sunul was driving when the sled approached the edge of the channel. He put the engine in idle and coasted to a stop about ten yards from the inclined passage leading to the depressed surface floor. Everyone was awake and asking why they had stopped, had something broken?

Sunul stood up and faced the group, "I'm afraid we have to lighten the load. The front strut won't be able to take the stress when the loaded sled hits the floor. We'll be in a bad situation of the strut breaks. I think it will take several hours to fix it. I'd like you all to don your EVA suits, climb out and let me take the vehicle down the slope."

Page asked, "Do you want us to walk to the other side of the depression? We could do that. It might be good exercise—most of us have been sitting for hours. What do you think, doctor.?"

Shania was already getting into her EVA suit and answered, "I believe that is a very good idea." She glanced at Sunul and he gave her a thumbs up sign.

"The dome is over twelve hours away, the exercise will tire some people out. We can have something to eat and get some sleep." Sunul retrieved his helmet from the recess above his head and mentioned, "Have a buddy help secure your headgear. You'll be outside for about twenty minutes." He allowed five minutes for everyone to seal their helmets and then said, "I'm lowering the internal pressure now."

The atmosphere inside the cabin was vented until the inside and outside pressures equalized. The two side doors slid open automatically. As the occupants were leaving the cabin, Sunul commented, "Please follow the tracks across the surface and climb to the top on the other side. I will follow with the vehicle." He watched as the others moved down the incline and began walking on the lower surface. He counted heads to make sure no one was behind the sled in danger of being killed by the nuclear exhaust.

Sunul decided to wait until everyone was across the depression before he added thrust to the engine and began to move the sled toward the incline. When the front runner struck bottom, Sunul rotated the gimbal ninety degrees, directing the exhaust upward and increased thrust. The sled lurched forward and began sliding across the sand toward the far side of the depression. Redirecting the gimbal and cutting power, the three runner sled skidded transversely over the 200 yards and climbed the opposite incline without Sunul having to redirect the exhaust.

The next twelve hours were monotonous, nothing to see but Martian sand and the lengthening shadows as the sun neared the horizon. It was dark when they reached the large surface rocks. Mike slowed the sled and followed the previous tracks without difficulty. Those sleeping didn't realize they were passing through a dangerous region. The passengers who were awake noticed the slowdown, but didn't ask for an explanation; they were now confident they would be reaching the colony before long.

Sunul took over for the last two-hour shift and the rescue vehicle arrived at the western gate close to midnight. Sunul, Mike, and Nate were the last to enter the dome and were greeted with an ovation from the rescued passengers and a number of colonists that had the day off or were in a celebratory mood. The joyous group drifted to Rose's to have drinks and thank their saviors. Sleeping was the last thing on the minds of the recued, they had dozed during most of the trip from the crash site.

Shania, Ed, and Sunul excused themselves after one drink and walked to the medical office. Shania knew how much Sunul wanted to recover the blood sample and she wanted to get the little cartridge in his hands. The door code hadn't been changed yet, so they went into the lab and Shania opened the freezing compartment. She pulled out the ice tray and ejected the ice cubes into a plastic bowl and began searching for the little black module containing her blood sample.

"It's not here, Sunul! Dr. Corcoran must have found it. Do you have another sample container?"

"Afraid not. It was unique. Rob only made one. Maybe Art found it. I'll ask him in the morning."

"I'm so sorry, Sunul."

"Don't worry about it. When you get back to Earth, you can give Gina a fresh sample. That might be better anyway. Thanks for coming over here to check."

When Sunul got to his residence, Art was still up reading an American Medical Association journal, but he had nodded off. He stood up and the journal fell to the floor.

"How'd it go?"

"We got everyone back—no injuries. Our vehicle worked as well as could have been expected. No breakdowns, even though we were loaded to the viewports. If we'd had two more people there would have been standing room only. I'm pooped. Those two- and four-hour naps have really messed up my sleep cycle."

"I can give you something for that."

"No thanks, doc. I'll be all right in a day or two. I like to avoid drugs. But I do have a question for you."

"What's that?"

"Did you find a small black module in the ice tray at the medical office lab?"

"I did. I tossed it in the recycling bin. I figured it was something left over when the refrigeration unit was installed."

Sunul sighed heavily, "Nope. It contained a blood sample."

"Who's blood?   And why was it in that container?"

"Shania's."

Sunul decided to confide in Dr. Corcoran and told him the entire story of the alpha group's experiences on 5K23m and their return to Mars and then Earth with the four children, two of whom were special. He mentioned Gina administered a small blood sample from the special children to Shania had cured her cancer. After Sunul mentioned his sister had cancer, Art immediately realized the importance of the cancer cure to Sunul and asked, "Why didn't you use a sample of the children's blood to fight your sister's cancer?"

"The children are grown now—they're young adults, and they've disappeared. We don't know where they are, but I've got an idea where to begin looking for them. I'm going to enlist at least one of the other members of alpha group to help me find them if Shania's blood chemistry doesn't allow Gina to produce a drug."

"Who else knows about this?"

"Including you, the alpha group, and the Winslows,—." Sunul didn't finish what he was saying.

Corcoran noticed Sunul was nearly in a trance, almost asleep with his eyes open, so he suggested they get some rest. Sunul lay down on his bed and was asleep before he could remove his clothes.

As Art closed his eyes, he thought, "That's eleven people plus the two children. But I'll bet someone in the government knows, too, and I know someone leaked it to the drug companies."

Chapter 12

Sunul was awakened at noon by a call from the colony's communications center. He was asked to report to the engineering office, site C-3, at 1:00 p.m. He showered, shaved, and while wearing a towel around his waist, ate a big meal. After snacking for nearly three days he needed a nutrition loaded brunch. It was ten 'til one when he was dressed and started toward engineering. He reached for his com unit, normally in his shirt pocket, but when it wasn't there. He remembered he had forgotten it when he left the com center several days ago. He was anxious to get a message from Gina and the kids, and find out how Priscilla was doing. He'd pick up his com unit after the meeting with engineering. But right now he wondered, "What does engineering want me for?"

He smiled when he entered the engineering unit, it was a self-serve system. He had to answer a couple of questions: name and International Space Agency ID number. The computer system greeted him and a female voice announced, "There are two jobs waiting for you, Mr. Burke. Would you like a hard copy?"

Sunul answered, "Yes," and a printout was ejected from a slit in the counter top. The two tasks were listed as to priority. The first was to meet with the oxygen gas production crew at their underground work site. The second was to help prepare a trailer to retrieve the failed transition ship and inspect it for damage. He was to work with Mike after returning from the O_2 generation facility. He folded the paper and stuck it in his left hip pocket.

He asked the computer, "How do I get to the oxygen production facility?"

"Take crawler N1. Select your destination. Sit back and relax. The journey will take twenty minutes. You will have two companions. Please arrive at the north gate before 2:00 p.m. The next crawl will be at 4:00 p.m."

"What is the current time?"

"The time is 1:27 p.m."

Sunul thought, "I'll pick up my com unit and while I'm walking to the north gate, I'll listen to any messages. Hopefully, something from Gina and the kids." He left engineering and walked slowly to communications trying to think of what problems he might help with at the oxygen generation facility. If there were nuclear generator problems, he could probably diagnose the difficulty. The experience he had gained working with Jar'l, Monel, and Rob on 5K23m and the flight back from the Kuiper Belt had built his confidence with nuclear power systems immeasurably.

As he began strolling from communications toward the north gate, he used Rob's app on his com unit to retrieve two messages from Earth. The first was from Gina about Priscilla. Her condition had worsened and she was flying to the states. Gina was going to meet her at Dulles. The kids would stay with the Patels while Gina went to D.C.

The second message was from Jar'l. He had found out through back channels that James Frieland and Evan Shiner were not to be trusted, confirming Sunul's suspicions about the two men. Jar'l and Monel hadn't heard from Adam and Eve since the young couple had said they were going farther south in Argentina. Sunul read the messages a second time and deleted them.

Toby Scott and Shania were waiting in their EVA suits when Sunul arrived at the north gate. Shania's presence surprised Sunul; he didn't think Dr. Winslow would still be working for the colony, now that her replacement, Art Corcoran was on site. The two companion travelers greeted Sunul and handed him an EVA suit and helmet.

"Aren't we going in a crawler?" Sunul wasn't fond of walking

"We still have to wear suits for the underground system. The atmosphere down there is nearly 100% oxygen." Shania explained that the air in the nuclear facility was not being mixed with Mar's atmospheric gases; it was too difficult to trap large amounts of nitrogen from the atmosphere and the carbon dioxide was too abundant in the outside gases. Therefore, EVA suits were necessary if a person was going to stay in the underground complex for any length of time.

"There's no danger of fire or explosion?"

"No, no flammables are present and all the equipment is shielded. There's no possibility of sparks and nothing to burn." Shania smiled and Toby accented her words with, "That's right. I've read all the specks and the reports. There's never been an accident."

Sunul had pulled on his suit and latched his helmet in place. He assisted his companions with their headgear and then pressed the exit panel. As they walked to the crawler, Sunul adjusted his sun shield, waited for the others to get in, and then climbed onto the front bench, taking the right window position.

Shania had taken the driver's chair and pressed the destination screen. The various sites flashed on the display showing the transit times. She pressed [O2 facility] and the crawler jerked into motion, shifted into moving smoothly, made a slow, sweeping right turn, and increased speed.

The twenty minute trip seemed very short. Sunul and Toby discussed the underground structure where the nuclear power generators were located. Toby had seen the original plans. Sunul was unaware of the actual structure, but he was aware of all the theoretical projections. The oxygen generators should be operating at 73% efficiency.

Shania had been at the site many times before and knew of the procedures and underground structures. She drove the crawler into a Quonset-like building and sealed the door behind the crawler. When the inside pressure was equal to the subsurface value, an elevator dropped the crawler sixty feet below the Martian surface. Upon exiting the crawler, they were met by a safety representative who attached a circular patch to their suits above their hearts.

Shania knew the worker and addressed her, "Hi, Anita. There are just three of us today." Shania introduced Sunul and Toby and mentioned why they were all at the O_2 facility.

"Monthly checkup time, huh? I heard you were returning to Earth." Anita was well informed, but didn't mention the crash. Most of the workers at the underground site worked a week and then had a week off.

"Yeah. Ed and I will be leaving on the next transition ship—in couple of days. Dr. Corcoran will be visiting you in the future."

"Okay. Well, have a good trip back home. Nice meeting you gentlemen."

"Thanks, Anita. Hope to see you back on Earth."

Anita turned and walked away, but looked back and waved.

Sunul and Toby were scanning the surroundings and noting the layered rocks. The solid rock walls were somewhere in the distance, the four-foot rectangular columns supporting the roof were a uniform ten feet apart, providing space for the excavators to move unhindered but able to carry the extreme weight of the strata above.

"I didn't think I would see anything like this, Toby. I expected granite or lava."

"I know what you mean. I just recently found that these layers are hundreds of millions of years old— that's in Earth years; Martian years are twice as long."

"Pretty good evidence of water having been on Mars in ancient times. Unfortunately, no fossils have ever been found—no record of life has been found in these strata, but maybe something will turn up near the poles."

Toby looked around but apparently didn't see what he was searching for. He asked Sunul, "Have you seen any indication of where the safety office might be located?"

"Come with me, Toby. I know where it is. I have to go there too; to check on oxygen sensors."

"I'll inspect the O_2 generators while you guys are in the safety office. Shall we meet here in about an hour?" Sunul was guessing at the time it would take for him to check the reactors.

Toby and Shania nodded and Shania said, "We shouldn't be gone that long. We'll wait for you here." She grabbed Toby's arm and guided him toward the crawler elevator.

Sunul decided to follow the sounds of excavators and the hum of the power generators. As he passed a few columns, he began to count them. He followed the columns in a straight line so he couldn't get lost. As he walked through the well-lighted cavernous underground, he noticed the columns were numbered. When he reached J-117, the noises were becoming much louder, and the vibrations were more intense.

He stopped for a moment, sipped some water from the reservoir in his helmet, and leaned against one of the columns. He could feel vibrations, so he knew the reactors couldn't be too far ahead. He had walked over 1,100 feet, assuming the distance between columns had remained constant at ten feet. The first equipment he saw was a small remotely-controlled crawler scooping up the debris on the floor of the man-made cave. Then he observed a worker guiding the loaded scoop toward the reactor. The orange EVA suit was unmistakable in the brightly lit complex.

There were two more figures, dressed in bright-blue EVA suits, crouched beside an access panel on a reactor assembly Sunul had never seen before, but he assumed was malfunctioning. About two-feet from the floor on one side of the cube, around eight-feet on an edge, was a bin over-flowing with crushed rock. The workers appeared to be arguing, but suddenly stood and looked at Sunul. One of the bright-blue units must have seen the outsider in his peripheral vision.

"Who the hell are you?" a male voice growled.

Sunul stepped closer and said, "Mind if I take a look?"

The other blue suit asked, "Who are you?" It was a feminine voice.

"Sunul Burke, troubleshooter. Please adjust your view windows so I can see who I'm talking to."

"Yes, sir," both voices replied. The face-plates became clear. Both workers were young nice-looking people with short-cropped hair, the male's was very short, creating a bald appearance. They were staring at Sunul.

Sunul laughed. "What are you staring at?"

The woman answered, "We never thought we'd meet you, sir. You are a legend on Mars."

"You can forget about that. I'm here to solve problems. What are your names?"

"I'm Julie Morgan, he's Matt. We're married."

"Okay, Julie. Tell me what the problem is."

It took about five minutes for Sunul to discover that the husband and wife team had been trained on an earlier oxygen generation model, the MO-82. The model they were trying to adjust was an MO-85. Sunul moved to the other side of the cube and popped open a circular panel about eight inches in diameter.

"Come here, Morgans. You need to know this about the newer models."

Julie and Matt joined Sunul and he pointed at the buttons for the different modes of nuclear processing. "These settings are for continuous or intermittent input and the setting selected here should agree with the setting you were looking at in the other panel. However, the processor will function, but at lower efficiency if the settings do not coincide."

Matt spoke up, "The other one is set on intermittent and this one is set on continuous. No wonder we haven't been producing O_2 at a higher rate. Julie, set the other one on continuous. We always have the feed bin filled to overflowing."

"Tell Joe to speed up the trips with the loader, we're going to need more feed for the converter." The excitement in Julie's voice was unmistakable; the improved output was going to be applauded back on Earth. She hoped they would receive some sort of accommodation; maybe a low interest loan on a new house, somewhere in the mountains back on Earth. They had been renting near the training base for over two years. But then she thought, "We'll have to mention

Mr. Burke in our report. He told us what the problem was."

"Thanks for the tip, Mr. Burke. I'll check with the other three converters and make sure they are at maximum output." Matt shook hands with Sunul and suddenly looked around. "Did you feel that, Julie?"

Julie hurried over to Matt and Sunul and latched onto Matt's arm. She was scared about being underground and having the roof cave in. "Was that a marsquake?"

All of the emergency alarms in their suits sounded simultaneously. A voice announced: "Please report to the safety office immediately. There has been a severe accident. Turn off any machinery."

Sunul reached over to the nearest access panel and pressed the standby button. Matt did the same to the circular panel on the opposite side of the cube. Julie had already begun the walk back toward J-7. Wearing EVA suits, it took Sunul and the Morgans about ten minutes to reach the safety office. A crowd had assembled and about twenty people were talking in small groups. The safety office door swung open and a man of about forty-five years stepped out. He was fairly tall and thin, unshaven and was frowning. His ID patch said Floyd Cooper. He made an announcement.

"There has been a cave in—centered around column C-17. It appears that Doctor Winslow has been killed. She was checking the oxygen pressure modules in that area. At least five of the columns gave way and tons of rock crushed her. I know you all knew the doctor, she was well-liked and served an important part of our mission on Mars. She will be missed."

Sunul couldn't believe what he was hearing. He worked his way over to the speaker and asked, "Are you sure the doctor is dead?"

"I'm afraid so. Her body patch shows no pulse. She didn't suffer, the patch suddenly showed a flat line response. I'll have to contact her husband."

"I can do that if you like. I need to talk to him anyway."

"All right. Thanks, Mr. Burke."

"You're welcome. When will you recover the body?"

"It will be some time before we can get equipment and some engineers down here. We might have to fill that area with cement to prevent any further collapse. This is the first death we've had at an engineering site on the planet. Very unusual."

"Could the collapse have been man-made?"

"You mean someone wanted to kill Dr. Winslow?"

"That's *just* what I mean. You know her transit plane crashed several days ago. That crash has yet to be investigated, but it appears to me that someone wants to get rid of the doctor."

"Come with me, Mr. Burke. Let's have a look at the cave in. You might be right."

Mr. Cooper and Sunul walked toward the rubble-strewn area and stopped at C-15. They were now on a first name basis, deciding it would be easier to communicate that way. The formalities were unnecessary.

Floyd knew what to look for if the roof had been forced to drop. "Let's inspect the intact columns near the collapse. I'm looking for particles imbedded in the adjacent columns. There shouldn't be any if it was a normal collapse due to column and strata failure."

Sunul assumed the explosive charges would have been placed near the top of the columns that failed. He eyeballed where the columns had been and began searching for projectiles of rock embedded in the intact columns near the mound of rocks that had plummeted from the ceiling. It didn't take long to find evidence. Almost simultaneously, both men found small chunks of rock that were out of place.

"Here's something, Sunul. This came from an explosion." Floyd held up a piece of rock that resembled a crude arrowhead.

"I've found some fragments that are out of place, too." Sunul showed Floyd two small wedge-shaped chunks of rock which he held in his right palm.

"We can check the seismic data and see whether there was an explosion or the collapse was of natural origin." Floyd added, "I'll go with you to talk to Mr. Winslow—he's a seismologist. He can verify what we suspect."

"Before we go back to the dome, Floyd, let's get a list of all visitors to the oxygen generation site in the last few days. Will you have a list here?"

"Only a partial listing. We'll get a comprehensive list from the colony—any member of the group will have to have travelled in a crawler. The physiological parameters of any member leaving the base are automatically transmitted from the crawler to the medical center. Dr. Corcoran will have those records."

Chapter 13

Work was cancelled for the remainder of the day at the oxygen generation station and the personnel were transported to the dome via four crawlers. At the north entrance to the dome, Sunul and Floyd removed their EVA suits and slowly walked to the Winslow residence discussing how they would give the disturbing news to Ed Winslow. Upon arriving at the door, it opened and Winslow invited the two men in.

"Please have a seat. I know why you're here— Shania was accidently killed at the O_2 plant. The security team informed me earlier."

Ed looked tired and his eyes appeared slightly bloodshot. Sunul felt sorry to have to bring up the suspicions he and Floyd had about the death. But the sooner Ed was in the loop, the more rapid the culprit or culprits would be found and dealt with.

"Can I get you men something to drink?" Ed asked.

Floyd and Sunul shook their heads and Sunul spoke up, "We think the roof collapse was done on purpose—it wasn't an accident."

"What?" Ed was shocked at the suggestion. "Who would want to hurt my wife? She always helped people—devoted her life to helping the sick and injured." He sat down and said, "Tell me what you're thinking."

Floyd filled Ed in on the details of Sunul's and his investigation.

"Well, the seismographic data can easily distinguish between a natural collapse and one caused by explosives. Let's check out the data. I've got to see this for myself. I'll help you find the killer, that's for damn sure."

Dr. Winslow stood quickly, his expression changed from one of sorrow to one of determination and urgency. "Come with me, gentlemen. We need to visit the seismology lab."

The replacement seismologist had not arrived from Earth yet, so no one had reviewed the data recorded during the collapse. The three men entered the lab and Dr. Winslow sat at the dedicated computer and replayed the most recent seismic events. He looked at his watch and asked, "When did the collapse occur?"

Sunul thought for a moment and commented, "About one-hour twenty-minutes ago."

Ed began scrolling back through the data until he came to a fairly large signal that corresponded to the time Sunul had estimated.

It took only a moment before he exclaimed, "You're right, it was an explosion! Someone killed Shania." He turned toward the two men and added, "But why?"

Sunul reminded Ed of Shania's experience with cancer and reviewed the worry the drug manufacturers would have if a cure for cancer was found—something cheap and 100% effective with no side effects.

"Oh, yes. Shania did mention that, but I didn't think she would be in any danger. I guess I've been very naive. I wonder if drug companies have killed before."

Floyd stepped closer to the monitor and pointed, "Explain what these squiggles mean, doc."

"Okay. If it was a natural collapse due to column failure, there would be some small signals at the beginning and the amplitude would build to a maximum rapidly and then fall off quickly, and irregularly, usually with smaller aftershocks, but this data shows a large initial signal and then a regular signal from the collapse, but with no aftershocks. That means someone used explosives to start the collapse. There's no denying it." He turned around to face Floyd and Sunul. "How do we find the bastard that did this?"

"We have to get some data from Dr. Corcoran. He should have the physiological readings from everyone using crawlers in the past few days. At least we'll know who our suspects are. Then we'll start the questions. Dr. Corcoran might help us with some drugs to get truthful answers." Sunul put his hand on Ed's shoulder and asked, "Are you up to pursuing this?"

"Yeah. I don't think I've ever been this pissed off before. I wish I had a gun."

Floyd replied, "I guess, right now, we would all like guns. Too bad they aren't allowed on Mars."

The medical office was as quiet as a tomb. The three visitors entered and Sunul approached the reception desk, normally occupied by Dr. Corcoran, unless he had a patient in one of the two examination rooms. Sunul called out, "Art?"

The doctor appeared from exam room one, right behind the front desk. "Sunul, what can I do for you?" He nodded to Ed and Floyd. "Gentlemen."

"You heard about Shania?"

"Sure did. What a terrible thing to happen."

"This is Ed Winslow, Shania's husband."

Art stepped toward Ed and shook hands. "Sorry about your loss, Dr. Winslow. Is there something I can do for you?"

Ed said, "Thank-you. Yes. We'd like to find out who has been to the oxygen generation site recently, other than Floyd and Sunul—and Shania, of course. You can forget about the regular crew members."

"Who are you looking for?"

"We don't know, but we do know the cave-in was not an accident. We think Shania was killed to prevent her from causing the pharmaceutical industry major financial losses."

"I see. Come with me to the lab. I can review the data from the crawlers and ID anyone that used one in the last week."

Art led the way to the lab and faced a large console. He said, "View four." Four holographic monitors appeared, one at each side of the island console. The three visitors took positions so each man could have his own view.

"Crawler data to subsurface oxygen generation facility. Identities of colony members visiting the facility during the last week."

Art's left eyebrow raised when he read what was on the screen—it was blank. A second later a message scrolled across the viewing area, "NO DATA AVAILABLE."

Sunul responded, "What's going on, doc?"

Art's surprise was obvious. He raised his left hand to his chin, paused for a moment, and said, "Someone has erased all physiological parameters recorded during the last week."

"How could that be?" Ed was irritated by the news.

"Don't worry, Ed. I've got a backup that no one but me knows about." He grinned and opened a locked cabinet drawer that contained a one-cubic-inch memory module. He held it up so the men could see the small cube. "This little jewel holds ten terabytes of data. All physiological data is automatically backed up on this baby. I call it my magic cube." He smiled and placed it on top of the console. He stepped back and commanded, "Copy data to console."

"DATA COPIED," appeared on all the monitors.

Art repeated the previous question and three names appeared on the displays: Mr. Sunul Burke, Mr. Toby Scott, and Dr. Shania Winslow.

"Well, I guess we know who killed Shania. Let's get him." Ed was rubbing his hands together, anxious to grab Toby and punch him into submission, or worse.

"Wait a minute, Ed. Who's the head of base security?" Sunul was unaware of any police force at the Mars colony.

Floyd answered, "We have a review committee that rules over any violations. I'm one of the members, the doctor is another; there are three more. We met two years ago for the first time when we established the committee, Sunul."

"Too bad this isn't in the 1800s. We'd have a sheriff or a marshal. When are the other members of the posse available?"

Ed remarked, "You like Westerns, Sunul?"

Sunul smiled and replied, "Western movies, not the books. Takes too long to read a book."

Floyd spoke up, "Dick Craft, Lenora Franks, and Joan Pemberton are the other members. I can get them after dinner—about 7:30 p.m. They should be in their residences then. Shall we pick up Mr. Scott and hold him for questioning?"

"I don't think we need to worry about him going anywhere. He can't run away." Sunul looked at the others.

Art commented, "He could commit suicide and prevent punishment. He could walk out one of the entrances without a suit."

"Dr. Corcoran?" A call issued from the front desk. "It's Toby Scott."

Art raised his voice and answered, "I'm back here. Come in."

The young geologist entered the room, surprising the four men. They all stood and turned to confront Toby. Ed had a venomous scowl, the others didn't know what to say, but just frowned.

Toby nodded and said, "I wanted to know if anyone other than Dr. Winslow was injured from the cave in."

Sunul moved his chair into the middle of the room and said, "Sit down, Toby. We have some questions to ask you, and we want some honest answers."

"Okay. What would you like to know?" Toby sat down and looked up at the four men. He didn't exhibit any nervousness. Then he said, "I don't know who you are." He pointed to Ed Winslow. "We've never been introduced."

"I'm Ed Winslow, Shania's husband." He didn't make any attempt to shake hands with Toby.

"I'm sorry about your wife. That was a terrible accident."

Ed answered while cracking his knuckles, "You know it wasn't an accident. You killed her!"

"What? I put those sensors just where you told me to place them! You said they would transmit warnings of any dangerous vibrations in the igneous rocks above the mining area."

"Those weren't sensors, Toby. They were explosive charges." Sunul watched as Toby reacted to the shocking details.

"What? Dr. Winslow here told me they were seismic sensors."

Winslow objected, "Now wait a minute, kid. I've never communicated with you about anything."

"You're lying. You told me where the sensors were and where to put them for maximum sensitivity. I put them just where you said."

Ed stared at Toby. "But I've never talked to you before. When and where did we meet?"

"You sent me a com message. Your picture appeared on my unit and I'm sure it was your voice telling me about the seismic units and where to place them."

Ed asked, "When did this so-called conversation take place?"

"Three days ago. Here, you can see the message. It's still in memory. I don't erase messages until a week has passed. Deletions are automatic." Toby attached his com unit to the computer so everyone could see the replay.

The replay was just as Toby had stated. Sunul asked Ed to use some of the same phrases and speak into the computer. After the recording was completed, Sunul said, "Computer, compare the same phrases. What is the probability that the same individual said both phrases?"

The men stood, waiting for the computer response. They were surprised when the result appeared on all the screens: 17%. The computer then showed a comparison of words analyzed. The complex analytical figures guaranteed that the two voices were not identical, despite the similarities of the audio.

"Well, Toby, it appears someone other than Dr. Winslow contacted you." About five seconds of silence passed before Sunul continued, "Now, who could it have been?"

Corcoran volunteered, "I'll start a speech analysis of all newcomers on Mars in the last two weeks. It will take some time, though. I'll have to do a lot of talking to get enough data for the computer to make a positive analysis. I'll contact everyone to update their immunization data. I don't think that will cause any suspicions."

While the investigation team in the doctor's office was continuing the discussion of Shania Winslow's murder, the water witch, Evan Shiner, was on his way to the oxygen generation facility, although travel to the underground excavations was supposed to be temporarily suspended. He had never piloted a crawler, but from what he gathered from talk by the colonists, it was a cinch. He had donned an EVA suit, climbed into a fully charged crawler, set the destination, and sat back to enjoy the short trip in silence.

Phobos and Deimos could both be seen in the dark sky, as well as thousands of stars, but moonlight from the mini moons was miniscule compared to that of Earth's moon and did not cast discernable shadows. Shiner switched the headlamps to high beam and watched the few irregularities in the surface features come and go. When he reached the facility, the lights dimmed automatically and the access door raised. The crawler moved ahead and parked without Shiner's assistance.

Chapter 14

The transition vehicle was parked on the elevator pad that lowered to the excavation cavern sixty-feet below the surface. Shiner punched DESCEND on the touch screen and the crawler began to drop below ground level. He moved around in the cabin to grab his divining rod and locate his extra compressed air bottles. When he both felt and heard his knee pop, he cursed, "Damn knee! I should never have gone on that damn rafting trip on the Colorado in '61." He sat back and massaged his knee.

When he reached the bottom of the shaft, the interior vehicle lights increased in intensity and the excavation cave lights came on. He squinted at the brightness when the crawler's automatic door swung open, the shaded vehicle's windows no longer dimmed the bright exterior lighting.

"Now to find the cave-in area." He made his way to the cavern office and scanned the plan mounted on the wall outside the office door. He was looking for position *C-15* on the chart, the location centered at the roof failure. Evan wanted to investigate the rock that had fallen from the roof of the underground complex of columns with the intention of learning more about potential sources of water or weaknesses in the overhead rocky structures.

He moved from the *H* file to the *C* file and began walking along the rough *C* file structures. At column *C-12*, Shiner noticed the litter on the floor was beginning to increase; the cave-in was near. Yellow caution-tape was wrapped around column *C-13* and extended into the dim reaches of the cavern. *C-15* did not exist, a pile of rubble covered the floor, extending into the void in the ceiling. Shiner maintained his distance for fear of further ceiling collapse, but his experienced eyes caught site of some rubble at the foot of the C-17 column. He glanced above the rubble to the ceiling, but no defects were observed. He turned and glanced back at the massive pile of rock that had fallen.

He stepped closer to the edge of the debris and directed his head lamp up into the emptiness above. Shiner suddenly stepped back from the rubble when he was surprised by a nearby noise. He swung around. The rubble at C-17 was moving!

"Help me. Please help me."

"Oh, my God. Dr. Winslow?"

"Yes. Can you get me back to the dome? Don't tell anyone that I'm still alive."

"Can you walk?"

"No. My left leg and arm are both broken. I need help to get to the infirmary and Dr. Corcoran."

"Well, I don't think I can carry you, but let's give it a try. If it doesn't work, I'll go back to the dome and get a gurney."

"No need. There should be one in the safety annex to the main office. Go get it. I won't try to crawl any farther. Do you have any extra air cylinders?"

"I brought some extras, they're in the crawler. I'll get one and be right back with it and the gurney. You just relax."

"Thank-you. Who are you?"

"Evan Shiner. I'm a water witch—of sorts." He smiled and said, "Hang on, doc. Five more minutes and we'll get out of here."

"Hurry, Mr. Shiner. My air supply is below ten percent."

Shania was thanking God for Evan's return to the cavern before her air ran out. She watched him disappear down the file of C columns. She had slept to conserve air since the explosion despite her aching left arm and leg. As she lay on the ground, after being thrown about twenty-feet from the column that exploded as she walked past it, she began to think what had happened was not an accident. She had disabled her tracking patch soon after the cave-in had occurred to make the suspect or suspects think the murder had been accomplished. But after diagnosis of her injuries and hearing the departure of the workers, she had crawled closer to the rubble in case someone might return and find her. She had hoped the person that found her would not be the one responsible for the explosion. Then she had slept, despite the pain.

She heard the rattling of the gurney as Evan pushed the device over the irregular floor.
He parked the transporting stretcher next to Shania and locked the wheels. Evan moved behind Shania, placed his hands under her arms and lifted so she could stand on her right leg while holding onto the gurney. She leaned over the mobile stretcher and Evan lifted and slid the rest of her body so she was lying face up. Evan replaced the nearly empty air canister in her utility package and released the gurney's break.

It took about ten minutes to get back to the crawler and another five to get Shania into the vehicle and return the gurney to its location in the safety annex. Evan walked back to the cave-in area and made sure there were no tracks left by the gurney.

Shania was able to relax for the twenty-minute trip to the dome. She sat in the air lock sanitary facility while Evan called Dr. Corcoran and asked him to come to the northern dome entrance. When he asked the doctor to bring a gurney, Art responded, "Are you injured?"

"No, but someone else is. Maybe you could bring a hovercraft—it would cause less pain to the patient during the ride to the medical center."

"All right, I'll be there in about ten-minutes."

Floyd, Sunul, and Art had gone to dinner and returned to the medical center to discuss what had occurred earlier. When Evan called, Art and Sunul were talking about the importance of Shania's blood specimen that had been lost. Sunul had just mentioned as soon as he returned to Earth, he would try to locate Licon and Miranda, AKA Adam and Eve. He knew their probable location: southern Argentina.

When Art concluded the call from Evan, he said, "I think you should come with me, Sunul. I might need some backup. This guy Evan sounds a bit like he's trying to launch without fuel." Art smiled and glanced at Floyd, "Floyd, you'd better get some rest. You'll be busy with the cleanup of the ceiling collapse debris tomorrow."

"Right. Good night, gentlemen." Floyd left the medical office and headed to his colony residence.

"What's going on, Art?"

"I'm not sure, but the water witch needs to transport an injury to the medical building. It sounds like a severe injury; he doesn't want the patient jostled around. There might be some lifting involved, you can give us a hand."

Sunul stood, clapped his hands and said, "Let's go. If the injury is that severe, Evan needs some immediate help."

The two men ascended the stairs to the roof and climbed into the hovercraft and lifted off. Fifteen-seconds later, the make-shift ambulance landed at the north-gate dome entrance.

Evan was standing beside the crawler, just inside the open interior airlock door. He approached Art and Sunul as they stepped out of the hovercraft, its two blowers still rotating at idle speed.

"Hello, doctor, Sunul. I'm happy to see that you brought some help. The doctor has a broken leg and a broken arm, both on the left."

Art quizzed, "The doctor?"

"Yes, doctor Winslow. She's in the bathroom."

There had been a short period of confusion in the minds of both Art and Sunul. They wondered how Ed Winslow had gotten severely injured in such a short time since they had earlier been talking with him.

Sunul suddenly remarked, "Doctor Shania Winslow is alive?"

Evan replied, "Yes. Who did you think I was talking about?"

Dr. Corcoran didn't bother to explain, he moved quickly to the sanitary facility and knocked. "Shania?"

"Come in, Art. I can't get up."

"Jesus, Shania, why didn't you call us? Your suit's com unit still functions doesn't it?"

"Just get me to the medical unit. I'll explain later. Take off my helmet, I can't remove it with only one hand."

Shania, in her dusty EVA suit was slumped on the toilet with her broken limbs toward the back wall. Art decided he couldn't lift Shania from the small facility without risking dropping her, so he called, "Sunul, you'd better lift Shania. You're a hell of a lot stronger than I am." Art backed out of the small room and Sunul took his place.

"All right, Shania, I'm going to lift you and back out to Art. He'll give some extra support. We don't want to hurt you, so let us know if we're doing something wrong. Okay?"

"Take off my helmet. Please! I feel trapped."

Before Sunul lifted Shania, he slowly and delicately twisted her helmet and dropped it on the floor. Shania took a deep breath of fresh air and sighed. "Okay, I'm ready."

Sunul was surprised how easily he lifted Shania. The Martian doctor's body structure was very similar to Gina's but she seemed much lighter. But then he realized the Martian gravity was only about 40% of the Earth's. Sunul knew Art had underestimated his own strength. Sunul moved slowly, turned, and walked quickly to the hovercraft with Art alongside to prevent any stumbling. With Shania reclining in the ambulance, there was only room for two others. Evan volunteered to stay behind and secure the north entrance to the colony.

Shania turned her head and said, "Thank-you, Evan. You showed up in time to save my life. Come visit me in the hospital, but keep my existence a secret for now. Okay?"

"Don't worry. I won't utter a word. Take care." Evan waved as Art wound the fans and the craft lifted twenty-feet into the air and then whisked away to the medical facility. Sunul leaned forward toward Art and said, "Land on the roof. We don't want prying eyes to see our patient. I'll carry her down the stairs, you prepare a bed. You want to x-ray her arm and leg, correct?"

Art nodded, thinking to himself, "Shania is the prettiest woman I've ever met. I wonder if she's in love with Ed. He didn't show much emotion when we told him of her death. Well, a slight amount, but he could have been acting."

He slowed the craft when they were two buildings away from the medical unit, slowly maneuvered to the roof landing pad, and shut down the electric engines. With the fans slowing, the craft dropped about a foot until the rubber undercarriage lost air pressure and supported the weight of the craft and riders. Ed swung out of the driver's seat and headed down the stairs to ready the x-ray equipment for horizontal scans.

Sunul stooped over Shania, carefully lifted her, and he carefully descended the steps to ground level.

"In here, Sunul." Art had called from the medical lab and said, "Let me help get her positioned for a couple of quick scans. You can place that shield over her torso, after we cut away the EVA suit. Are you wearing clothes under the suit, Shania?"

"Yes, although I wouldn't be embarrassed if you saw me naked. You *are* a doctor."

"Just checking. I could have had Sunul step out of the room. Some of my female patients have hesitated to disrobe in front of me—an unmarried physician. I'm going to cut off the EVA suit—at least the left half."

"Go ahead and take the whole thing off. I'll be more comfortable."

Art had to use a pair of shears to cut through the tough EVA suit material. When Shania was lying in her undergarments, he covered her with a warm blanket.

"How's that?"

"Great. I was going to ask for a warm blanket." She looked at Sunul. "Sunul, please cover my torso with that vest shield. I still want to have some children when I get back to Earth." She pointed at the old-fashioned shielding that looked like something a baseball catcher would wear.

"Nice equipment, huh? They give us the best." Art's sarcasm was evident in his voice and facial expression.

Shania exhibited a faint smile and said, "Whatever works, doc." She closed her eyes and commented, "I believe you'll find that my fibula has a clean break and the radius is cracked, but not broken through. The blast threw me against one of the adjacent columns. I was knocked unconscious but came to and crawled away from the debris."

The x-rays validated Shania's diagnosis of her injuries. Corcoran turned away from the monitor and moved beside Shania. He held her right hand and said, "You were right about your injuries. I'll put a brace on your forearm and put a support cast on your leg. We have the latest stimulation casts, so your fracture should heal rapidly. I'll give you a calcium supplement, too."

Sunul spoke up, "We'll notify your husband. He can come and get you and take care of you for a week while your leg mends."

"No! Whatever you do, don't tell Ed that I'm alive. Can I stay with you gentlemen? All I need is a foam cot with a heating pad." She winced when she adjusted her position slightly to see both Sunul and Art. "I don't eat very much, never have. I'll pay you for your trouble."

Art and Sunul were slightly amused by what Shania had said. Neither man was concerned about her lodging expenses, but they were interested in her reasons for keeping her husband from knowing she was still among the living.

Chapter 15

Ed Winslow made his way to residence location L-7, dimly lit by the corner lamp two buildings away, dimmed during the late night hours. He tapped lightly on the door. There was a wait, but only a few seconds passed before he heard, "Come in."

Ed pressed the illuminated entry pad and the door swung open. The room was pitch-dark except for stray photons coming from the outside walkway. Ed couldn't make out any features of the man standing to his right about ten feet away.

"What did you want to see me about, Ed?"

"Have the arrangements been made for me to receive the quarter-million credits you promised?"

"I sent a message an hour ago that the project was complete. Your account should be bulging right now. You did just what we wanted. Good job."

"I just wanted to check. I'll be returning to Earth on the next flight."

"Next return to Earth is in three days. Will you have time enough to pack your things?"

"No problem. I don't want anything of Shania's. I've just got some clothes and books."

"I found some seismic recordings over at the Eastern dome access port. Do you want them?"

"I must have forgotten them when we returned from that last surface excursion. Where are they? I'll pick them up."

"Why don't I show you? I have to leave the dome anyway. A new search light was installed and I have to make some adjustments. I'll put on my helmet and we can go."

Ed heard some rustling and asked, "Need some help?"

"No thanks, I've got it."

Ed didn't know who his associate was, but they walked together to the eastern dome entranceway. Ed hadn't paid much attention to his companion in the EVA suit, except he carried a large, long-handled, adjustable wrench. They didn't meet anyone on the way to the access port. Ed's curiosity about the seismic records built as they approached the inside door to the airlock.

His companion checked the atmospheric pressure in the lock and opened the inner door. Ed stepped forward and asked, "Where did you see the tracings?"

"They're in that upper cabinet beside the outer door—they're in a tube."

Ed frowned and stepped toward the cabinet and opened the doors. That was the last thing he ever did.

The associate had hit Ed's head with a crushing blow. The seismologist was probably dead before he contacted the ground. The inner door to the dome was closed and the outer door was opened. Ed's body was dragged from the dome and placed in a sitting position against the outer dome wall as if he had taken a stroll and sat down to take a rest. If the blow to the head hadn't killed him, he would die quickly in the rarified and toxic Martian atmosphere. No one could live for more than a minute or two in the low-pressure carbon dioxide envelope surrounding the red planet. Holding his breath was not an option for Ed, or anyone else.

The associate re-entered the airlock, sealed the outer door, closed the open cabinet, wiped fingerprints from the cabinet handles and left through the inner entranceway door. He met no one on his way to his alternate residence at M-4. The killer removed his EVA suit and repaired the suit's automatic transmitter which he had disabled for the brief extra-dome exposure. He was confident this murder of a Winslow on Mars would undoubtedly never be solved.

It was after 11:00 p.m. when Sunul and Art transported Shania to their bachelor quarters. They had accomplished the move from the medical center without detection. The two men had taken turns carrying the injured doctor to their residence. Fortunately they didn't have to travel far.

Art volunteered his bed for Shania to use for her recovery. He had given her a spinal to prevent pain when they realigned the bone in her lower leg. A slight twist was necessary to get the broken bone in the proper orientation for rapid bridging of the bone separation. When the fractured bone was in exact alignment, Art fit an isodynamic-form-fitting cast to Shania's leg.

Sunul cooked dinner that satisfied the tastes of the three individuals. Shania hadn't eaten in twenty-four hours and was famished. She was barely able to keep her eyes open, despite having slept several hours after the cave-in occurred. She excused herself, visited the bathroom and went to bed. Fortunately, the bedrooms were separated by the sanitation facility.

Art set up his cot adjacent to the wall of Sunul's bedroom and sat down. Sunul cleaned up the kitchen area and sat beside Art.

Sunul commented, "You've been awfully quiet. What are you thinking?"

Art ruffled up his full head of nearly black hair with both hands and grinned. "I think I'm in love, Sunul."

"I figured as much. I've been watching you taking care of your new patient. She is a gorgeous woman, but you have to realize she's married."

"Yeah, I know. But did you hear what she said? She didn't want Ed to know she was alive."

"I heard. I'm not sure what that means. Maybe she'll give more information tomorrow. Let's hit the sack. I'll take the cot tomorrow night so you don't have to do all the suffering."

"That's a deal! It's been a long time since I spent a night on a cot. Maybe the technology has advanced since then."

"Gentlemen! Could one of you please help me to the bathroom?"

Art was standing up before he was awake, and nearly toppled over the cot obstructing his movement at knee level. He rubbed his eyes, frowned, and realizing he was standing in his underwear, said, "Just a moment, Shania, I'll pull on some pants."

Sunul's bedroom door was still closed, he hadn't heard Shania's call for assistance. As Art lifted Shania to carry her to the bathroom door, his com unit rang. It was the emergency call booming throughout the residence. He had to finish one task at a time. As soon as he was sure Shania was able to stand and move about in the tiny bathroom, he smiled at Shania and said, "That's my emergency call. I've got to take it. I'll check on you in a minute or two."

Shania answered, "It will be more than a few minutes, Art. Thanks for answering my call so quickly." She shut the door and Art moved to the cot, picked up his com unit, and answered.

"Doctor Corcoran here. What can I do for you?"

"This is Floyd Cooper. I was just contacted by Evan Shiner. He found a body outside the dome about ten minutes ago. He told me it's Ed Winslow."

"You're sure about the identity?"

"Yeah, positive. Shiner new him because they had talked about locating deep subsurface water. I think you need to check the body. I believe he was struck on the head and he wasn't wearing an EVA suit."

"Where's the body? Sunul and I will be there in say—fifteen minutes. We just got up."

"We're at the eastern entrance. Shiner's with me and the body."

Art knocked on Sunul's bedroom door and said, "Get up Sunul. We've got a job—fifteen minutes." Art heard movement behind the door and stepped back when the door cracked open.

Sunul was blinking, trying to focus his eyes. "Morning. What's the problem?"

Art whispered, "Ed Winslow has been murdered. Shiner found him outside the dome without a suit."

"Have you told Shania?"

"Not yet. She's in the can."

"Okay. You want me to help with the body?" Sunul was still whispering.

Art nodded and said, "We'll take the hovercraft and bring back the body for an autopsy. Floyd thinks he was struck in the head and placed outside."

Shania came from the bathroom, balanced herself against the wall, and looked at Art. "What are you guys whispering about, something concerning me?" She smiled, thinking she had caught the men discussing her.

Art watched Sunul enter the room aligning the Velcro on his shirt, the last thing he needed to be fully clothed. Art had only looked at him momentarily, and then turned to Shania. "I just got a call from Floyd Cooper. Evan Shiner found your husband outside the dome. He's dead."

Shania turned her head as if she hadn't heard correctly. "Ed is dead? I know he wouldn't commit suicide. Why would anyone kill him?"

Sunul reacted quickly, "He must have known too much."

"About?"

"Killing you. He must have been involved in some kind of plot, probably initiated by a drug conglomerate on Earth. That's the only thing I can come up with. They must know your blood contains the mimicry cells to make the anti-cancer agents that Licon and Miranda possess." Sunul continued, "We've got to keep you alive and get you back to Earth. You can stay with Gina and me and my children. They can keep a secret."

Art was concerned. "We need to find out who killed your husband, and then figure out how to get you back on Earth without anyone knowing."

Sunul responded, "I have a suspect in mind, Jim Frieland, and I think I know how to smuggle Shania back to Earth. I'll have to call a friend of mine to get some assistance."

Shania still hadn't shown any emotion about Ed's death, but she was tuned into Sunul's every word. "How can you contact a friend on Earth without the communications people knowing what is going on? They read every transmission coming and going."

Sunul smiled, "I have my ways, don't worry about that." At this point in Sunul's evaluation of the crew on Mars, he wasn't going to divulge how he was covertly sending and receiving messages from Earth. Although he trusted Art and Shania implicitly, he was never sure who else might be listening or surreptitiously recording his conversations. Whoever was causing the deaths or attempted assassinations had left little evidence of their activities. Sunul had to get in touch with Rob; he could probably dig into the prime suspect's background and find out who Jim Frieland's employer is.

Shania hobbled into the bedroom, left the door open about an inch, and said, "You men had better go. I can take care of myself. I won't be answering the outside door or any com units. My existence has to remain a secret. I'll explain more about my life when you return. I'm sure you have some questions."

Art and Sunul exited their quarters and headed for the medical facility to fly the hovercraft to the dome's east exit to retrieve Ed Winslow's body. As Art piloted the craft, the two men discussed Shania's lack of emotion about Ed's death. By the time they landed, Sunul came up with an idea. Floyd Cooper would have to be involved in the plan. Sunul had yet to mention his plan to Art.

When they arrived at the exit, Floyd greeted the two men. Evan had returned to his quarters to get some breakfast. The body was in the airlock out of public view. Art gave the body a close visual inspection and then looked more closely at the patch of dried blood in the head wound. After less than a minute, he stood and commented, "His skull is fractured—something irregular and very hard caused the damage. I doubt if he ever regained consciousness when he was outside. He didn't suffer asphyxiation—probably dead before he was placed outside."

Sunul looked at Floyd. "On the way over here, I thought of something, but you'll have to go along with it."

Floyd looked up from the corpse. "What is it?"

"Have you started cleaning up the debris from the cave-in?"

"Not yet. I have to get the engineers' permission to let workers in that area."

"That's good. I'd like you to put Ed Winslow in an EVA suit and bury him in the debris. Tell the workers not to open the helmet. The body should go directly to the medical lab."

Art stood up and smiled at Sunul. "Aha! They'll think the suit contains Shania's dead body."

Sunul nodded and then proposed, "The Winslows' bodies will be shipped back to Earth for burial, but that's only what we want people to think. One coffin will contain food and compressed air—enough for at least a week, to support Shania as she is transported alive in the other coffin. That way we can get her back to Earth without anyone knowing. She won't be at risk."

"Damn, Sunul, that sounds like a great idea. I can use a loader and bury Mr. Winslow before the engineers get down there to investigate. They won't be there until tomorrow morning."

Art was ready to help any way he could. "You'd better get Ed in an EVA suit and take him to the mine. Make sure there isn't a tracker badge in the suit. We'll help you load him in the crawler."

"That's all right. I can handle everything myself. You gentlemen should get some breakfast and take care of your patient." He winked at Art and Sunul.

Chapter 16

The hovercraft was returned to the infirmary roof. During the short jaunt, Art had asked Sunul what his next step was going to be. As they descended to the medical office floor, Sunul whispered, "I think I should tell Shania my plan—unless you want to take the lead."

"No. You tell her what you're thinking, I'll listen and back you up if necessary."

"No more whispering, gentlemen. Let me hear what you're saying, I'm not some delicate flower that won't understand the facts." Shania was sitting on the cot with her leg elevated on a pillow, looking up from reading a medical journal. She had moved the cot to the wall of her bedroom and was leaning against some pillows behind her lower back. "I rearranged some things." She was grinning, waiting for some criticism, but it never came.

Art sat down cautiously at the end of the cot being careful not to cause any movement of Shania's broken leg. "You look much better today. You're feeling all right?"

"Much better, thanks." She smiled at Art and started to lean forward to touch his hand, but the splint and the cast restricted her movements, so she sagged back and asked, "What did you find out about Ed?"

Art related what they knew about Ed's death and then Sunul took over the conversation.

"I have a proposal to present to you." He thought about what he had just said and almost stuttered, "Not that kind of proposal," he grinned. "That was a poor choice of words." Both Art and Shania were laughing. "What I meant to say is I have an idea of how to get you back to Earth covertly and in contact with Gina. Only a handful of people would know—and they're people we can trust."

He had gotten Shania's rapt attention. "I suppose you're sending me home in a box."

"Exactly."

"Wait a minute, I was just kidding. You'd better fill me in on your little proposal," she grinned.

"Okay. But first Art and I need to know why you aren't broken up about the death of your husband."

"I've been wondering when you two were going to ask about that. I bet you've been talking about my lack of tears."

Both men nodded.

"We were never in love. We married in order to come to Mars; it was a contract. We were hardly ever together and never had relations. Ed was a confirmed bachelor and I had broken up with my fiancé. All Larry wanted me for was sex. That wasn't enough for a meaningful marriage. He was very shallow and stuck on himself. I'm sorry it took me so long to figure that out; we had been together for three years. I had to get away, so I signed up for another tour on Mars. Ed and I located each other on the Internet and made a deal." She looked down at her cast and then said, "I am sorry he was killed, but we hardly knew each other."

Shania glanced at the men and then focused on Art. "I'd like to get to know you much better, doctor. But I'll be returning to Earth in a short time. Perhaps you will look me up when you return from Mars?"

Art was smiling and said enthusiastically, "You can bet on that, doctor. Say, what was your maiden name?"

"Shania Ann Estwick."

"What a pretty name for a beautiful young woman." Art was staring into Shania's light-blue eyes."

"Thank-you, Art." She blinked twice, grinned, and stared back at Art. "Now, explain about stowing me in a box."

Art grinned and glanced at Sunul. "Join us, Sunul. Tell Shania what you've hatched."

Sunul grabbed the back of a chair, reversed it and sat facing Shania and Art, leaning into the back of the white plastic seat. "Art and I will make two coffins, one for you and one for Ed, however, Ed will remain on Mars. Floyd will incinerate Ed in one of the nuclear oxygen generators. We'll stack the two coffins—you'll be in the bottom one laying on a soft cushioned bed and the top one will be loaded with food and air for you to breathe. I'll weld the two containers together and we'll mark them so you won't be inverted during the trip home."

Shania volunteered, "I'm not claustrophobic, if you're wondering." She looked like she was going along with the plan. "Tell me more."

"Well, I haven't figured out the waste problem yet. Art?"

Shania and Sunul both looked at Art. He smiled, "I think I have that figured out. How about a preflight enema and a catheter? You'll have liquid foods, carbohydrate, fat, and protein supplements. You won't have to go for the entire trip." He looked at Shania and said, "I'm sorry to put you though this, but Gina will get you out as soon as you get back to Earth. Right, Sunul?"

"Exactly. Rob and Gina will get you out of your coffin as soon after you land as possible."

"Who is Rob?" Shania had never met Rob or ever heard his name mentioned by Sunul.

"Rob is Rob Griswalt. He's a mechanical and electrical genius. He was on the trip to the Kuiper Belt. I'll be sending him a message this afternoon. He'll give me tips on constructing your coffin home. I've never seen him make a mistake—he's brilliant."

Shania shook her head. "Jeez, Sunul, is everyone you know a genius of some sort?"

Sunul laughed, paused a couple of seconds, and replied as he nodded, "That's about right, but the jury's still out on you and Art."

She smiled. "I'll try not to say anything stupid."

"I wouldn't worry about that. What comes out of a person's mouth isn't always an accurate sign of their IQ."

Art went to work at the medical facility and Sunul composed a brief, but fact-filled message to Gina and Rob. Sunul made sure Shania was able to care for herself and then left for the communications center. Shania was going to compose a list of items she would need when confined to the coffin enclosure. As she worked on the list, she wrote down questions that popped into her mind as she thought of passing a week's time in the metal boxes.

Sunul sent a regular message to Gina. He decided not to wait for a return message, left his com unit near the broadcast units and started toward the medical center. He had gone about half-way when he heard a voice from behind.

"Sunul Burke, I have a question for you."

Sunul spun around and saw Evan Shiner jogging toward him, but still twenty feet away. Suspicious of Shiner ever since he found that Shiner claimed to be a water-witch, Sunul was on guard.

"What can I do for you, Evan?"

Out of breath, Evan asked, "How is Shania doing?"

Sunul gave the surrounding a quick glance and replied in a whisper, "Keep your voice down. You know we don't want anyone to know she's alive."

"Oh, yeah. Sorry." Evan looked around and whispered, "Can I see her?"

"About?"

"She's a beautiful woman. I feel sorry for her. I wanted to offer my condolences."

"When I see her, I'll tell her what you said."

"She's not nearby?"

"She's in a safe place."

"Not on base?"

"Look, Evan, she's in a safe place." Sunul was tiring of Evan's persistence. "I'm trying to keep her alive. I have to go. I'll tell her you asked about her." He turned away from Evan and resumed his direction toward the medical center. When he had taken about five paces, he looked back, but Evan was out of sight. He thought, "Evan is climbing the ladder of my suspects, but Jim Frieland is still on the top rung."

The short walk to the medical facility took only a couple of minutes. Art was in the emergency room just inside the entrance, bandaging some fingers that had been pinched when the colonist was cleaning the three rooms in her residence. Art introduced Sunul to Sharon and he sat in the waiting area until Sharon left. Sharon had volunteered that she was trying to clean house while her husband was away on a mining expedition and in her haste, she mashed two fingers when a kitchen cabinet door closed unexpectedly. She was very embarrassed.

Sunul was slightly curious, "Anything broken?"

"In Sharon's hand? Nope, she'll have a couple of blood blisters, that's all. I gave her some antibiotic ointment. She'll be fine."

"What do you know about this Evan Shiner fellow? You know who he works for?"

Art shook his head and said, "I don't know much about him, probably as much as you do. He's supposed to be able to locate water, but I think that's a bunch of hocus-pocus."

"Has he been in for any kind of treatment?"

"No. Why are you interested in Shiner?"

"I saw him a few minutes ago. He has a strong interest in Shania."

"Well, he did save her life. Maybe he just wants to know how she's doing."

"Hmm. Maybe you're right. Do you think it's a romantic interest? He's about thirty years older than Shania. He mentioned she is a beautiful woman. I wonder where he saw her before. He couldn't have seen her in her EVA suit, the visors are tinted and hers was badly cracked."

"He did see her, Sunul. He was there when we took off her helmet before transporting her here."

"Oh! You're right. I forgot about that. So I guess he's just concerned about her well-being."

Art smiled and commented, "I'm not worried about any competition from him. I think Shania is interested in me."

"Can't argue there. I noticed you and Shania seem to have a connection, but can you be sure she won't find someone else while you're stuck on Mars? I have to admit she's a dynamite looking woman—and very smart. She and Gina are going to work together nicely on the cancer medication. I hope their work comes to fruition before my sister passes away."

The room was silent for about ten seconds and then Art replied, "I might have to void my contract with the agency and return home sooner than I had originally planned. I don't want her to get away."

Sunul had listened closely and Art's last utterance sounded like something a detective would say about a criminal more so than a suitor would say about the woman he is pursuing. Sunul dismissed his thoughts assuming he was over-analyzing a few words and being picky. He had developed great respect for the new medical doctor on Mars. Sunul was waiting to hear back from Gina about her and the kids and from Rob about Jim Frieland and Evan Shiner, suspects one and two. At the time he composed the message to Rob, it hadn't occurred to him to include Art Corcoran in the inquiry.

Art's com unit suddenly came alive with a loud ring. He had turned the volume up so he wouldn't miss a call from Shania.

"It's Shania, Sunul. Someone's trying to break in our residence."

Sunul was headed out the door before Art had finished his sentence. It took him less than ten seconds to cover the fifty-meters, having to only make one turn from the medical center to the living quarters. He skidded in the sand near the front door, put his hands up to keep from smashing against the entrance, and circled the building. He didn't see anyone. Whoever had been there must have heard him coming and fled.

Using his com unit, he opened the door, slipped into the living area, closed the door, and summoned, "Shania, are you all right?" Although Sunul was troubled by the distress call, he couldn't raise his voice above that of normal conversation, fearing the noise would carry and give away Shania's hiding place.

"Yes, Sunul. I'm here—in Art's closet."

Sunul entered Art's bedroom and helped Shania from behind the doctor's clothing, picked her up, and carried her into the living area.

When she was sitting on the cot and combing hair back from her face, she exhaled and said, "How did you get here so fast?"

Smiling, Sunul said, "When I heard you say breaking, I ran as fast as I could to get here. I didn't know if someone had gotten in and was threatening you."

"Well, thank-you. You're in very good shape. You're not even out of breath. My heart is probably beating faster than yours is." She adjusted her leg cast and leaned back against Art's pillows. "I'll be all right now. Whoever was pounding on the door must have decided no one was home. Did you see who it was?"

"No. They must have heard me coming and took off. I didn't see anyone."

"What is Art doing? I thought he would come."

"He was on the com with you when I left the medical facility. What did you hear at the door?"

"It was a pounding, like a fist hitting the door. It wasn't a normal knock. The wall vibrated—I hid in the closet and called Art. I was more surprised at the noise than I was scared." She reconsidered, "Well, maybe equal amounts of both."

"How does your leg feel today?"

"It's fine, so is my arm. I won't need the splint after another day or two. I'll be glad to get rid of that thing. I feel almost like I had a stroke and my left side is paralyzed."

Chapter 17

Priscilla wore a stocking cap over her bald head to hide her lack of hair due to chemotherapy drugs and to try to keep warm in the late September cloudy weather. It was 9:00 a.m. on the gray, wet, Friday morning. As she left the oncologist's office and stepped into the vestibule, she gathered her coat around her neck, fastened the topmost button, and wrapped a red knit scarf around her neck. She took advantage of a gentleman's polite holding open the outside door for her. With both hands on her umbrella, she stepped onto the wet sidewalk and began the three-block trek to her apartment.

Priscilla's purple umbrella shimmied slightly as the light wind swirled and removed a few leaves from the small trees that lined the avenue near her doctor's office. The usual pedestrian traffic was almost nonexistent, the misty rain had kept people indoors that gray morning. The weatherman had announced that the sun would make an appearance in mid-afternoon. Then the sidewalk cafes would be populated by tourists and citizens alike, drinking café au lait with their croissants.

Disappointed with her doctor's pronouncement that the chemo was not working, Priscilla stared ahead, avoiding any of the usual acknowledgements to shop owners on her way home. She couldn't exhibit her normal cheery disposition. She dreaded having a mastectomy and worried even more about the cancer metastasizing. She crossed the avenue diagonally, hardly aware of the traffic, though it was light. She heard a bell ring and a bicycle rider whizzed by avoiding a collision by a few centimeters. An unintelligible oath could be heard from the rider who was undoubtedly exceeding the speed limit.

When Priscilla entered the apartment, she found the lights off and the furnace was turned down to sixty degrees. Francois wasn't home. As she walked towards the efficiency kitchen to make some tea, she dropped her umbrella, scarf, and coat on the living room floor. There was a note beside the teapot: "Darling Priscilla: I have been called to the office. Will return ASAP. Francois."

She thought, "I wonder what he had to do. He's usually off on Friday. I'll have some tea and take a nap. We have to talk."

Ten minutes later, she added a pinch of cinnamon to the hot tea and transferred the pot to a trivet on the sofa table. With a blanket covering her legs, she poured a cup of tea and added a teaspoon of honey. As she sipped the sweetened liquid, she wondered what Sunul's home was like. She hoped Gina had decorated. She knew Sunul was a minimalist, meaning the walls would be white and bare if he was in charge of home beautification. Priscilla smiled and then snickered almost inaudibly.

It was almost one in the afternoon when Francois returned. The rain had stopped and the sun was occasionally hidden by clouds, but the weather forecast had been correct for once.

Priscilla heard the lock click and the door swing open as Francois entered the apartment. Before he had removed his coat and beret, Francois bent down and gave Priscilla a kiss on the forehead. She was wide-awake now.

"How are you feeling?"

"Not so good," she frowned.

"Upset stomach from the chemicals?"

"No, bad news. The doctor said the chemo is not working. I think I'll go to the US and see if Sunul and Gina can help me. They offered to help once before."

Francois dropped his beret on the sofa and shrugged out of his coat. After hanging it up, he asked, "What about Gisele? Is she going with you? She will miss school."

"I've been thinking about her. I think she should come with me. She has never been to the states. Seeing the US would be a good education for her. If she misses anything, she'll make it up; she's very smart." She smiled at Francois and laughingly said, "She's only in kindergarten, dear."

Francois grinned and then turned serious, "When do you want to go?"

"I need to talk with Gina. Last time she was expecting me, I had to cancel because of my doctor's appointment. But now I don't think I'll see my doctor any longer, the chemo she has had me on isn't working. She recommended I go to the United States for immunotherapy. The US program is the most advanced. I think I'll call Gina after I eat something. Would you like to have some lunch?"

Francois was walking into the kitchen. "What if I cook for you? What would you like?"

"Oh, Francois, I don't know. Just make us some sandwiches—something light, some cheese, and a bit of wine; some of that Oregon claret. It's very good."

She watched her husband, tall and thin, even taller than Sunul, eight-years older than herself, busy himself in their efficiency kitchen. She was admiring his wavy black hair, wishing her cancer was in the past and her silken-blonde filaments were back. Combing her shoulder-length hair in the morning had been an important aspect of her daily routine. Prior to the cancer, when Francois left for the architectural firm in the early morning, she would sketch, paint, and develop new approaches to the colors of subjects beginning to appear on her canvasses from the tip of her charcoal pencil. It had been six months since her creative juices had been expressed with much enthusiasm.

"Is Sunul back from Mars?" Francois asked as he placed sandwiches on the table.

"I don't think so, we would have gotten a note by now if he had returned."

"Sunul's comments sounded as if he knew of a cure. Gina seemed to have the same opinion. I wonder what they know."

"I've been thinking about what they said in their last letter. I had the feeling that Sunul was going to Mars to get something, but what could he be after that would fight cancer?"

"Come to the table, dear. Let me tell you about my new project while we eat, then you can arrange for your flight to Florida. I wish I could go with you and Gisele, but I can't go now. Maybe I'll be able to take some time off in November."

Priscilla's call to Gina was encouraging. Sunul would be back in about a week. He was accompanying two caskets containing the Winslow doctors. Instead of cremation, they wanted to be buried in their family plots in Lincoln, Nebraska. The space agency was making the shipping arrangements and Sunul would ensure their safe travel. Gina told Priscilla to fly to Orlando, only an hour's drive from the Burkes' home. Gina, Sunul, and the kids would meet her and Gisele at the airport. Priscilla made a reservation with Aero-Europa for October 7. She and her daughter would leave Paris in nine days.

A dust storm began in the mid-summer early afternoon on Mars, but as usual, it didn't amount to much. In fact, the atmosphere is so thin, the pressure on the dome was slight, but the sunlight was dimmed for about an hour. During the blow, Sunul walked to the communications center and retrieved his com unit. He returned to the medical facility after listening to Rob's voice telling him the rest of the transmission was a plan for constructing the live-in coffin. Art was in the lab processing some patient body fluids when Sunul entered the building and asked, "Art, are you with a patient?"

"No, Sunul, we're alone. My last patient left about five minutes ago."

"Good. I need to use the lab computer. I've got the plans for Shania's living quarters while on her trip back to Earth."

"Come into the lab. The computer is idle; go ahead and run your program."

Art put down his samples and joined Sunul at the display as the holographic image began to appear above the lab bench. As they studied the growing image, Art commented, "That friend of yours has thought of everything I was considering and then some. He knows how to construct something from nothing, doesn't he?"

"Yeah, he's amazing. I didn't expect to get this back until tomorrow. He must have developed this entire plan in a couple of hours."

Art and Sunul began accumulating the materials to fabricate the container for Shania. The carbon dioxide absorbers were to be made from the replacement units for EVA suits. Water and food were easily obtained from the medical supplies and from the two men's living quarters. Diapers were taken from the EVA supply storage unit so Shania wouldn't have to wear a catheter. A pressure equalization valve was removed from an EVA suit and installed in an inconspicuous location in the upper casket wall. Foam rubber was installed to fit Shania's body and LED lights for reading, writing, and eating activities were wired inside the container and connected to batteries.

Rob had commented that the total weight of the two joined caskets and contents should agree with the weights of the empty caskets and the two Winslows. Art checked the medical records for Ed Winslow's body weight. They didn't want to wait for the discovery of Ed's body under the cave-in debris before they prepared the large shipping container.

In spite of a few interruptions due to patient care, Art and Sunul had the apparatus nearly completed in less than a day. They used the storage area at the back of the medical lab for their construction site. The next afternoon, when they were satisfied with the preliminary assembly, there were only two things remaining. One was to have a rehearsal with Shania safety-belted inside, the other was to install an environmental control package. That afternoon, Lloyd recovered Ed's body from the debris pile and brought it to the medical lab.

Some decomposition had begun, but the men didn't open the EVA suit, they just weighed the body and subtracted the weight of the EVA suit. Sunul removed the environmental control backpack and installed it in the shipping container. Because of Shania's lack of physical activity while in the coffin, a single temperature controller was all that was necessary for the container. Art swapped the partially used contents of the salvaged pack with new inserts. They were ready for a trial run. Rather than try to smuggle Shania to the medical facility, they decided to use the hovercraft and fly the container to their quarters.

When Art and Sunul arrived at their quarters, they unloaded the container and carried it into the living room. Shania directed the rearrangement of the lightweight furniture to accommodate the container yet still allow movement through the room. She surprised the men with dinner. While they ate, Sunul told them what Rob had found out about Jim Frieland and Evan Shiner.

"Guess what I found out about Frieland."

Art answered, "He's working for the pharmaceutical corporation."

Shania nodded in agreement, but was shocked when Sunul said, "Nope. He's unquestionably a CIA operative. He has nothing to do with any corporation. He's government all the way, straight as they come."

She resumed chewing her meat substitute, swallowed, and asked, "What about Shiner?"

Sunul frowned, "He's the one I don't understand. He works for a company that does the shady contract-work for the pharmaceuticals."

"What?" Art was taken by surprise. "How could that be, he rescued Shania from the cave-in site."

"I know. He was trying to pry some information from me about where Shania was recovering. I think he was trying to break in here."

Shania commented, "But he could have killed me at the cave-in site. Why would he rescue me?"

Art answered. "We would have gotten his physiological data which would have incriminated him."

"Could be something else, Art."

"What's that?"

"What if he has the hots for Shania?" Sunul grinned, but then followed with, "I'm serious. Shania is very good looking." Both men looked at her.

Shania blushed and said, "Now you *are* kidding. Why would he think I could be interested in him? I'm married, and he's at least fifteen years older than I am. She suddenly realized Ed was dead, she was single. She glanced at Sunul and Art. "So you think Shiner killed Ed?"

"A very strong possibility, Shania. Now he's looking for you when his physiological parameters aren't being monitored. We don't monitor anyone inside the dome."

"You can't do that?" Sunul was disappointed with the information from Art.

"Oh, we could do it, but it never has been necessary. As soon as an EVA suit is inside the dome all parameters are dropped from the computer." Art looked at Shania and she nodded.

"That's correct, Sunul. It's always been that way on Mars. Otherwise we'd have data coming out our ears—most of it useless. We'd also have to have a more elaborate computer system for receiving and storing data." She grinned, "The Agency wouldn't fund it."

Sunul changed the subject. "Are you claustrophobic, Shania?"

She didn't answer immediately. A few seconds passed and she said, "I don't think so. I guess you want me to try out my shipping carton. Let's clean up the dishes first and then I'll get acquainted with my travel home." She laughed and tried to hobble toward the kitchen, but Art grabbed her around the waist, guided her to the cot, and ordered, "Sit! Sunul and I will clean up. You just relax."

Chapter 18

With Art's and Sunul's assistance, Shania climbed into the shipping carton and pulled the hinged upper portion down. The men heard two clicks as the coffins locked together. Sunul wanted to ask Shania how she felt when sealed in the container, but he was afraid his com unit would transmit too far. If someone intercepted a communication, the secrecy of her being shipped alive to Earth would be lost. She stayed in the compartment for about ten minutes before popping the seal and opening the coffin.

"Surprise!" Shania sat up in the container and looked around smiling, and said, "Is the party over?"

Both men laughed and Sunul reacted, "Jill-in-the-box?"

"You are certainly not a puppet, Shania. How was it in there?" Art was smiling.

"Not at all bad. I tried all the conveniences—except for the diapers," she grinned. "I think I'd better not wear any kind of pants; I'll have trouble applying the diapers if I wear anything on my lower half. When I get back to Earth, Gina can help me get dressed and Sunul can lift me out of the enclosure. What do you think, Sunul?"

He answered, "That should work." He grinned, "You know, I've seen naked women before."

She grinned, "Well, don't plan on seeing this woman naked."

Art laughed, "Never?"

Shania didn't answer, she just said, "Would one of you—gentlemen, help me out of here?" She looked at Art and smiled.

Art bent down into the funerary box, hoisted Shania out, and placed her on the cot. He stepped back and asked, "Can you think of anything else for your trip?"

"Let me think about it. When do we leave Mars?"

Sunul was looking at the arrival/departure times displayed on his com unit. He stuck the unit in his pocket and said, "We leave tomorrow at 4:00 p.m. The departure following that will be eight days from now. Will you be ready in sixteen hours?"

Shania sighed, glanced at the coffin, then the two men, and replied, "Let's do it. I want to get this experience behind me. This trip home will conclude my last visit to Mars."

"One last thing, Shania. If I can get into the cargo hold, I will be checking the coffins daily. I'll tap on the container with this code: tap, pause, two taps, pause, one last tap. If you are all right, give two short taps back. Oh, we need to leave here two hours before liftoff. Art and I will load you into the shuttle cargo bay. The transfers might be a little noisy. Also, I checked on the cargo hold, it will be pressurized to one Earth atmosphere."

Art added, "I'm going to put biohazard decals on your carton. No one will try to open your coffins. If your box gets pried open, you can scare the shit out of them by sitting up and talking. I imagine whoever it is will faint." He grinned.

"I wouldn't even think about that happening. The chances are damn near this big." Sunul held up his hand with his thumb and index finger forming a zero. "The reason I say that is I'm going to put two metal bands around the coffins to make sure they don't separate. If I don't hear a response when I tap on the coffins, I'll cut the bands and open the container."

"That makes me feel better, Sunul. I'm not going to worry."

At 1:00 p.m. the following day, Shania mentioned to Art, "I just thought of something. I need a muscle stimulator; it only weighs about half-a-pound."

Art, Sunul, and Shania had just finished lunch and were killing time until two o'clock, when Shania would be sealed in the two-coffin container. She had decided to wear under garments until she was secure in the large container. She had never been an exhibitionist and though she knew the two men had seen unclothed women before, she still possessed modesty. She understood it was the nature of a man to sneak a look at a beautiful woman's body, clothed or unclothed. Of course, an unclothed female figure was a much greater temptation. Shania was aware she was an attractive female and she had worn a pair of Art's briefs. She would insert the diapers into the undershorts when she was isolated so the diapers could be worn.

As the minutes ticked away, approaching 2:00 p.m., Shania went into the bathroom, then the bedroom, and removed the cast. She changed to a T-shirt and briefs and reapplied the leg support. She then called to the men, "I'm ready to get in the coffin."

Sunul laughed and glanced at Art. "First time I've ever heard a body ask to be placed in a coffin."

He grinned when he saw Shania and said, "I hope you put on a clean pair of my briefs."

She gave him a dirty look and replied, "I borrowed the cleanest pair I could find. I'll return them on Earth if you like."

"That won't be necessary, just burn them."

Sunul picked up Shania and lowered her into the bottom of the shipping container. She wiggled around for a moment and then said, "Close the lid and thank-you both. I hope to see you again on Earth."

Art walked over to the coffins, leaned down and kissed Shania on the forehead. "Have a good trip. Oh, your com unit is fully charged, but don't transmit anything until you're back home. I updated the books and movies for you."

"Thank-you, Art. You're a good man. See you on Earth." She winked and dropped the lid on the container. The men could hear the internal lock click, sealing Shania in the coffin for the next week.

Art assisted Sunul with the loading of the coffins onto the hovercraft. Sunul flew to the western dome entrance and loaded the coffins into a crawler. After climbing into his EVA suit, he started the engine, opened the outside door and began the short excursion to the launching terminal cargo area. The doors opened automatically when the crawler approached the building and Sunul drove onto the receiving dock.

Sunul's audio link came to life, "How can I help you, sir?"

"I've got cargo bound for Earth—two coffins. I'd like them banded so there's no chance of them being separated. If you show me the tools, I'll take care of it."

"That's not allowed. I'll get the tool and be right with you. I have to suit up, the cargo area is not pressurized."

It took about five minutes before a freight packager appeared carrying a hand-held device shaped like a gun with a cylindrical attachment approached Sunul. Sunul had already removed the coffins from the crawler.

"This the package?" The EVA suit inquired.

"Yes, sir. Two bodies going back to Earth. I'm going, too, but I wanted to make sure the package goes as a unit. I don't want to be looking for a coffin back on Earth. The bodies haven't been processed by an undertaker. Seems like there isn't one on Mars."

"That's right. Normally, after the physician has examined the body, we cremate the remains. Then we spread the ashes outside the dome. Ashes make good fertilizer, you know."

"Can you band the coffins together?"

"Yep. That's what this is for." He held up the banding tool. "It'll just take a minute. If you tip the package on one edge, I'll shoot the band under and then if you'll tip the other way, I'll snare it and fuse the ends together."

Sunul watched the ribbon snake out of the hand tool and seek an opening between the coffins and the shipping dock. "How does that work?" he asked.

"It's got an optical sensor that seeks an opening using piezoelectrics. If the tip doesn't find an opening, we have to tip the carton from the other side, then the ribbon shoots through and we can fuse the ends together."

"Can the band be cut with a knife?"

"Nope! You have to use a laser cutting tool. That ribbon only comes apart at a temperature of three-thousand-degrees Celsius. Those old-tech Nylon and steel bands are a thing of the past."

Sunul was relieved that the coffins were going to be secure from tampering. He thought, "But why would anyone want to open a coffin on its way to Earth?" A few seconds later he answered his question, "Someone looking for Shania expecting she's still alive."

The container was loaded on a forklift and the driver said, "You can check in upstairs—just follow the purple dashes."

Sunul watched the small vehicle with the coffins speed away to a lift. After the elevator doors closed, he followed the floor markings to the departure desk two floors above the cargo area. He was amused as he ascended two flights of stairs. He smiled as he followed the purple trail through an airlock at the passenger level. He was thinking that whoever designed the terminal thought the cargo was more important than the comfort of the passengers, and in this case he was right.

He secured his helmet to his utility belt and walked to the checkout desk. The clerk appeared from an opening behind the counter and said, "You're the passenger with the coffin cargo?"

Sunul nodded and replied, "Correct. I'm Sunul Burke, travelling to Earth. I don't have any luggage to check, just the coffins. I'd like a shipping receipt."

"I'm Andy Sanders, Mr. Burke. Glad to meet you. You have quite a reputation on Mars."

Sunul shook hands with Andy and asked, "When do we lift off?"

Andy glanced at the console and mentioned, "About fifteen minutes, sir. Your cargo has been loaded. There will be one other passenger, a Mr. Shiner. He hasn't arrived yet."

Sunul was somewhat startled when he heard the other passenger's name. Shiner was the chief suspect in Dr. Winslow's murder. Did Shiner suspect Shania was in the coffin and alive? Sunul had a question for the shipping clerk, "Can a passenger get into the cargo hold during the flight back to Earth?"

The young mister Sanders replied, "You'll need to access the coffins?"

"No. I'm just curious about access if there's an emergency."

"There's an emergency access panel behind seat number four. If it is opened, an alarm signal will be activated. Breaching the inner cargo wall is not a good idea, the outer wall of the ship is not fail-safe in the cargo area."

"Thanks, Andy. That's good to know." Sunul rejected the idea that Evan Shiner would be trying to enter the cargo hold with the intent of opening the coffins. Sunul was confident that Shiner had pounded on his quarters' door when Shania was there alone.

Sunul was assigned seat three and Shiner was assigned seat two, diagonally ahead of Sunul. The other two seats were vacant. As Sunul took his seat and watched Shiner make himself comfortable in seat two, Sunul wondered who the other two passengers would be. When the outside cabin door slammed shut, Sunul realized the other two seats would not be occupied, the weight of the coffin accounted for the other two travelers. The cabin illumination changed from white light to red and the pilot made an announcement.

"This is your pilot. I will be taking you to the orbiting station where you will be transferred to the ship returning to Earth. I will also be piloting that ship. My name is Captain James Frieland. My copilot will check your seating; her name is Bethany Franklin."

Sunul had less than a second to digest the pilot's announcement when the forward cabin door slid open and the copilot appeared. Sunul read the ID badge above her left breast pocket. His thoughts shifted back to the pilot's name: James Frieland. That had taken Sunul completely off-guard. Sunul knew Frieland worked for the CIA, but that didn't prevent him from being a qualified interplanetary ship pilot. But why was Sunul unaware of that?

Miss Franklin stepped into the cabin and gave a fleeting smile and a quick wave to Evan and Sunul. Her head was shaved and she sported bright-crimson lips, purple eyebrows, and light-blue eyeshadow. The Transportation Bureau encouraged the garish adornment of the stewards as long as they avoided piercings. A study had determined facial decorations tended to relieve anxiety of passengers on long space flights. Sunul felt like he was in a dream and had gotten on a carnival ride.

But Bethany was very businesslike and announced, "Please don your helmets and fasten your seat belts. We'll be off in four minutes. The countdown can be seen on the forward bulkhead. It will be a few minutes to the orbiting station. I'll see you then." With that, she disappeared into the forward part of the ship. The cabin lights changed to green and the digital countdown panel glowed with red digits. The time read 3:11.

Sunul leaned back into his cushioned seat and exhaled. He closed his eyes for a moment and wondered, "What is Evan Shiner doing on this journey to Earth? As soon as we're off the shuttle and on the ship to Earth, we're going to have a talk." The time read 2:41.

The centrifugal force was typical for the three revolutions around the circular runway as the ship accelerated before the rocket engines took over and powered the transition vehicle through the rarefied atmosphere. Escape velocity was attained in less than fifteen seconds and the vehicle reached the stationary orbiting station in about five minutes. The docking maneuvers were automatic and were completed in less than ninety seconds. Bethany reappeared with bronze-colored lip gloss and ushered Evan and Sunul off the ship and into the station's airlock. They hadn't had to wear their helmets.

The men were encouraged to use the toilet facilities prior to their week-long excursion to Earth. Sunul felt no urges but washed his hands and face. When he exited the bathroom, he glanced out an observation window and watched the coffins being transferred to the earthbound ship. As soon as the ship left the orbiting station, Sunul wanted to check on Shania. He had to move into the cargo hold and tap on the container to make sure Shania was healthy.

Following that, Sunul was going to have a talk with Evan Shiner.

It had taken ten minutes to transfer all the earthbound cargo. In addition to the coffins, there was a large box. Sunul was just able to make out the label from thirty meters. The label read 'electronics for repair.' Sunul wondered what items the box contained. It seemed to him that most damaged equipment was normally buried or fed into one of the nuclear power plants as fuel. The only thing he could think of was the rare-earth elements and precious metal contents were going to be salvaged. So far, only trace quantities of those elements had been discovered on Mars.

Bethany joined the two men and escorted them down the curved hallway   to the airlock.

"Please don your helmets, the ship has not been pressurized. Following our departure from base and the sealing of all mooring site connections, the ship will be pressurized to one atmosphere. You may take any position you like in the passenger compartment, it is not necessary to assign seats. The distribution of mass is not important in the larger vessel."

Sunul stepped next to Evan and prevented him from raising his helmet. Evan tried to move away, but Sunul had a tight grip on Evan's neck plate.

"What's going on?" Evan's sharp tone demonstrated his annoyance. He tried to brush Sunul's gloved hand away, but quickly realized Sunul was too strong. He relaxed and said, "What do you want?"

"I want to have a frank discussion with you as soon as we get on the ship."

Sunul's menacing look caused Evan to reply, "Okay, but you can't force me to do or say anything. They'll throw you off the ship. I don't know what your problem is."

Sunul released his hold on Evan's suit and put on his own helmet. He watched Evan trying to lock his helmet in place. Evan was noticeably affected by Sunul's confrontation, and on the third try, was able to engage his helmet on his neck plate. Sunul was almost ready to offer his assistance, but refrained.

"Are we going to have difficulty with you men on this flight?" Bethany grabbed Sunul's left arm and turned him toward her.

Sunul answered very calmly, "I don't think so. Don't worry, I won't start anything. I want to talk to Mr. Shiner about some serious business, that's all."

"I hope you're right. Fighting on a ship to or from Earth is a major offense—minimum prison sentence of ten years."

"You might remind Mr. Shiner of that fact, Miss Franklin."

Chapter 19

Shiner was securing himself to his seat and didn't bother to look up when Sunul sat beside him. Bethany quickly checked the seat straps and commented, "Two minutes to launch. We won't bother with the countdown. The forces will be negligible during our smooth acceleration period, then we will be coasting for about four days. Of course, we will be picking up additional velocity due to the gravitational attraction of the sun. Let me know if you need anything. The flooring is magnetic so you won't have to float to the bathroom." She gave the men a wink.

Watching both men, she backed to the hatch leading to the cockpit. A few seconds after the hatch closed, Sunul could hear the release hooks disengage and could feel the ship floating away from the satellite. After a thirty-second delay, the engines fired and the earthbound ship was on its way. Sunul felt a small initial force pushing him back into the cushioned seat and then the information screen on the back of the seat in front of him displayed a message in green indicating it was safe to remove his headgear.

A second notice in yellow appeared: Please slide your helmet under your seat. Sunul noticed Evan following the instructions. Sunul ensured his helmet was fastened in the storage location and sat back to relax. He sat quietly for a couple of minutes and then decided it was time to begin questioning Evan.

"Why did you kill Doctor Ed Winslow?" Sunul turned toward Evan and waited for a reply.

Evan raised his voice, "You think I killed that guy? You're crazy, Burke. I was hired to watch you, not kill anyone. I've never disposed of anyone in my life, even though I felt like it a couple of times."

"You've been watching me?"

"That's right. I lost track of you the other day. I went to your quarters and knocked on the door. No one answered, so I left."

"I was at the medical facility talking with Dr. Corcoran. Why have you been watching my activities?"

"Orders. I was told to keep an eye on you. Something about locating some children that were born in space. My handler didn't explain the details. I do what I'm told. They said you might try to contact the children."

"So you haven't been after Shania Winslow?"

Evan smiled and squirmed a little. "I've been after her all right, but not to cause any harm. I wanted to get to know her—she's a real beauty, isn't she? After I found her hurt, I guess I did a bit of stalking. Where in the hell did you put her? Is she all right?"

Sunul was beginning to think Evan Shiner was telling the truth. Evan *did* have romantic ideas about Shania. Apparently, Shiner didn't suspect that Shania was alive and sealed in the coffins. "Well, Evan, she expired from her injuries. She had some internal problems that Dr. Corcoran couldn't deal with. We kept her alive a few days and when her husband was killed, she lost the will to live. It was her wish to be buried with her husband in their family plot in Nebraska. I'm escorting the bodies back to the Winslows' estate."

Shiner frowned, "God, that's too bad. She was a gorgeous woman. I had hoped she might want to thank me for saving her from that cave-in by granting me a special wish or something."

"I doubt that you would ever have had a chance of that happening, Shiner. She was devoted to her husband."

"Yeah, you're probably right about that. I hoped there might be a chance for me after I found her husband's body outside the dome. I didn't think they had much of a marriage."

Shiner shrugged and tilted his seat back. "You married?"

Sunul thought, "Maybe Shiner isn't such a bad guy after all. I might as well get to know him, we're going to be riding together for seven days. Maybe he's a chess player."

Sunul glanced at Shiner and said, "Yes. We have two kids."

"I've never married—been too busy doing other people's dirty work. I'm getting tired of it. I'm forty-five now. I need to find someone and settle down."

"Any prospects?"

Shiner paused a few seconds and replied, "No. I had hoped to ask Dr. Winslow for a date back on Earth, but that was a pipe dream. Ah, she was too pretty for me anyway."

"You're not homely, Evan, but she was a medical doctor and had a PhD in psychology."

"Yeah. I knew she was very smart, but I have a MS in mining technology. I'm not a dummy. It might have worked."

"Shania was about fifteen years younger than you are—that's quite an age difference."

"I know, but my dad married a woman that was twenty-eight years younger than he was. Their tenth anniversary is coming up in December. They were married Christmas day."

Sunul smiled, "So your mother is younger than you are?"

"Uh-huh. It seems like she's my sister. People think she's my wife, not my mother. They're always surprised. It's kind of funny sometimes." Evan grinned, "I like to see the look on people's faces when they figure it out. One time an elderly lady gasped and almost fainted. My dad, mom, and I had a big laugh about it."

"What happened to your birth mother?"

"She died in a car wreck, but my dad recovered. He tried to avoid the accident, but the other driver had a heart attack and hit them head-on. It was a real mess."

"That was before the lane-guidance system was invoked?"

"Yeah. Head-on crashes can't happen anymore."

"I believe the highway departments also installed electronic speed control on all roadways about then."

Evan laughed, "I know a lot of drivers that are irritated that they can't exceed the speed limit any more."

"Only if you have a permit. A friend of mine can speed whenever he has to—to reach someone in need."

"Yeah, cops too." Evan looked at his com unit and then back at Sunul, "If you don't mind, I'm going to take a little nap. We can talk some more over dinner."

Sunul responded, "Sounds like a good idea." Sunul tipped his seat back, sighed, and closed his eyes for about five minutes. When he heard snoring from the adjacent seat, he signaled for assistance from Bethany. He didn't want to rouse Evan, so he got up and moved forward to be able to talk with Bethany out of earshot of Shiner.

Bethany was startled when she came through the door and encountered Sunul leaning against the bulkhead.

"Sorry to scare you, but I didn't want Mr. Shiner to hear our conversation."

"What can I do for you, Mr. Burke?"

"I'd like to check my cargo. I want to see if anything has shifted."

Bethany thought for a moment and then said, "Follow me, please. I'll show you to the cargo hold. I don't believe there has been any shifting or damage to the cargo, but you can certainly check."

Sunul was admiring Bethany's figure as she led him about twenty-feet through two small hatches and stopped at a larger door marked CARGO. She swiped her ID card across the playing-card-size panel mounted on the door and it slid open.

"Here you are, Mr. Burke. Will you need any help?"

"No. Thanks, Bethany. I see the carton. It will just take me a minute. You probably have other duties to perform. I'll seal the door and go back to my seat when I'm finished. Thanks again."

Sunul watched Bethany turn and walk away. He moved to the coffins and tapped the code. There was a slight delay, then he heard two muffled taps and could feel the vibrations with his hands. Shania was all right. He wished he could remove her from the container, but thought better of it; she was safe where she was. Besides, he would have to use a laser cutter to remove the straps. Cutting through the wall of the coffin might injure Shania.

Sunul exited the cargo hold and sealed the door. As he was returning to the passenger compartment, he still had lingering suspicions of Shiner. Evan Shiner could have been lying to him about not trying to kill the Winslows. If Shiner hadn't disposed of Ed Winslow, who would have struck the fatal blow? The space agency was going to have to send an investigation team to Mars; the killer would not go unpunished. Of the over two-hundred scientists and support personnel on Mars, someone was guilty. Sunul's report about the murder would cause anyone returning from Mars to be under suspicion until the crime was solved.

Evan woke up when Sunul returned to his seat. He stood there for a moment looking at Evan.

"Is there a problem?" Evan was blinking his eyes and smoothed his hair back from his forehead with his left hand.

"You're a lefty?"

Evan raised his left hand, "Guilty as charged. I write and throw with my left hand but I bat right-handed. Kind of strange, huh?"

"I suppose—never thought much about it, I'm ambidextrous." Sunul was thinking about what Art had said about Ed Winslow's killer; the murderer was probably right-handed.

"When I woke up, you were standing over me. What's going on?"

"Don't worry. I just came back from the cargo hold. Bethany let me in to check my shipping box. I wanted to see if it had shifted or tipped over."

"Something important in it?"

"Yeah. I'm taking some rock samples and maps to the Smithsonian for some expert examination. Some of the rock samples are very fragile."

Evan just nodded and closed his eyes.

Chapter 20

Sunul waited nearly twenty-four hours before making his next check on Shania. Evan's sleep cycle had been initiated with his first nap after arriving on the ship and was continuing as Sunul had hoped. The two men had little more conversation and carried on as if the other was not present. Except for one game of chess, which Sunul won easily, they seemed to live in separate universes. Sunul enjoyed the solitude and recalled all the experiences he had while on Mars.

The remainder of the travel week passed uneventfully. On the morning of the last day, Sunul asked Bethany if he could join the pilots for a view of the Earth as the ship approached. She disappeared into the cabin and when she reopened the door, she motioned for Sunul to enter the operations center.

"Take the copilot's chair, Mr. Burke. We're on autopilot until we are within 15,000 km of the moon base."

Sunul slid into the form-fitting chair and took a look at their heading. The half-moon looked very small when compared to the nearer marble sized sphere of the Earth. Sunul was estimating the time left before he would be back on Earth kissing Gina, and hugging Libby and Miles. He was hoping he could leave trips to Mars in his past. As he watched the moon and Earth hanging in the black of space, Captain Frieland commented, "Happy to be nearly back on Earth?"

Sunul glanced at the pilot and said, "Yeah. I think that was my last trip to Mars. I'm going to stay on good old Earth after this. You know, I thought you were in cahoots with the pharmaceutical industry. You had me fooled for a long time. When did the CIA begin hiring interplanetary ship pilots?"

Frieland laughed, "Years ago when I first met you on Mars, I was very intimidated, Mr. Burke. After I studied your report on the trip to the Kuiper Belt, I decided to train for space travel. The agency was all for it, so I spent a year in New Mexico and six months on the moon cramming everything I could get about space travel into my brain. I still don't know how you accomplished your return to Earth from the outer region of the solar system."

"I was too young and foolish to know the slim odds back then. My crew made a big difference between success and failure. I had some ideas, but the crew carried out most of the important work."

"Well, it was an amazing trip. Every student of space travel reads of your exploits. You are a hero to many people and I imagine every new cadet. Your piloting was top-notch."

"Thank-you, captain. What's the procedure for moon landing?"

"It's all automated. Bethany and I have to make a few minor adjustments to thrust vectors, but that's about it. The computers instruct us what to do. The days of manual landing are in the past. A well-informed child could land these ships." Captain Frieland looked away from the viewing port, smiled, and extended his hand to Sunul.

Sunul shook hands, stood up, turned, and motioned for Bethany to return to the copilot's chair. As he backed out of the cockpit, he saluted and said, "Thanks for the view."

Three hours later, Bethany announced, "We're an hour from lunar landing. Make sure you have all your belongings gathered and labeled. There are containers, labels, and marking instruments in the panel marked miscellaneous at the front of the passenger cabin. You should be secured in your seats when the interior lights switch to red. You will have an hour wait at the lunar landing site. You may make contact with any location on Earth using a secure line during that time. Before you are transferred to the Earth-bound ship, make sure your cargo is loaded. If it is not retrieved within one hour of landing, it will be warehoused and inspected within forty-eight hours. The agency does not want to store off-world materials for any length of time."

The touchdown at moon base Grimaldi was uneventful. As soon as the ship was pulled into the underground facility and the red caution lights were extinguished, Evan and Sunul slid their helmets from under their seats. Facing each other while holding their headgear, Evan spoke, "I'm still going to be watching you, Mr. Burke. Don't be surprised if you see me again—but maybe not this close."

"Watch all you like, but if you interfere with me, my family, or my friends, you will regret it. Believe me."

Evan replied, "Fair enough. I'll be doing my job." He extended his hand but Sunul ignored the gesture. Evan was on notice. They would never be friends.

Bethany waited for the men to don their helmets then escorted them through the cavern to the waiting area. In the eight years since Sunul had been at the base in the Grimaldi crater, little had changed, except perhaps a fresh coat of paint. The walls, previously gray, were now a light-yellow and the direction stripes on the floor were now dashed lines instead of the original solid colors. Sunul mused, "The agency is trying to save costs." He smiled and looked for the secure communication lines in order to place calls to Gina and Rob.

He entered the shielded bubble and pressed Gina's picture on his com unit. She answered on the third ring, "When will you be home, honey? We've missed you so much."

"Tomorrow, but I haven't found out whether I'll come into the base in Florida or California. I have a large cargo box containing things that need special handling. I'll call Rob after we get through talking. How are you and the kids doing?"

"We're fine. Miles and Libby have been missing your help with their homework. I've offered to help, but they want you, especially Libby. The Patels are still with us but they say they will move out when you get home. I'll advise them tonight."

"How's Hugh doing with his prosthetic?"

"He's learning all kinds of tricks with his new hand. He's been using it a lot for removing lids from jars and cracking nuts. He seems to enjoy performing. He delights with crushing glass bottles and aluminum cans. He's been asking about your experiences on Mars. Of course, I haven't been able to tell him much."

"I'll tell you the whole story when I see you and the Patels. I'll call you again when I find out my itinerary. Oh! Guess what! Jim Frieland was my pilot from Mars to the moon. He's one of the good guys."

Gina laughed, "He sure had me fooled. I thought he was body waste. Funny how perceptions are. Well, we'll be waiting for you. Have a safe trip and take care of that cargo."

"Okay, will do. Bye dear."

"Bye for now, Sunul."

Sunul was happy to have heard Gina's voice after three weeks off Earth. Now he had to find out the destination of the return flight to terra firma: California, Texas, or Florida. He used his com unit and called the Grimaldi central office. In a few sentences he found that the Earth-bound ship was scheduled to set down at Earth landing strip Canaveral, ELS-4, at 9:00 a.m. the following morning. The next step was to place a call to Rob Griswalt.

"Hey, Griz, know anyone in the mortuary business that can be trusted?"

"Sunul! Good to hear your voice. Yeah, I have a contact I can call. He's helped me before. When will you be coming in?"

"Tomorrow at 9:00 a.m., ELS-4. Can you meet me with a truck and a mortician to sign the papers? Oh! I'll need a laser torch to cut the security bands on the container. Please call Gina for me and tell her the details. I've got to get on the ship in a couple of minutes."

"No problem, buddy. I'll be there with the equipment so we can air out the container."

"Sounds great, Rob. I'd like to get some air in there ASAP."

"You want to take the contents to your place?"

"That's right. I want Gina to look at the bodies."

Rob laughed, "I'd like to see the bodies, too."

"I'll bet you would. All in good time, my friend. See you at nine o'clock. Thanks, Griz. Bye."

"Radar out."

Sunul smiled at Rob's comment about seeing the bodies. Rob knew there was only one body in the coffin and Shania certainly wasn't dead. Although Rob had never met Shania, he had heard of the pretty doctor.

Sunul exited the secure communications bubble and moved to the passenger loading area where he could observe cargo being placed on the Earth-bound ship. He hadn't checked with Shania since the day before, but it was too late now. He decided to wait for eight hours until they were back on the landing strip in Florida. But if he was provided an opportunity, he would check on the doctor when they docked with the orbiting satellite in geostationary orbit, ninety minutes before touch down.

Evan Shiner was sitting in the waiting area reading when Sunul arrived. Shiner didn't bother to look up from the novel he had purchased at the boarding kiosk. There was no longer a boarding pass, a retinal scan was all that was necessary. Sunul leaned into the scanner and saw the green acknowledge light blink. The computer voice stated, "Thank-you for checking in, Mr. Burke. Your ship will be leaving in five minutes."

Sunul moved to the viewing port and watched as the ship's cargo hold was receiving the large coffin containers bound together. Knowing everything was moving as planned, he relaxed and sat down next to the space-way that led to the ship. In less than a minute, a buzzer sounded, a blinking green panel was illuminated and Bethany appeared at the space-way hatch.

She motioned to Sunul and Evan and said, "Gentlemen, please come with me."
Bethany waited until the men were standing and shuffling toward her when she instructed, "Please secure your helmets. The space-way is not pressurized. When seated aboard the ship, and the light turns green, you may remove your headgear."

Bethany swung her helmet into position, twisted it until the mechanism locked, watched as Sunul and Evan followed her arm movements, led them through the tunnel, and into the Earth-bound ship. After checking the three sets of seat straps, she spoke into her suit's com-link, "Ready for travel, Captain."

The cabin lights dimmed from bright-white to a rose-colored glow and Sunul could feel the ship uncoupling from its harness connections. A small vibration occurred as the ship began accelerating, moving rapidly from the Grimaldi base toward rendezvous with the geostationary satellite over the Pacific Ocean.

Sunul fell asleep soon after they left the moon base, and when he woke up four hours later, his helmet had been removed. He turned and looked to his right at Evan. Evan was smiling and said, "You snore heavily, Burke, but it didn't bother me. I've been enjoying Mozart and Beethoven while you sounded off."

"Glad I didn't bother you, Shiner. I would have been embarrassed, maybe even upset a little." At this point in Sunul's relationship with Shiner, he really wasn't concerned about how loud he had been snoring.

"Bethany was going to rotate your seat, but I told her not to bother, you weren't bothering me."

"If she had done that, I'm sure I would have awakened. Thanks for the assist. I guess I was more tired than I thought. When I get home, everyone will be up so I'll resume my regular biorhythm."

Those were the last words Sunul had with Evan on the moon to Earth ship. Their seats were behind one another on the glider to Earth's surface and when they deplaned, Sunul lost track of Evan when Gina and Rob appeared to welcome Sunul back home. Gena nearly launched herself into Sunul's waiting arms and they hugged and kissed while Rob stood by watching.

Rob laughed and commented, "Wow! That collision must have been like a large asteroid striking the moon millions of years ago."

As the Burkes uncoupled from their celebratory embrace, Gina asked, "Where's the coffin? We've got to get Shania out of there and more comfortable. It's going to take her a couple of days to recover from a week in bed and the increase in gravity."

Rob stepped between his friends and with his arms around their waists said, "Come with me and meet a friend of mine, Mr. Ollie Stiffend."

Sunul glanced at Rob with a quizzical look and Rob reacted, "That's his real name, Sunul."

Gina, Sunul, and Rob climbed onto a golf cart-like base excursion vehicle and sped off to the incoming cargo dock. As they approached the long single-story blue building, Sunul saw the coffin shipping container sitting next to a medium-sized panel-truck labelled "The Remains of Frames— Stiffend and Sons." When the cart pulled up alongside the truck, the driver got out and greeted Rob with a handshake and a pat on the back.

"I've signed for the package, Rob, but we need a signature from an MD as well."

Gina stepped forward and said, "I'll sign off on it."

The driver, Ollie, was introduced to Gina and Sunul, and escorted them into the warehouse office where the official papers were signed.

Chapter 21

Ollie Stiffend was a former college football lineman and had not changed his eating habits much since playing ball. He still weighed nearly 300 pounds and was physically fit. Six-foot six-inches tall, he could intimidate nearly anyone, but he possessed a Teddy bear personality. He was wearing a blue T-shirt stretched thin over his chest and enormous biceps. His black work pants and steel-tipped work boots suggested he was a lumberjack. He was prepared for some heavy lifting. Beads of sweat were forming on his forehead just below his hairline.

"Mr. Griswalt, Mr. Burke, let's get that container loaded and get off this base. I don't like it here."

The three men moved to the coffins and Ollie directed, "You little fellers pick up that end, I'll take this'un." Coworkers had no choice but to follow his directions.

Ollie pushed up the rear loading door of the truck, grabbed the coffins and slid them toward the vehicle. He pointed at the container and after a couple of seconds to allow Rob and Sunul to get a grip, Ollie said, "Lift." Without much effort from his helpers, Ollie slid the coffins into the back of the truck. He turned around and asked, "Any of you want to ride with the deceased?"

"We will," replied Sunul and pointed to Gina. "Rob, why don't you ride up front with Mr. Stiffend?"

Ollie picked up Gina and propelled her into the truck and Sunul swung into the back like he was mounting a horse. The door closed, blocking most of the sunlight, except for the small windows in the truck's roof. Sunul moved to the container and tapped the code. After a short delay there were two taps in response. Shania was all right.

Gina and Sunul grabbed onto the security bands on the coffins to steady themselves as the truck lurched forward and then began moving smoothly.

"Does Rob know we want to go to our place?" Gina had a concerned look.

"Yeah, he knows. I asked him to get us a laser cutter to remove these bands, they can't be cut with hand tools."

"The cutter is probably in his truck at the house. Ollie and Rob picked me up this morning for the trip to the base. Rob parked his security vehicle at the curb." Gina was anticipating the reunion with Shania. It had been seven years since they had seen each other. "It will be great to see Shania again and get her out of this ugly container."

"I agree. I've worried about her ever since Art and I sealed her in there. I'm sure she'll be damn glad to see sunlight again."

It took fifteen minutes to get to the Burkes' driveway. The truck was turned around and backed up to the garage at the side of the house. When Ollie cut the engine, Sunul raised the truck door and dropped to the ground. After helping Gina down, he used his com unit to open the garage door. The men unloaded the coffins and thanked Ollie for his assistance. He would receive credits to his account, even though he said it wasn't necessary, he was happy to have been able to help them.

They watched Ollie drive away, smiling and waving as he started down the block toward the city business district. Rob brought the laser cutter into the garage and Sunul shut the door.

Rob made short work of the security straps and Sunul yelled at the container, "Unlock the box, Shania!"

Gina dimmed the garage lights. They all heard a mechanical click and the coffin top began to fold back. It was almost like an old-time horror movie as the vampire rose from a coffin to suck the blood from another victim. An arm appeared, then a shoulder, a head of hair, and Shania sat up grinning. "Get me out of here. Please!"

Gina was the first to react and saw the soiled nature of Shania's scanty clothing. "Sunul, get one of my bathrobes. Rob, turn on the bathwater in the hallway bathroom." While the men were out of sight, Gina helped Shania stand up and steadied her so she wouldn't fall. It was going to take a few hours, or longer, for Dr. Winslow to get used to Earth's gravity. Sunul returned with one of Gina's pink robes. Gina shielded Shania from view and motioned Sunul to toss the robe. "Now, you guys go away. I'll take care of her until she can get cleaned up."

"Does she need to be carried?" Sunul asked with some concern.

Shania shook her head, thinking she would be able to walk without assistance. Sunul did an about-face and went into the house.

"Okay, we're alone now. Strip off that soiled underwear and slip into this robe. I'll help you to the bathroom. You can soak for as long as you want—there's no shortage of water or soap."

Gina escorted Shania down the hallway and into the spa-like bathroom and helped her into the tub which was large enough for four people. Gina turned on the jets and Shania dropped her robe and slid her svelte sexy body into the bubbling, swirling water.

"Oh, my God! This is almost as good as having sex!" Shania disappeared beneath the water for a few seconds and then sat up, water streaming off her head and upper body. With her eyes closed she reached out to Gina and said, "Shampoo, please."

Gina laughed, "You were isolated from eligible men for too long, Shania."

Rob and Sunul had adjourned to the living room and were having a beer, but could hear the voices coming from the bathroom. Rob motioned toward the bathroom with his bottle and said, "I think there's a pool party in there, Sunul."

"Yeah. I'm wondering what I would be doing after a week in isolation."

Rob looked around, "Where are Hugh and Triel?"

"They must have gone shopping or are in the backyard garden. I'll check and see."

Just as he stood up to move to the kitchen to check outside, the kitchen door opened and Libby ran in yelling, "Daddy! Daddy!" She ran and jumped into Sunul's outstretched arms. He lifted his three-year-old high in the air and said, "Hi, Libby! You look beautiful!"

"So do you, daddy. Where's mommy?" Libby looked around and only saw Rob.

"Say hello to your uncle Rob, Libby." Libby waved at Rob.

"Hello, nuncle Rob." Libby squirmed and said, "Put me down, daddy. I hear mommy in the bathroom."

"You can't go in there, Lib. Mommy's helping a lady take a bath." Sunul hoisted Libby onto his lap and circled his arms around her.

"She was all muddy?"

Sunul laughed and replied, "That's right. She was very dirty, but she'll be pretty when she gets cleaned up. I think you'll like her very much."

Hugh and Triel had been right behind Libby, following her into the house, but they stopped at the kitchen archway to watch the father-daughter reunion before interrupting by coming into the living room. As the Patels came in the room, the doorbell sounded, and the male robotic voice announced, "Guests are at the front door. Robo-taxi drove them from Orlando. They are Priscilla and Gisele Girard. They arrived in the United States from France an hour ago."

Sunul stood, holding Libby on his right hip, rushing to the door, pressing the green open-door panel as he moved down the short hallway. When the door swung open, a robot valet holding two large suitcases asked, "Is this the Burke residence?"

"Yes, it is. We have been expecting the Girard family." Sunul hadn't known when his sister and niece were going to arrive, but decided to cooperate with the android. He could not see Priscilla and Gisele, they were out of sight behind the large humanoid. The valet set the bags just inside the door, backed out onto the porch, and motioned for Priscilla and her daughter to come forward. Sunul lowered Libby to the floor and braced himself when Priscilla ran into his arms. They kissed each other on their cheeks and had a second, prolonged, hug.

"Oh, I'm glad you're back from Mars. It's so good to see you. You know, you're more handsome in person." She stepped back and pulled Giselle forward with her hands on her daughter's shoulders. "This is Giselle, she's five."

Sunul introduced Libby similarly. "This is Libby, she's three. Libby, this is your aunt Priscilla and your cousin Giselle. Why don't you show her your room?"

Libby grabbed Giselle's hand, pulled, and said, "Come with me." The little girls climbed the carpeted stairs holding hands and disappeared down the second floor hallway.

Sunul took Priscilla's hands and held them to his chest. "How are you feeling, Cilla?"

"I'm a little tired from the flight, but I want to find out what Gina can tell me about new cancer treatments."

"Before we get into that, I want you to meet Rob Griswalt and the Patels, Hugh and Triel. The Patels have been staying with us while recovering from some injuries. They were all on the trip to the Kuiper Belt with Gina and me." During the introductions, Sunul's com unit sounded. Miles was calling from school.

"Dad! You're home! I hoped you'd be there. I think I'm being followed. I just talked to Juni Griswalt and she thinks someone is watching her, too. What should I do?"

"I'm sending you a picture. Tell me if this is the guy shadowing you. Ask Juni, too."

"That's the guy, Dad. Juni says that's the guy she saw, too. Who is he?"

"His name is Evan Shiner. If he gets close enough, tell him to remember what Sunul Burke told him. He'll leave you alone, or he's in real trouble. He knows better than to mess with me. Oh, Miles, tell Juni to come home with you. Her parents will be here for dinner."

"Okay. See you after school, Dad."

Following dinner, the group began to thin out. Leanne had joined Rob and they were the first to excuse themselves; they both had to work the next day and daughter, Juni, had school. Hugh and Triel gathered their belongings and moved back to their home, which had been cleaned and updated with advanced security features.

Shania wanted to discuss cancer research with Gina and Priscilla, but she couldn't concentrate or keep her eyes open. It was going to take her a day or two of adjustment to Earth's gravity before her mental processes and physical stamina would allow her to contribute to the research. She had excused herself and gone to bed before the Patels and Griswalts had returned to their homes.

After the children were in bed, Gina, Priscilla, and Sunul sat at the kitchen bar discussing Priscilla's flight and the smuggling of Shania from Mars to Earth. Priscilla said her two-hour flight with Giselle was very comfortable, even the hiring of the taxi had been easily negotiated, but the hour-long ride had been boring.

"You must have been anticipating the sight of my smiling, handsome face."

Priscilla laughed and replied, "It wasn't that, dear brother. Giselle went to sleep and I didn't have anyone to talk to—I had many questions about the automated highways and if the French credits had the same value as the ones in the United States. I should have checked on values of credits before leaving Paris."

"The android taxi drivers speak twelve languages, Cilla, and the credits are the same, worldwide. The banking system is finally universal."

"That's good to know. I think the chemo has dulled my brain and I haven't kept up with things. I was afraid the driver wouldn't speak French and my English isn't so good anymore. Francois and I speak French at home and I have forgotten much of my English from the past. Giselle speaks both languages in kindergarten. Gosh, the last time I was in the US was over fifteen years ago."

Gina asked Priscilla about her chemotherapy and found that the French oncologist was several year's behind in procedures. The cancer cure rates were as high as 93% for all forms of breast cancer.

Gina explained what the plan was to use Shania's blood to generate a drug with 100% effectiveness, but the pharmaceutical industry had anticipated that possibility and had tried to kill Shania on Mars.

Sunul was listening intently and said, "I believe there will be a resurgence of activity to find Adam and Eve and eliminate them when it becomes known that Shania is dead. Evan Shiner should have spread the word by now of what he considers a fact. If someone discovers that Shania is alive and working on a cancer drug, we are all in danger. If you receive any messages from people unknown to you, you can't let on that Shania and Gina are working together. Just make sure no one knows Shania is here. Okay?"

Priscilla looked down at the floor and then quickly eyed Sunul, "What about Gisele? Who shall we say Shania is?"

Sunul looked at Gina for some help.

"Tell her Shania's name is Erica Grossman and she's a lab-tech working with me on a hospital project. I'll have Shania dye her hair and wear some gaudy earrings. We'll give her some temporary tattoos, also."

Sunul smiled, "And have her wear some loose clothing so she's not so sexy."

Gina quipped, "I've got an old agency sweatshirt and a pair of work pants that will fit her. That should keep eyes off the ripe fruit."

Priscilla was smiling, entertained by Gina's and Sunul's comments. She had a serious question, "Sunul, who else knows that Shania is still alive?"

"Only two people. They're both on Mars: Art Corcoran and Floyd Cooper, but I trust both of them."

Priscilla asked with great concern, "With our lives?"

Chapter 22

Gina had set the alarm for 5:00 a.m., but silenced it immediately so not to awaken Sunul, and dressed quickly. She wanted to get Shania into disguise before the children got used to seeing the real Shania. She had to transform Shania into Erica and start the strategic subterfuge. She tapped on the guest bedroom door and entered, moved to the bed, and checked Shania's pulse. It was normal. When she sat on the bed, Shania's eyes flickered and opened wide.

"Oh, it's you, Gina. I was dreaming. A man was sitting on my bed removing his clothes. I couldn't see who it was."

Gina grinned, "I don't know whether you were being lucky or someone was going to attack you."

"I think I'd like to know what man is climbing in to bed with me." Shania sat up, glanced at her clock, and said, "Why are you here? It's so early. It's still dark out, isn't it?"

"We have to transform you into a lab tech named Erica. We'll make you blonde, give you a nose ring, and a few tattoos. Sunul said you should wear some loose-fitting clothes so you wouldn't look so sexy."

Erica grinned, "He said that?"

Gina nodded and answered, "I'm not jealous. He shares his thoughts quite often."

"You've got a good man, Gina."

Gina smiled and said, "Downstairs bathroom, make it quick. I'll get the bleach ready. Bring your makeup kit, we might need it."

An hour later, Erica appeared in all her glory. Short blonde hair, two nose rings, neck tattoos below her ears, and a pair of glasses worn on her forehead made Shania into a new person. When all was done, she looked into the mirror and commented, "Oh, my God. My parents would kill me for looking this way. I feel like three people are in this room."

"Only one more thing; we have to get you some clothes that are too big." Gina smiled, "Remember, Sunul's orders."

The two women went to Gina's and Sunul's bedroom and Gina entered, but not quietly.

Sunul turned over and motioned for Gina to come to him. She sat next to him and he pulled her toward him and kissed her. "Good morning, favorite wife. What's going on?"

"Good morning. I want you to meet someone. She's going to help me in the lab."

Sunul frowned and said, "I thought Shania was—"

Gina interrupted by putting a hand over Sunul's mouth. "Come on in, Erica."

Shania entered the bedroom and moved to the bed with her hand outstretched. Sunul didn't know what to think at first, but when Erica spoke, he recognized her voice immediately.

"Good morning, Mr. Burke."

"Jesus, Shania, your new look will fool anybody, but not your voice." Sunul glanced at Gina and said, "Can you alter her voice?"

Gina smiled and answered, "You want it higher or lower?"

"Higher, dear. If her voice is any lower, she'd have hair on her chest and would be singing baritone in the choir."

Gina laughed, "Okay. We can cause some tightening of her vocal cords and raise her voice about an octave. We've got to be careful though, we don't want her to be too squeaky."

Erica volunteered, "I'll do it, but we might have to order a drug that I can take orally. I don't want any injections into my throat. I'll use a falsetto until we can obtain the drug."

"I'll send a prescription to EC Drug over on Coast Avenue. Sunul can pick it up."

"I'll go for it before the kids get up. It's only fifteen minutes round-trip." Sunul started to get up but hesitated. "Ladies," he motioned for them to leave the room. He wasn't wearing any pajama pants or underwear. As the women exited, Gina was laughing and pushing Erica out the door. As Sunul pulled on briefs, his com unit signaled a long distance call was coming in. It was a short message, followed by three pings, signaling an off-world communication. He put the message on audible: "Hi, Sunul. Just wanted you to know all the debris from the cave-in has been removed and fed into the reactors. Nothing left but a small pile of ashes. There were some elevated carbon dioxide readings, but the CO_2 was not released to the atmosphere. Hope your trip was successful. Floyd Conners."

Sunul smiled at Floyd's confirmation of Dr. Ed Winslow's cremation. Sunul's emotions were buoyed to the highest level since he had returned to Earth. Other problems could now move up the worry-ladder in his mind. He completed dressing, headed for the garage, pushed the coffin package against the east-side wall, and made sure it was secured so children or other curious individuals could not access the interior. He would begin cleaning the interior of the shipping container when the kids were in school. As far as he knew, the agency had no work for him until after the Christmas holiday season.

The drug Erica needed was administered daily with breakfast, but occasionally caused her voice to break like an adolescent boy's transitioning to maturity. Erica explained the occurrences to the children as an allergy to kelp which washed ashore a few miles from the Burkes' residence.

Gina and Erica worked tirelessly for the next three weeks with occasional administration of trial drugs to Priscilla. When she was not taking part in the trials, she baby-sat Giselle and Libby, which was, by far, the majority of the time.

Sunul began renovating the two coffins to prepare them for inhumation at the Winslow family's plot in Lincoln, Nebraska. After removing the living accommodations from the coffins, he added the appropriate weights for Shania and Ed in the separate containers. He repainted the exteriors, fused the tops shut, and attached brass identification plaques to the lids.

After the women inspected the exterior of the coffins and didn't find anything abnormal, Sunul called Ollie Stiffend and paid him to ship the coffins to Nebraska for burial.

Now he could relax and help the children get ready for Halloween, only five days away on Friday.

The experimental lab work had looked promising for a change, but the last few steps in the isolation of the effective agent for the destruction of cancer cells proved to be negative. The three women had a meeting with Sunul on October 30, the day before Halloween.

"I can see the frustration on your faces, ladies. Why do you think it's not working and what's the next step?"

"We think the residual antibody mimicry has been lost because of time. We can only get so far and then we get nothing but vegetable soup; we can't isolate anything that has any potency for fighting the cancer. We are stymied." Gina raised her hands as if she were giving up. "Erica and I think the only avenue remaining is to find Licon and Miranda. Their blood holds the secrets to annihilating the cancer cells. We need their blood."

"Gina's right, Sunul, but where do we start looking for the children?"

"Erica, I don't think you are aware that the children, even though they are only eight years old, are fully grown adults. They appear to be in their twenties—and they are very intelligent. They were in Argentina the last time we had contact and we don't know where they are now."

Sunul hated to say those words; he feared Priscilla would begin to suffer from depression. He was sure she would think there was no hope; it was just a matter of time before she succumbed to cancer, still dreaded world-wide. He expected Priscilla to ask if he and Gina would take care of Gisele. Of course they would, but only after consulting with Francois.

During dinner that evening, Sunul came up with a proposal. There was a lull in the conversation when Miles asked a question, "Is Gisele going to go to school here in Florida?"

Priscilla said, "She'll be ready for the first grade next fall. We should be back in France by then, so probably not." No one spoke for nearly a minute and then Sunul slid back his chair and stood up. "I've got an idea, but I think I'll mention it after the kids are in bed. Anybody for dessert?"

It was nearly ten o'clock when the adults relaxed in the living room with goblets of wine. Gina brought up the subject, "What were you thinking, Sunul?"

"I've been mulling something over. I'd like to know what your impression would be if Hugh Patel and I go to South America and try to find Adam and Eve."

"Adam and Eve?" Erica was unaware of the names Licon and Miranda had chosen instead of the names given them by their parents. Gina explained that the two older children had left a note and exited the alpha group after the four families had lived in Colorado for nearly seven years.

"So that's why you don't know where they are?"

Sunul nodded, "That's right. They said they would be going farther south, but we don't know where. We'll have to go down there and track them. Hopefully, we'll be able to find them and bring back a blood specimen."

"I'll go with you, Sunul. I'll assist you with the blood sample, and I can address any medical issues that might arise in a foreign country. I believe we all have up-to-date immunity to all common diseases." Erica was determined to go on the journey.

"I don't oppose you joining us, but you'll have to change your disguise. Unless there is a celebration taking place in Argentina, you'll stick out like a sore thumb. We don't want any unwarranted attention. I have to talk with Hugh and find out whether he wants to go with us. I think he'll want to go—maybe strangle someone with his new hand." Sunul grinned.

"New hand?" Erica had only briefly met the Patels and didn't notice that Hugh had a prosthetic right hand. She listened intently as Sunul told her what had happened at the Patels' home. "My God, I was thinking the only mayhem had been on Mars. These guys are really playing for keeps. They must not care about the penalties for lawlessness. Maybe they like the penal colony on the moon; that's where their friends are. Do we have any defensive weapons?"

"Rob got Triel and Hugh Patel stun guns, model SG88s. They can only be fired by their owner. They have finger print and retinal recognition so they are useless to anyone else." Sunul grinned, "I'll have Rob get two more, one for each of us for use on our journey."

"Anything else?" Erica was obviously concerned about travelling without several weapons—for different emergencies.

Sunul hadn't thought much beyond the stun guns; his and Hugh's physical strength were also weapons, and Hugh's artificial hand could crush anything short of hardened steel alloy. He glanced at Gina and then back at Erica, "What about some drugs—a fast acting injectable for paralysis? I don't want to kill anyone on foreign soil. We might never return home. Foreign penitentiaries can be death traps."

Erica smiled at the thought of carrying a paralytic drug. She had a good idea for carrying something non-lethal and able to use it in tight situations. "An insulin pen! What do you think, Gina?"

Gina laughed and said, "Good idea, Shania! Oops, I mean Erica. No one would question you carrying an insulin pen. Actually, you might carry more than one."

"You ladies work on the pens. I'll talk with Hugh in the a.m."

Halloween morning was busy for Sunul. He talked with Rob about getting two more SG88 stun guns and then drove to the Patels' and had breakfast with them while Gina, Priscilla, and Erica fed the kids and readied their costumes for trick-or-treating. Gisele had never taken part in Halloween and was very excited, but a little wary of ghosts and scary costumes. Miles hadn't helped; he told Gisele the headless horseman story and when he realized he had scared her, he said he would be with her so nothing would happen, and if she was a little frightened, the candy they would get was worth it. Gina told Gisele no one rode horses any more.

Sunul returned from the Patels' at ten o'clock with the knowledge that Hugh was looking forward to accompanying Erica and him to South America. Hugh and Triel wanted to know if Miranda and Licon were all right. They knew that the children were being pursued by supporters of the pharmaceutical companies. The drug companies had one of two intentions: either monopolize the drugs to cure cancer or eliminate the certain cure by disposing of Licon and Miranda. All members of the alpha group were concerned about the latter possibility.

As the sun was setting, a few early trick-or-treaters were moving from house to house. Rob arrived in his security truck with the stun guns and showed Sunul and Erica how to personalize the weapons. He left for home fifteen minutes later in order to have dinner and go trick-or-treating with Leanne and his two girls. Collecting candy from their immediate neighborhood was a family affair. Rob had waited all year long to wear his gorilla costume.

Chapter 23

The kids were going through their haul of goodies from the neighborhood trick-or-treat activities, the outdoor lights had been extinguished, and the adults were having hot toddies and discussing the up-coming journey to Argentina.

Erica suddenly asked, "What am I going to do for a passport? Shania Winslow is officially deceased."

Priscilla looked at Erica curiously, "Didn't you need a passport to go to Mars?"

Gina laughed, "An astronaut is not required to have a passport. Have you ever been out of the country, Erica? Sorry Priscilla, I'm not laughing at you. I just thought it was a strange question."

Priscilla replied, "I was thinking that if a rocket didn't reach orbit and fell back to Earth, an astronaut might need a passport."

Gina said, "You know, I have never thought of that. Your question wasn't so strange after all. I apologize."

Erica said, "Well, I've never had a passport, but I'll need one. Where do I get a passport, and what should I look like? Oh, what name should I use?"

Sunul volunteered, "I'll take you to the county courthouse tomorrow; they'll prepare the documents. I'm a little worried that they'll run your prints and turn up your true identity, Shania Estwick. But maybe they won't check with the space agency. They'll just run a standard ID to see if you have ever been in prison." He looked at Erica questioningly.

"Never even been arrested, Sunul. No traffic infractions either."

"Pure as the vacuum of outer space," Sunul smiled, then said, "Get rid of the nose rings. Miles told me you look like you have boogers hanging from your nose. I can understand his interpretation." Sunul grinned and stuck his right index finger in his left nostril. The women laughed and Gina hit Sunul's arm, pulling his finger out of his nose.

Gina thought for a moment and then suggested, "We can shave your head and give you several wigs; different colors and hair lengths. You can also use different colors of eyeshadow and lipstick. You can keep the fake tattoos. They don't attract too much attention and they photograph well, drawing attention away from your attractive features."

"I didn't like those damn nose rings anyway; good riddance."

"Let's go in the bathroom. I'll seal those septum punctures and the pierced-ear holes. You'll be a new woman—ten years younger. No one will ever think you were on Mars." Gina grinned, grabbed Erica's wrist, and pulled her toward the master bath where some surgical equipment was kept in a lockbox.

In the morning, after Miles had gone to school, Sunul and Erica left for the courthouse where they met with Hugh Patel. They were gone for about an hour and returned with an updated passport for Sunul and entirely new documents for Erica. Hugh had also gotten a new passport, never having had one before. He admitted to Sunul and Erica that he illegally crossed the border into Mexico when he was a teenager. When he returned, he was no longer a virgin.

During the last eight years, the passports had become completely digitized and contained retinal images for identification. When entering another country a retinal scan image had to agree with the one stored on the passport which was the size of a credit card. The international community had adopted the new form of passport identification in 2082. The entire system was linked by satellites to computer centers in the United States, Ecuador, and New Zealand. There were currently 579 million records on file and the data bank was growing at roughly one million every two weeks. New data was being generated primarily by criminals and travelers to Africa and China.

That afternoon, Hugh joined Erica and Sunul at the Burkes' residence to plan their trip to South America. Gina and Priscilla had lay down with their girls to take a nap while the three travelers began preparation for their journey.

Erica and the two men had been discussing their travel plans for about five minutes when the front door computer announced the arrival of law enforcement personnel.

Sunul asked, "Identities of arrivals, please." His voice was broadcast through the speaker at the door and a voice came over the intercom system.

"This is Officer Sandborne and Lieutenant Max Webster. We're here for an inquiry. It should only take a few minutes."

Rather than have the door opened by the automatic doorman, Sunul went to the door and let the police in the house. He greeted Officer Sandborne warmly and she introduced her fellow officer as Lieutenant Max Webster, a member of the international security force.

"What can I do for you this evening, Miss Sandborne?"

"We're sorry to have to interrupt your evening, Mr. Burke, but Lieutenant Webster reported an irregularity in the identification of someone you knew on Mars, Dr. Shania Winslow."

"Yes, I knew Dr. Winslow. She was killed on Mars when the roof of the underground mining gallery gave way. I returned her body and that of her husband to Nebraska to be buried in the family plot."

Lt. Webster, a man of about 35-40 years old, was watching Erica as she and Hugh moved away from the kitchen table and approached the officers. The lieutenant was about two inches taller than Sunul and looked as if he had been an athlete, perhaps in college, or even a member of a professional football or soccer team. He smiled and took a step towards her as Erica came closer.

Sunul had just begun to introduce Erica and Hugh to the officers.

"I'd like you to meet my friends, —."

Lieutenant Webster interrupted, "Hello, Dr. Winslow. It's nice to know you are still among the living. The retinal scan of Erica Grossman is an exact match to that of Dr. Winslow."

Erica had extended her hand toward the lieutenant but suddenly withdrew it and held her distance about five feet from the officer. She frowned, thinking how this officer could have discovered so soon that Erica was Shania. Will their plans to find Miranda and Licon have to be changed, or will the search have to be carried out without a vital team member?

There was no use in denying her true identity, she said, "Okay, I confess, I'm Shania Estwick. Am I under arrest?"

"Not yet. I'd like to get some questions answered. Can we sit down and discuss what is going on? Officer Sandborne and I have been talking, and from what she has told me, I believe I need to know the whole story. This enterprise you have planned is much more complicated than what it appears to be on the surface."

"Good idea. Let's sit and explain the situation to the officers." Sunul motioned for the group to move to the table. "Would anyone like a beverage: coffee, tea, water, or something with a little kick to it?"

Shania volunteered, "I'll make some coffee."

Lt. Webster looked at Officer Sandborne, she nodded, and said, "Coffee would be fine, thanks."

Shania put some of the children's Halloween candy in a cereal bowl and set it on the table, gave everyone a mug, and brought the full coffee maker to the table. Sunul brought a plate full of cookies to the table and sat down.

"Well, I guess I'll start the report of our activities over the last eight years. Hugh can fill in any details he thinks are important; anything I overlook."

Sunul began with the journey of the alpha group to the Kuiper Belt and about fifteen minutes later he turned to Shania and let her relate the details about the cancer treatment using small amounts of blood from Miranda and Licon. Hugh discussed the years on the run and some details of life in the mountains of Colorado. He hesitated a bit when he told about Miranda and Licon leaving the group so everyone could resume their normal lives.

Sunul noticed Hugh was getting a little emotional when he began to relate the torture of his wife, Triel, and the mangling of his hand. Sunul asked Officer Sandborne to explain what had happened when the Patels were attacked.

"I've already mentioned this to Lieutenant Webster, but I'll go over it again very briefly—for continuity." When she concluded, she glanced at the lieutenant and asked, "Do you have any questions, Max?"

He shook his head. "I can't think of anything right now. Fortunately, the candy and cookies have supplied my brain with some calories to process all the information, and the caffeine is going to keep me alert."

He smiled, primarily at Shania, and asked, "What's next?"

Shania looked at Sunul and offered, "I guess I can take over and explain how I got back to Earth."

Sunul nodded, "Go ahead and tell them about the cave-in and how you got back to the dome. I'll explain the shipping container and your husband's demise."

As Hugh and Max listened, they consumed several cookies and a second mug of coffee. Gina was flabbergasted at what had taken place on Mars. She patted Shania's left wrist and gripped Shania's left hand as the doctor told of the week-long confinement in the coffins.

"I was feeling a bit claustrophobic a couple of times, but I watched the time, slept, and read a book, and when I heard Sunul's taps on the outside, I knew everything was all right. I tried watching a movie, but I fell asleep, and I didn't want to watch it again. I played solitaire, which I thought was appropriate for my situation." She grinned and then commented, "Now that it's over, it wasn't so bad, but I wouldn't want to do it again. A week of isolation was almost more than I could take."

Max commented, "You possess amazing self-control and mental fortitude. I'm glad to have met you. Well, now I see why you don't want anyone else to know you are alive. What are your plans now? Are you going to expose the drug companies?"

Sunul reacted before Shania could answer Max's question. "Floyd Conners, back on Mars, has disposed of Ed Winslow's remains in a nuclear processor. We don't know who killed him, but I have an idea. Unfortunately, I don't have any evidence to support my suspicion, so I'll keep it to myself. Shania has already told you about the outfitted coffins, so I'll skip that. Our next step is try to find Miranda and Licon for a blood sample to save Priscilla. We have to travel to South America; Argentina to be more specific."

"So that's why you got your passports earlier today." Max nodded his head in realization. "Considering the gravity of the undertaking, and the secrecy involved, I want to accompany you to help clear any international regulations or other formalities. I can also carry a firearm across international borders, no questions asked."

Sunul, Shania, and Hugh glanced at each other and gave affirmative nods. Shania seemed pleased that another strong man would be going along, especially because he would be armed with a handgun that delivered more punch than the stun guns they would be carrying or her drug pens. She had a momentary thought—wondering if Max was a married man; a furtive glance told her he didn't have a wedding band. But these days the absence of a ring was not conclusive evidence of bachelorhood; Sunul didn't wear a ring. When she glanced at Max a second time, she almost smiled, but held it back, she was still thinking about Art back on Mars, wondering when he would be returning to Earth.

"From the responses of my friends, Max, we'd be grateful to have you with us." Sunul extended his arm and shook hands with the bigger man.

Max shook hands with Hugh and then using both hands, engulfed Shania's right hand delicately. He wasn't quite sure which arm Shania had broken; she didn't seem to be favoring either one, however, she still wore a walking cast on her left leg. He thought she would be easy to carry; she couldn't weigh much more than 120 pounds. He outweighed her by nearly 100 pounds. He held her hand for longer than a normal handshake, gradually releasing the pressure of his hands, and smiling as she withdrew hers. Despite the overdone makeup, he couldn't help noticing her beautiful blue eyes. He would hate to have to arrest her.

"When do we leave for South America?" Max wanted to know the details; he didn't want to be left behind by the trio he hardly knew. As soon as he got back to his office, he was going to dig up as much data as possible about his three traveling companions. He assumed they would be investigating his background, too. He hoped they would be able to access his FBI dossier; it contained information about his entire life of thirty-six years on planet Earth. He would be notified if anyone was checking his background in the next twenty-four hours. He would have to be optically clean with them; absolutely no lying could occur.

Following a minute of consultation with Erica and Hugh, Sunul spoke, "We'll leave at 8:00 a.m. day after tomorrow. That will give us time to get our things together and do a little planning. Can you meet with us here tomorrow evening—about seven o'clock?"

"No problem, I'll see you tomorrow. It was nice meeting with you. This should be an interesting journey." He guided Officer Sandborne to the door and they left without any further communication with the three astronauts.

"That was interesting. I kind of like the idea of having an armed officer along with us. He looks like he could take on a small tank." Hugh leaned back in his chair and popped another cookie in his mouth.

Sunul commented, "He seemed to take a great deal of interest in you, Erica. Did you notice?"

"I did, but I didn't want to encourage him. We have a job to do. When our search for the children is complete, I might encourage his attention. I kind of like what I saw tonight. He's quite a specimen." She smiled and blushed, looking away from the men. "I think I'll get some rest. We'll be busy tomorrow getting ready to leave the states. Good night."

Chapter 24

Sunul contacted the space agency in the morning and arranged for a sub-orbital flight to Argentina. The four passengers to Buenos Aires would leave the Florida flight center Wednesday morning at 9:00 a.m. and arrive two hours later in the Argentinean capital city. The ship carrying two return-from-altitude gliders and eight passengers would climb to 120,000 feet and the four-man gliders would descend to airfields in Argentina and an ice-strip in Antarctica. Sunul would copilot the first glider, assisting a computer pilot if necessary, and land the small ship at the Buenos Aires space port. The other four-man crew, copiloted by an astrophysicist, would land on a runway near the South Pole. The expended mother-ship would come down west of Australia in the Indian Ocean to be recovered by the US Navy.

Since Hugh and Sunul were former astronauts, transportation was free, but Erica and Max had to pay for their passage. Max received a reduced fare because he was an international police officer, but Erica could not claim her astronaut status and maintain her secret identity. Sunul and Hugh dickered with the agency and arranged to use one quarter of their wives' free status. The remaining half-fare for Erica's passage was 2,000 credits which Sunul arranged to pay in four installments.

Max met the others at the spacecraft launch facility an hour before takeoff. His only luggage was an overburdened gym bag. Erica was amused and began to laugh when she saw what Max was carrying to the ship. He frowned when he noticed Erica watching him and asked, "What do you find so funny, doctor?" Max's voice betrayed his mild irritation.

"Please call me Erica, Officer Webster. Remember, I'm still travelling incognito."

Erica's rejoinder surprised him. "I'm sorry. I forgot your situation for a moment when I saw you laughing—apparently at me."

Erica was still smiling, "You look like you're going to gym class, not 4,800 miles for who knows how long."

Max's displeasure suddenly changed and he smiled. "I'm going to buy some new clothes in Argentina; then I'll need a suitcase as big as yours."

Erica looked at the three large suitcases belonging to Sunul, Hugh, and herself. They had each brought enough changes of clothing for a week before any laundering would be necessary.

When they were seated in their glider, which was latched toward the center of the booster, and opposite the aircraft destined for the South Pole, Sunul leaned over to Erica and said, "I think he likes you, but I also think we are intimidating to him. He knows we have all had brain implants and our IQs are twenty points above his. We'd better be careful and not make enemies of our own people."

Erica looked at Sunul and commented, "Thanks for the tip. I've been isolated from the regular population for so long I've forgotten what normal life is all about. I kind of like Max and I don't want to run him off. I'll try to be more discreet." She grinned and crossed her fingers.

Max and Hugh sat behind Sunul and Erica and had leaned back and tightened their restraints. Max asked, "No flight attendants?" and grinned. "I could use a stiff drink—never been on a plane or rocket before."

"Just relax, Max. Sunul is an expert pilot, and besides, the ship is completely automated. We don't have to do a thing." Hugh smiled and continued, "Unless there is a malfunction of some sort."

"And then what?" Max had a strangle hold on his arm rests and white knuckles betrayed his concern.

"Sunul will take over and guide us down to the landing strip. Don't worry, he's the best pilot that has ever existed on or off Earth. I'd trust him with my life any day."

"Why are our fares so low for going so far south?"

"We're not the reason for the flight, Max. After the gliders are released and separated a good distance from the ship, two satellites will be sent into orbit. They are communication satellites for the World Communication Industry. The launch costs WCI about eighteen million per satellite. Our fees are insignificant. Sit back and listen, you'll hear sounds you've never heard before. Parts of the ship will disconnect, we'll be pushed away, and then start descending for the remainder of the travel time."

"When will the noises start?"

Hugh glanced at his watch and said, "Any second now."

Hugh was correct, a vibration began as the gantry moved away from the fully loaded booster engine that carried the gliders and two satellites. The rumble sounded like a large truck moving down a small town street rattling windows as it passed by. There was a moment of silence and then the booster began to move slowly and then accelerated rapidly, forcing the passengers into their cushioned seats. When the vibrations ceased, less than two minutes later, the ship was coasting upwards above 110,000 feet, the acceleration had halted and gravity had nearly ended the vertical motion. The motion south along the great circle route was only opposed by the very slight friction of the upper atmosphere.

A thump occurred, followed by a vibration, and then a small jolt shook the glider as it separated from the booster. The whine of an electric motor sounded as the floor in front of Sunul opened and a pilot's station swung up from the opening. Erica was startled and reached over to grab Sunul's right arm, but when she saw what had rotated into positon, she smiled, released her grip and sat back in her chair.

"You could have warned me, Sunul." Her frown dissolved into a grin.

Sunul laughed and began scanning over the control surface display. His eyes locked onto the altimeter and then he shifted his vision to a ten-inch screen which showed the glider's position superimposed on the continent below. "We're over Brazil, folks, and starting our descent. As soon as our velocity drops below Mach 3, I'll open a viewport so you can watch the sights below. It will be a few minutes before the sky turns blue. The ride will be very quiet. If you hear anything, we're in trouble, but don't worry, I've done this before—once." He grinned and located the pad he would have to press if he had to take over from the computer system and land the glider manually.

Max leaned as far forward in his chair as possible and gave Erica's chair a thump with his fingers. Her head swiveled and she frowned at him.

"Aren't you just a little bit concerned, Erica?"

"Not with Hugh and Sunul in control. They have my complete confidence." Erica wasn't being completely honest with her statement, but she didn't want to exhibit any weaknesses to Max. She wanted him to trust what the astronauts were doing and not be skeptical of their every move. The team had only begun their journey and none of them knew where it would lead.

Twenty minutes later, the glider was twelve miles in altitude moving at Mach 2 over the border between Bolivia and Paraguay. Sunul watched the controls and the flight path making sure the computer-controller was keeping them on the predefined flight path. When the velocity of the plane went sub-sonic, all but Sunul were surprised by a new sound, the folded wings were being extended to increase lift and allow the glider to make the final distance to Buenos Aires without dropping like a rock as it cut through the thicker atmosphere.

"Relax, guys. We've just sprouted wings to extend the range of our little ship. I'll let you know when we're fifteen minutes from Buenos Aires airport. I'll call them when we are ten minutes out so they'll be ready for us. They'll hold the jet traffic until we're on the ground."

Erica commented, "Is that because they know you are arriving, or is that because of rules and regulations?" She smiled and Max said, "I was thinking the same thing."

"Thirty-five more miles until we're on the ground." Sunul announced as he watched the metropolitan area of Buenos Aires creeping onto the edge of his display screen. He then began conversing with an aircraft controller who had already picked up the glider on his terminal screen. "You are at 8,000 feet. Please drop to 2,000 feet and reduce speed to 100 knots."

"Will do. GF-2 out."

Sunul watched the controls and the display. The computer system was responding to the instructions from the controller at the airport. As the glider slowed and dropped in altitude a green light flashed on and the wheels began to drop from the fuselage slowing the little plane further. The plane was now at 1,200 feet above ground and appeared to be dropping too fast. Sunul's brain was telling him they would be about 500 yards short of the runway.

With only a few seconds left to make a decision, he reacted from instinct and disengaged the computer. He pressed the wheels up sensor tab and Erica said, "What's that sound?" She reached over and touched Sunul's right arm.

"The landing gear is coming up. We have too much wind resistance and we'll land short of the runway if I don't cut our rate of descent. We still have to make a turn to land on the runway we were instructed to take. The computer made a slight mistake."

"Don't worry guys—Sunul knows what he's doing. Relax!" Hugh leaned back and smiled, but his white knuckles showed that he was concerned.

Seven seconds later, Sunul put the landing gear down and three seconds later, the plane touched down 100 meters from the edge of the 3,000 meter-long asphalt landing strip and coasted to a stop near the terminal at the 1,500 meter position. A small tow-machine that looked like an old-time golf cart sped out from under the wing of a passenger plane and attached a hook to the glider's nose wheel. The operator waved and began pulling the glider off the tarmac to a small storage area where two other gliders were parked.

There was a small jolt as the glider was parked. A few seconds later, a voice came over the plane's intercom. "You may deplane now. You have been cleared and do not have to pass through the customs area. Have a nice stay in Argentina."

All four passengers replied, "Thank-you!"

Erica was the first on her feet and popped open the exit door. "I've got to get out of here! This flight has reminded me of travelling in those coffins. I'm so glad it was only a two hour trip and I had some companions."

The travelers were on their own, two hundred meters from the main passenger terminal. They extracted their luggage from the storage compartment and took a look around. No facilities were evident, but Sunul had his eyes on one of the towing machines. He walked to it and placed his suitcase on the rear ledge. He unbuckled the tow bar and said, "Here's our taxi, want a ride?"

Max grabbed Erica's suitcase and handed her his gym bag. She smiled at him and said, "My hero! Do you mind if I scoot your bag across the tarmac?"

Max laughed, "You can do whatever you like. That bag is on its last legs anyway."

When Sunul loaded a map of the area, Tezeiza Airport appeared on the screen and showed exits to highways and rural roads. They were sixteen miles south of Buenos Aires, but didn't want to go north into the city. Convinced Miranda and Licon had travelled farther south, they had to find a bus or taxi. The young people had stated in their letter they were going farther south.

Since Erica's locomotion was still hampered by her cast, the group sat on their luggage beside the south-going highway lanes waiting for a vehicle driver to stop and offer them a ride. Cars and large trucks were passing by, some occupants waving, some horns beeping, but no one stopping to pick them up. After fifteen minutes, Max grabbed Erica around the waist, picked her up and started walking. Sunul lifted Erica's suitcase with his left hand and with his right hand grabbed his own luggage and followed Max. Hugh watched for a moment and then followed, a little reluctantly.

At first, Erica was surprised by Max's actions, marveling at his strength, and rather than say anything, she decided to enjoy the ride. She knew it wouldn't last long; Max would have to put her down in less than a quarter mile.

"How long do you think you can carry me, Mr. Webster?"

"Please, call me Max, but not Mr. Webster. Aren't we getting along quite well? I don't think I will be carrying you very long. Argentineans are very compassionate, someone will stop before I run out of muscle power."

"You're sure of that?" Erica grinned and held on a little tighter. She could feel the tautness of his well-developed muscles and began to imagine seeing him without a shirt.

Before Max could reply, a horn sounded and a small flat-bed truck passed, began slowing, and pulled over to the side of the highway. Thirty yards ahead, the cab door opened and a middle-aged man wearing overalls and a long-sleeved plaid shirt stepped down to the road. The travelers could hear the flip-flop of his rubber sandals as the driver approached.

Sunul activated his com unit and set it for Spanish-to-English, but it wasn't necessary, the driver spoke English with only a hint of accent.

"Can I give you a ride?"

Sunul put his com unit back in his pocket and answered, "Yes, we would be thankful for that. We have an injured woman with us and some heavy luggage."

"Yes, I see. But you have no guitar."

"Oh, we are not musicians, sir. We are looking for someone from the United States, a young woman and young man."

"We must get off the side of the road. The police will come before long. I am Juan Sylvan Oberon, a farmer from Las Flores. That is 100 miles from here. In the city I just bought some fertilizer for my vegetables. I am on my way home."

Juan shook hands with the travelers and each gave him their first name. He took one of Sunul's suitcases and tossed it on the bed of his truck and the others followed his actions. Max boosted Erica onto the truck, but Juan, yelled, "No, señor. The señorita rides up front with me, it is much softer and not so stinky. Please." He was going to help Erica down, but Max reached over him and Erica slid off the truck bed into his arms.

"Let me assist you, señorita." Max grinned and Erica swung her left arm around his neck. He carried her to the cab and helped her onto the seat.

"Thank-you, señor Max," she smiled.

"You are very welcome, señorita. It is my honor." He grinned and shut the door.

Erica watched Max in the review mirror as he vaulted onto the truck bed. She thought, "Maybe I have misjudged him. He does have a sense of humor."

"You are looking for someone, señores?" Juan was looking up to the men on the truck. Hugh slid over to the edge of the truck bed, pulled out his com unit, and leaned down, to show Juan a picture of Miranda. "She is with a young dark-skinned man."

"Oh, yes! I have seen them. Ebony and Ivory! That is what I call them. They were at my farm some time ago. They ate dinner with my family and left the next day. They are very nice people. You are relatives?"

"Yes. The señorita is my daughter. I need to find her—medical reasons. It is urgent."

Juan looked at the traffic and back at Hugh, "We must go. Later I will tell you more." Juan climbed into the cab and waited for a car to pass, stepped on the accelerator, then swerved into the closest lane and accelerated to what Sunul estimated was fifty miles per hour.

Sunul leaned over to Hugh and talked above the noise of the air passing over the truck, "What luck, Hugh. In two hours, we might get some leads to finding Adam and Eve."

"I hope so. I'd sure like to see my daughter again." Hugh blinked a few times to prevent tears from running down his cheeks. "I hope I don't pass out from the fumes." He motioned toward the eight bags of fertilizer tied on the back of the truck bed. "We'd better sit as close to the cab as possible. Whew!" The three men scooted forward and sat with their backs against the cab, giving them a massage with every bump.

Two hours later, the truck took an off-ramp that transitioned to a dirt and gravel road. They travelled about 200 yards to a nicely groomed single-story farmhouse. The brakes squealed as the truck came to a stop near the front porch. Juan sounded the horn and three children came running from the front door, two little girls, apparently twins, and an older boy about ten-years-old. The girls looked to be about six and were smiling, holding hands, and laughing. As soon as Juan hit the ground, the kids swarmed him. He bent down, kissed the girls, saying each of their names: Emilia and Teresa. He put his arm around the boy and gave him a high-five with the other hand.

When the men dropped to the ground from the truck, the children suddenly became quiet, the little girls moved behind their father's legs and peered around to watch the men. Erica opened the passenger-side door and swung her legs out. Max moved quickly and eased her to the ground.

"Juan! Who have you brought home, some help?" A middle-aged woman with a round pretty face and glistening brownish-black hair to her shoulders appeared on the porch. She was wiping her hands with a small white towel bordered in red. She was smiling.

"Some guests, Magdalena. They will have dinner with us."

Chapter 25

The children were captivated with Erica and Hugh. The girls wanted to know all about Erica's cast, and Juan, Jr. discovered Hugh's artificial hand when Hugh reached into a pot of boiling water to retrieve a spoon that had slipped from Maggie's hand. Hugh explained to the Oberons an accident had badly damaged his hand and it had been replaced. Hugh was relieved when they didn't press for details. Erica's explanation was not very inventive, but was adequate. She was carrying a basket of laundry and had fallen down a flight of stairs breaking some bones.

Juan recollected the family's meeting with Ebony and Ivory during the evening meal.

"The señorita was very tired but the señor not so much. They say they were going south to see more of the country, but they were walking and it was still cold outside. Spring was not yet here. They stayed overnight and left in the morning. My cousin, Jose, who lives farther south was here then and he gave them a ride in his pickup. The señor, Adam, gave us some credits. I say it was not necessary, but he made me take it. He say it was only fair."

"They were only here that one night?" Hugh wanted more information.

"Yes." Juan nodded. "May I see the señorita's picture again?"

Hugh retrieved Miranda's photo and held his com unit out.

"The señorita is much younger in the picture, no?"

"Why do you say that? The picture was taken about a year ago."

"But the señorita is much older now, I would guess she is thirty to thirty-five and the señor looks like he is maybe forty, almost my age. I am forty-two."

Hugh ran his fingers through his hair and frowned. He looked at Erica and asked, "Could Adam and Eve be ageing prematurely?"

Erica hesitated, turned to Sunul and questioned, "Has Gina mentioned anything about premature ageing to you?"

Sunul shook his head, "If she did, I don't remember."

"That means she hasn't mentioned it. You would remember that; you remember almost everything said to you. If it is true, we need to find them as soon as we possibly can. Their immunological systems could be wearing out. Their blood might not react as effectively as it did on Mars."

Juan's head swiveled quickly to look at Erica. "Mars? You have been on Mars? Where are you from? Should my family be worried? I have heard much about aliens; many people are frightened when they hear those words. Have people really gone to other planets?"

"Don't worry, Juan. Sunul, Hugh, and I have been on Mars. There is a scientific community there and there is a prison facility on the moon. Mr. Webster hasn't been in space; he works for law enforcement in Florida. We are all United States citizens."

"I don't understand about the blood. You need the blood of Ebony and Ivory?"

Erica explained what had happened on Mars to treat her cancer and Sunul told Juan about Priscilla's cancer. Juan nodded, understanding the need for the blood sample.

"I will call Jose Rojas, my cousin. I am sure he will give you a ride south—as far as you want to go. He has a very fast vehicle."

Sunul could hear Juan talking to his cousin, but he didn't have his com unit active to interpret the rapid fire Spanish. When Juan hung up he came into the living room and said, "Jose will be here in the morning to pick up his fertilizer. You will go with him—another 100 miles to the south, maybe more if he isn't too busy. He also saw the ebony and the ivory. He thinks he knows where they went."

"That's wonderful, Juan. How can we repay you for your kindness?" Erica didn't wait for his reply. She moved into the kitchen to help Maggie with the dishes. The men sat together watching the late news while the women and girls chattered away in the kitchen amidst the clatter of dishes. As the men discussed the news, Juan Jr. asked if he could go to his bedroom to memorize music for the next mass. Junior was in the boys' choir. Juan excused him and he said goodnight to the travelers.

Jose Rojas pulled into the parking area at 9:00 a.m. He had driven his customized Humvee the 107 miles from his Chillar repair-shop/general store in ninety-five minutes. The red with silver trim pickup looked massive; taller and longer than Juan's little farm-weary faded-green flatbed truck. A three-step ladder dropped to the ground, the driver's door swung up, and a blond-haired, heavily muscled young man, about the height of Sunul, descended to the clutches of the Oberon children.

He said something quietly and the children extended their hands. He placed a piece of hard candy in the palm of each right hand. Juan barked an order and the kids scampered off behind the house laughing as they ran. The cousins shook hands, hugged, and Juan escorted Jose to the porch where the travelers were standing.

After a minute of introductions, Jose was invited into the house. Everyone had something to drink while Jose listened to Hugh explain the search for Adam and Eve. When Hugh showed Jose the picture of Miranda, he nodded and said, "I remember them very well, but the señorita is much older than in that picture. I am guessing she is about thirty years old, a little older than I am." He smiled and said, "I am twenty-eight now at my last birthday. My mother says I should be thinking about getting married. I told her I would think about it." He laughed, "I don't even have a girlfriend." He looked at Erica and said, "Do you have a boyfriend?" Everyone laughed and he turned a light-sunburned-red.

Jose told the travelers about his businesses and mentioned he had come for four bags of fertilizer Juan had brought from Buenos Aires, so he could offer them a ride at no expense. Then he made a comment, "Two men, a tall one and a short one, were asking about the ivory and the ebony ones. They asked when I saw the young couple and which direction they went when they left my business. The shorter man called the taller one Doc. The one called Doc got angry. He said, 'Don't call me Doc.' I don't know why he didn't like it."

Sunul asked, "Do you remember the name of the shorter man? Was it perhaps Evan?"

Jose scratched his head for a moment, dropped his hand, and grinned, "Yes, señor, that was the name. I was thinking it was Eben, but that would be a strange name, wouldn't it? It was Evan. I'm sure of it."

"Damn! That's Evan Shiner. I warned him what was going to happen if he got in my way. He's working for the drug companies and the doc must be, too."

Erica stood and exclaimed, "Oh, my God! Do you think Doc could be Art Corcoran?"

"If it is Art, he knows you're still alive, and that means Evan knows, too. Evan has a thing for you, Doctor. I doubt he would allow Art to hurt you, if that's what he has in mind. But I was under the impression that Art wanted to pursue you for marriage. He sure had that look in his eyes." Sunul paused for a moment and then continued, "We're going to have to watch for those two. But the 'Doc' guy might be someone else that we don't know."

"You are a doctor, señorita?" Jose had been listening closely.

"Yes, Jose. Does that surprise you?"

"A little bit. You don't look like a doctor to me. You look like a hippie."

"I don't normally look this way, Jose. It's a disguise for this trip. I don't want anyone to know who I really am. I hope you won't tell anyone that I'm a doctor from the Martian colony."

Jose grinned, a little sheepishly, "I will say nothing—my lips are—stapled." He made a hand motion against his lips as if he were pressing on a stapler. Jose stood up and asked, "Could one of the señores help me load the fertilizer? I have little time to waste, although the traffic is not bad today."

Max chugged down the last of his beer and volunteered, "Let's do it. We don't have any time to waste either."

The goodbyes to the Oberons took a few extra minutes due to the numerous hugs and good wishes. Maggie had prepared a lunch for the travelers and handed Sunul a basket with some advice, "Señor, do not let Jose be first to eat," she grinned, "there won't be any for the rest." Sunul thanked her and gave her a kiss on the forehead. "I hope we see you again in the future. Maybe you can travel to Florida."

A half-hour later, the fancy red pickup, carrying four extra people and four bags of fertilizer was speeding south on highway 3 toward Chillar with eighty-three miles to go. Hugh had joined Erica in the cab with Jose and was trying to find out as much as possible about Adam and Eve. Hugh thought he might jog Jose's memory for some latent facts concerning his daughter and her companion.

"I'm sorry, señor, but except for the first few minutes, they rode in the back. They say it was too warm in the cab with me. They did as they pleased and paid me for the charging of the batteries. I took them to Bahia Blanca. That is 167 miles south of Chillar. They stayed in the back all the way. I gave them blankets, but they didn't use them."

Max and Sunul unloaded the heavy bags of fertilizer at Jose's general store, located on the northern edge of the little town, while Hugh and Erica used the bathroom facilities. While Max and Sunul waited, Max commented, "Any possibility of renting a plane? I feel like we are moving too slowly."

"I'd like to move faster, too, but if we fly we'll probably lose their trail. We know they were here. I think we should continue on the ground. Hitching isn't too bad; we've met some nice people and covered over 200 miles." Sunul's reasons were sound.

"I suppose you're right. We don't want to risk losing their scent, although I feel like we're chasing after some ghosts."

When Erica and Hugh rejoined Sunul and Max the group went outside the store to a picnic bench and opened the basket Maggie had packed for them. Jose declined an invitation to join them; he was already gnawing on a large candy bar the size of a hotdog. The travelers were discussing their next move when Jose came from the store and animatedly said, "Señores, señorita, I cannot drive you any farther. I must make deliveries and go to the hospital to visit a friend. I am sorry."

The foursome accepted his apology graciously, bought a few snack items, said goodbye, and made their way out to the highway.

"Señorita, it is time for me to carry you again. It won't be long—we'll get another ride."

Erica smiled at Max's grinning face and let him sweep her off her feet. "You're very warm, señor. What have you been doing?"

"It might be because I was anticipating carrying you, but more realistically, I think I might be allergic to the fertilizer Sunul and I carried into the store from the truck. If you don't squirm around, I will cool off before long. You're not heavy, but please don't breathe on my neck."

Erica laughed and said, "That hadn't crossed my mind." She was looking over Max's shoulder and grinning."

Sunul and Hugh, a few yards back, noticed Erica's broad smile. Hugh commented, "I think the doctor is breaking down and beginning to have some thoughts of romantic involvement."

"You've got something there, Hugh. A few sparks seem to be forming."

The travelers had walked about a quarter mile when two older sedans, one black and the other a dark-blue with a damaged right front fender, slowed and turned onto the shoulder about 100 yards ahead of them. The passenger-side doors opened and two men stepped out, but left the doors open.

Max slowed until Sunul and Hugh caught up. "I don't have a good feeling about this. Those two coming toward us have bad intentions. I can tell by the way they walk." He put Erica down and felt for the gun in his belt above his right buttock. He had turned side-on to the two men to conceal his reaching movement.

The closest man yelled above the noise of a passing semi as it buffeted the hikers and the vehicles on the shoulder, "Hey! Do you need a lift?"

Max indicated he couldn't understand what had been said and stepped farther onto the shoulder, moving away from his fellow travelers. "Erica, get behind the luggage! Down! Everyone!"

As the men came closer to Max, their cars began backing, matching the walking speed of the two Angels of Death wearing loose-fitting leather jackets concealing what Max knew to be guns. Max watched their faces, and as they drew nearer yet, their eyes. There was no fear.

At fifteen yards, Max drew his gun, dropped to his knee, and yelled, "Stop or I'll shoot!"
The men continued walking, calmly reaching under their jackets. A rapid series of shots rang out, all from Max's gun. Both men fell to the ground dropping their hand guns. They screamed in pain and reached for their knees. They hadn't had a chance to discharge their weapons.

Max took three long strides and stood above the closest man, kicked the loose gun away and pointed his gun.

Erica screamed, "Max, don't kill them!"

Max pulled the trigger, moved to the second man and took another shot at point-blank range. The second bullets caused the downed men to roll on the ground in agony, but they weren't dead; Max had shot each one in the foot on the same leg that already had a wounded knee.

When Max's first shots had rung out, the cars' engines had revved, but there was nowhere for them to escape, the traffic formed a solid wall on the near lane, the shoulder sloped down about a meter, and the depression was strewn with basketball-sized rocks. The drivers cut their engines and sat waiting, knowing their fate had been determined.

Chapter 26

"Hugh, disable those handguns." Max pointed his pistol at the guns that had been kicked away from their owners.

Sunul picked them up and handed them to Hugh after removing the clips and extracting the chamber rounds. "Crush the handles and the trigger guards."

"This will be fun, better than squishing beer cans." He took each gun and twisted the handle 180 degree and then bent the trigger guard against the trigger so the mechanism couldn't possibly function. He tossed the disabled guns about ten yards from the shoulder to the other side of a barbed wire fence. The crippled gangsters would have a difficult time retrieving their useless weapons if they were dumb enough to try.

Erica had opened her suitcase and gotten bandages to wrap the gunmen's knees and feet. Their pants legs were soaked in red and Erica thought Max would be in trouble if one or both of the men succumbed from blood loss. Hugh cut off the trousers at the knee on the injured legs and helped the men remove their shoes. Erica cleansed the wounds with alcohol despite the shrieks of pain and wrapped them tightly to stem the blood flow and prevent the wounds from becoming infected.

Max was watching as the doctor bandaged the bullet injuries, but didn't give a whit if the bozos lived or died. He started toward the nearest car to yank the driver out for questioning.

"Why did you shoot them a second time?" Erica was using forceps, trying to extract a bullet from one of the wounded men, and she had to ask.

"I want them to change their profession. Their type is no longer relevant. They just didn't know it—now they do. Do you want them to keep following us?"

Erica didn't answer, knowing Max had made a good point. She pulled a slug from the man's calf muscle and tossed it toward the mutilated firearms. The unconscious man had passed out from the pain. Erica quickly wrapped the leg and gave him a shot of antibiotics.

Max jerked the driver's door open, reached in, grabbed the man around the neck, and dragged him from the car. The driver didn't resist. Max shoved him toward the two men on the ground where Erica was kneeling, having finished first aid. Max noticed the man was looking toward the field adjacent to the road as if trying to avoid eye contact with Erica. Max yelled, "Slime, look at the doctor!"

Erica stood up as the driver swung his head toward her.

"Art! What the hell are you doing with these assholes? When did you get back from Mars?"

"I had to come back to protect you. I care for you too much to see you killed, Shania."

"How long have you been working for the pharmaceuticals?"

"They got their hooks into me about a month before I went to Mars. They wanted you dead. After I had the explosives planted, I realized I couldn't do what they told me to do anymore. Fortunately, you weren't killed by the cave-in, so I began helping you."

Sunul had pulled his stun gun and was approaching the lead car as Art and Erica were talking. The driver watched the display from the rearview camera and recognized the man closing in on him. He had nowhere to go. He briefly considered stepping out in traffic, but his cowardice didn't go that deep. He waited, expecting a beating, but no worse.

Sunul stayed on the passenger side of the car and cautiously leaned down to peer into the front seat. "Shiner! You son-of-a-bitch! Slide over here and get out before I shoot you."

"Okay! Don't shoot me, I'm not armed."

Sunul opened the door violently and pulled Evan Shiner from the vehicle. Shiner fell to the ground and rose to his knees with his hands up as shields as if he would be protected from the stun projectile. Sunul reached down and grabbed Evan under the arm and lifted him to his feet.

"Get back there with your buddy, you good-for-nothing slime. You don't get it, do you? I told you what would happen if you hurt my family or friends. Max! Shoot this idiot in the knees. Maybe he'll quit following us around if he can't walk."

"No! Don't shoot me, Sunul. I have some information you can use. I'll tell you if you promise not to shoot me."

"Let me talk to my friends. They might want to shoot you—just like the others."

Evan looked at the two men on the ground wincing in pain, bloodied legs wrapped in gauze.

Sunul spoke with Max, exchanging only a few words before returning to Shiner.

"Okay. What have you to tell us?"

"The two children you are looking for, Ebony and Ivory—they went to the Falkland Islands—to Stanley."

"You're sure? If you're feeding me a bunch of crap to get away from pain for a short period, it'll be twice as bad when I find you are lying. You realize that, don't you?"

"Yeah." He nodded that he understood the consequences. "Ask the doc, he'll verify what I just told you."

"I'll do that. One last thing, Shiner. Do you know who killed Ed Winslow?"

Shiner nodded, "It was the doc. He's in love with Shania Winslow—same as me. He wanted to get her husband out of the way, but then he was ordered to kill her. He almost did. He knows there's no way to prove he's guilty. The body was burned up in one of the nuclear oxygen generators. No body, no crime."

"Sit down, Shiner—over there beside your buddy." Sunul pointed at Art with his stun gun.

The four travelers huddled together and Sunul filled them in on what Shiner had divulged. "Hugh, what is the closest city on the mainland to the Falklands?"

Hugh spoke into his com unit and answered, "Comodoro Rivadavia. It's a little over 700 miles from Bahia Blanca. We're three hours out of Bahia Blanca. We're in bad need of a plane."

Sunul clenched his teeth, his mind putting evaluating the present situation. "Okay. We've got wheels to Bahia Blanca. We'll find a plane there; it's a large city of 300,000. We'll trade the cars and some credits and rent a small plane. Erica, put our two friends out of commission for a couple of hours. That'll give a good head start. I hope they won't be able to catch us."

The doctor questioned, "You think they'll come after us—after this?"

"I know Shiner and you know the doc. What do you think?"

"Right. I'll incapacitate them for about three hours." She withdrew one of the pens and adjusted the dosage, walked over to Art and stuck the pen against his neck. He collapsed to the ground. She made no attempt to ease his fall. Shiner knew what was in store for him. He lay down and waited to feel the pinch of the injection, which was completed in a couple of seconds.

Sunul and Max pulled the bodies off the shoulder out of possible striking by vehicles. Max stuck one of his international police ID cards in Art's shirt pocket. Sunul motioned toward the cars, "Let's get out of here. Hugh and I will lead, you guys follow. If we get separated, I'll send you a message and we can regroup. Okay, let's hit the road."

Traffic had thinned and pulling onto the road was not a problem. The occasional bumps in the road were hardly noticed in the comfortable cars compared to the trucks they had ridden in previously, of course, the cushioned seats helped. Max was an excellent driver, never drifting more than a few car lengths behind Sunul and Hugh. They made good time. Three hours on the road and they were on the outskirts of Bahia Blanca, population 304,873, according to the automated road sign. Hugh laughed as they passed the sign; the last digit increased by two.

"Two newborns today, Sunul."

"What?"

"The sign just went up by two as we passed."

"We just entered the city limits, Hugh. It counted us." Sunul stated the obvious.

"I don't think so. You actually think the road sign is that sophisticated?"

Sunul was smiling and Hugh noticed. "You had me there for a minute. I didn't think you would be joking around after our confrontation with those four turds. Do you think we'll see them again?"

"I don't know. Maybe not those guys; maybe someone else. We'll have to be aware of the people around us. When in a crowd, we should probably take some panoramic photos and watch for tails. See what you can find about leasing an aircraft. We should stop and get something to eat. My water pipe is about to burst, too."

"Don't talk about it; it only makes it worse. If I heard some running water, I'd probably have a major accident. Find a place for us to take care of things—quickly."

A quarter of a mile later, Sunul exited the highway and pulled into a charging station. It was a twenty-four-hour service facility and had all the necessities for travelers. Sunul didn't bother to watch for Erica and Max to join them. His plumbing call was urgent, as was Hugh's.

The lobby was busy but the travelers joined forces and bought something to eat. Two young men sitting at a bench-like table were closely watching the four travelers. Hugh noticed their attention first and mentioned it. Max walked over to them and asked some questions in Spanish with the aid of his universal translator. He returned with some good information.

"They aren't watching us any longer. What did you say to them?" Erica asked, curious about the two men lacking any further interest.

Max grinned, "They wanted to know more about you. They like the way you move—a woman with confidence. I told them we had just gotten you out of police custody for crashing a motorcycle into a women's apparel store. You didn't like the sexy displays."

"Thanks a lot, Max. What information did you get?"

"There's a vehicle rental establishment about a half-mile from here. The owners rent cars, boats, vans, buses, trucks, and airplanes—just about anything for credits. They sometimes trade. The three brothers are wheeler-dealers—they'll take advantage of us if we're not careful."

"Well, I think we've found the right place. Let's see if we can rent a small plane." Sunul stood up, brushed some crumbs from his trousers and started toward the door. He glanced back and said, "Buy us a dozen soft drinks and some candy or cake. I expect we'll have at least a two-hour flight."

The triple "A" sign was mounted about fifty feet above the surroundings at the top of a flagpole. It was much like the age-old sign from the US for the Automobile Association, but as the two cars got closer, the real reason for the three A's was revealed. The sign stood for Adolph, Adrian, and Alfred, the three brothers and owners of the business.

There wasn't much of an office at all, but a small ramshackle building, slightly bigger than an outhouse from the mountain woods, was located in the center of a large lot containing numerous vehicles of all shapes, makes, and sizes. There were three concentric circles of cars, trucks, and boats before disarray became the organization's style. On the edge of the lot, near the entrance, were two small planes.

Sunul's attention was drawn to the planes; they were both capable of carrying the foursome and their luggage. His greatest concern was for their range. The hydrogen and oxygen fuel tanks had to be able to fuel the engines for over 700 miles. Most small planes running on Aqua-Pure fuel could easily travel 500 miles without refueling, but 200 miles farther could be a problem. However, if Sunul could find an airport to refuel, the problem would be solved. He would consult with the renters; they would know the area and the capabilities of the aircraft.

Max and Sunul followed arrow signs to the main office; the remodeled outhouse as Sunul called it. One of the brothers, Adrian Kramer, was on duty; his name was displayed on his shirt.

"Señores, how might I assist you?" Adrian was not a big man, but he spoke with the authority of a business owner. He extended his hand and shook with Max and Sunul.

"We'd like to rent an airplane. We need to fly to Comodoro Rivadavia. There are four of us and our luggage." Sunul had supplied basic information.

"Whoa! That is over 700 miles! You will have to refuel. Do you have a good pilot?"

Sunul smiled but didn't comment. Max replied, "Probably the best in the world."

"Very good, because the coastal winds can be dangerous this time of year. They are unpredictable in the spring. You will refuel at Trelew; that's the half-way point." He was watching Sunul very closely. "You are the pilot?"

"Yes, sir. I'm only concerned about the cost. What will you charge us?"

He smiled, "A special price for you and your companions—just 2,000 credits. Can you afford that?"

"I would like to make a trade instead of credits. I have two cars to give you for the 2,000 credits. Will that be satisfactory?"

Adrian's eyes widened. "Two vehicles? Let me look at them before I will trade. Where are they?"

"Right outside, the black and blue sedans. They're in pretty good shape—no bullet holes. Take a look." Max grinned when Sunul said there were no bullet holes.

Adrian grabbed an info pad and marched outside to the cars. Hugh and Erica were leaning against the blue sedan concealing the dent. Adrian walked around the cars, kicked a couple of the tires and looked inside. He pulled his head from inside the black sedan and spoke into his IT-pad, observed the results, walked over to Sunul and said, "They are worth 2,350 credits, no more."

Hugh and Erica were talking while searching on their com units. When Erica heard the 2,350 number she came over to Sunul and stated, "Hugh and I have another dealer. He'll offer us 2,500 for the cars and he has a newer model Air Hawk 79 plane available for 2,150. Let's go talk to him."

"I'll give you 2,550 for the cars and a voucher to Aqua-Pure for refueling. That's a total of about 2,750 credits. That's my last offer. Take it or leave it."

The foursome huddled together and Erica confessed, "I didn't get an offer for the cars, the guy said he'd have to see them first." She smiled and followed with, "Let's deal with Adrian and get out of here, okay?"

Sunul broke the huddle, stepped over to Adrian and shook his hand. "You've got a deal, Mr. Kramer."

"All right. I'll need the documents for the cars. They should be in the glove compartments."

Sunul found the papers for the black sedan, but not the other car. He gave what he had to Adrian.

"I need papers for the other vehicle."

"We don't have them, sir. What can we do?"

"But I need some papers for both autos, Mr. Burke, otherwise the deal is off."

Max stepped up and said, "Will this do?" Max flashed his international police badge.

"You are die Polizei, um—the police?" He looked at Max and frowned.

"Yes. Use my badge number on the papers. I will also provide a signature and a number you can call for verification. There won't be a problem."

"That is fine, gentlemen. No problem at all. I will get the transfer papers for you to sign. I will need two signatures."

Ten minutes later, the travelers were loading their belongings on the newer of the two planes, a Wind Slicer-281 capable of carrying six passengers up to 500 miles. Sunul had the key code from Adrian and was inspecting the control surfaces as the others watched.

"Where's the runway, Sunul?" Hugh was scanning the area, taking a 360 degree view, shielding his eyes from the sun. "It's got to be close."

"I presume that's it—right over there." Sunul pointed at the freeway.

Max's eyes followed Sunul's finger and said, "You're kidding me."

"Nope. Get in the copilot's chair, big guy. Erica and Hugh, climb in the back. You can choose any seat you like, but not on the same side."

Hugh glanced into the plane and mumbled, "Big choice." Erica laughed and climbed in directly behind Sunul. Hugh swung up and behind Max. Sunul turned sideways and directed Hugh to put two of the suitcases behind Erica to balance the load.

"Fasten your belts—we're going to taxi over to the highway and wait for a clear path to emerge."

Adrian motioned for Sunul to slide open the window and said, "I'm going to stop traffic for you, just wait a minute. Go ahead and start your engine."

Sunul got comfortable, tightened his harness, and passed the key-code magnetic strip over the steering column and waved to Adrian that he understood. He pressed TAXI on the display and the engine came to life. Sunul released the breaks and the Slicer-281 began to move toward the highway. Adrian could be seen with a vehicle blocking the road ten yards from the plane's entrance to the paved highway. Sunul guided the plane onto the road, checked to make sure the path was clear and pressed TAKE-OFF. Sunul held the brakes until he got the signal to release them. The Slicer accelerated down the highway and knifed into the air. Next stop: Trelew.

Chapter 27

Sunul took the plane to 5,000 feet and checked the radar. Air traffic was light and he set the destination to Trelew and let the automatic pilot take over. "Keep your belts on; the system says there's some rough air ahead. The coastal winds will toss us around a bit. I hope none of you get airsick. Check under your seats for barf-bags. The computer says it's a two hour journey to Trelew. Enjoy the ride; it's better than riding in those sedans."

Erica remarked, "I'm going to snooze. I didn't sleep well last night."

Contrary to the rough air advisement, the two hour ride was uneventful and Sunul took over from the autopilot ten minutes from the Trelew airport.

"How big is Trelew, Sunul?" Max was looking down at the outskirts of the city.

"According to the data I received, it's about 120,000. Its population is fairly stable—hasn't changed more than twenty percent in the last 60 years."

The radar image from the airport showed three military aircraft lining up to land. Sunul had to circle the airport three miles out for about seven minutes. He was now second in the landing que, behind a jumbo cargo carrier from Europe. Erica was watching the enormous plane approach the runway. The Slicer-281 was making its fourth go-around at 1,000 feet.

"Is that thing going to crash?" Erica had a look of deep concern.

"Why do you say that?"

"Isn't it going too slow to make the runway?"

"Deceptive, isn't it. It's moving faster than you think. There's no reference for you to judge the speed in the sky. It's probably going more than 120 miles per hour and the engines are ready to howl if it slows too much. The pilot will goose it a bit if necessary when he nears the ground. He's undoubtedly landed hundreds of times, if not thousands. Watch when he touches down; it'll be very smooth."

It was just as Sunul had said. Erica watched the gigantic plane kiss the runway and the flaps flare out. She could faintly hear the sound of the engines applying reverse thrust to help diminish the big plane's kinetic energy. She relaxed and stretched her neck, having tensed her muscles while watching the cargo plane land.

"We're next. We'll be at the terminal in about two minutes. Use the facilities while I get more fuel. It will take at least fifteen minutes. Grab us some more snack food."

As the three passengers deplaned, Sunul contacted the tower and asked for the location of the refueling bay. He taxied about fifty yards, pulled to the edge of the tarmac, and shut down the engine at the refueling station for small planes. While the oxygen and hydrogen spheres were being changed out, he had a brief discussion with one of the attendants. He asked about travel to the Falklands.

"Hardly anyone goes to Stanley from here anymore, unless they're British. You don't sound British, you must be Canadian or American."

"American. I'm trying to find someone. I was told they went to the islands."

"This plane won't get you there; you'll need something bigger, more substantial. The winds can be a problem over the ocean."

"We're going to Comodoro, then to Stanley. Is there much traffic to Stanley from there?"

"Not much that I've ever heard of, just some scientists headed to the Antarctic. The British and the Americans have a new plane for travel to the frozen south. I heard the other day there would be a flight soon. Springtime allows more planes to go south with supplies and manpower. Someone is developing more tourist activities, too."

"Thanks for the information. Here's a voucher for the fuel."

The attendant took the slip from Sunul and commented, "Those guys are still in business?"

"Yeah, why?"

"I heard one of the brothers had pulled some shady deals and the authorities nailed him."

"We only dealt with Adrian."

The attendant laughed, "He's the youngest. The other two are probably in jail."

Two hours later, the Slicer-281 was on the ground in Comodoro. Sunul found the rental desk in the terminal and turned over the key card, joined the others, and went to dinner. They were tired from the day of travel and confrontation and checked into an airport hotel for the night.

Max was the first of the travelers to arise in the morning. He dressed, had a cup of coffee in his room, and sat looking out the large picture window which needed washing. He wondered why the others seemed to take travelling so easily. His senses were being bombarded with a flood of information and he was having some difficulty distinguishing the inconsequential from the salient details. He thought, "Am I so different than the others? They have been in space, lived on Mars, returned to Earth in rocket ships. Does that account for how they seem to accept things so easily?"

He heard water running in the adjacent room where Erica was staying; he assumed she was in the shower. "I'll give her ten minutes and then knock on her door—see if she wants to have breakfast with me. God, I'm hungry." He smiled, "I wonder what the doc looks like in the morning?" He flipped on the wall screen and sat down to watch the local news.

Erica was showering, cleaning off the accumulated grime from riding in trucks the day before. She washed off the simulated tattoos and scrubbed her face to remove the gaudy makeup. She thought there was no good reason to maintain her disguise. Who would be after her on the Falkland Islands? If the men thought she should continue to conceal her identity, she would reapply the fake layers. Ten minutes is all it took.

Wrapped in a towel, she heard a knock on her door. The knock was nothing special, just some knuckles against wood. She pulled on a blond wig and went to the door.

"Who is it?"

"Max. Would you like to have breakfast with me? Sunul and Hugh aren't up yet."

"All right. Give me five minutes. Come in and wait while I get dressed."

Max heard the magnetic lock click. He pushed the door open, expecting to see Erica, but no one was there. She had run to the bathroom when she released the lock.

Her voice came from the bathroom. "Sit down, I'll be right with you."

Erica's suitcase was open on the bed; the contents were organized. Everything was folded to take up the least possible space. Max looked away quickly; he didn't want to get caught peeping. He felt a little embarrassed that he had even scanned over the contents, but he hadn't noticed any pink or black underwear. The bathroom door swung open.

"Who is this woman?" Max had a hard time standing up and keeping his eyes glued to this beauty simultaneously; he couldn't help himself. She looked like a model—right out of a fashion advertisement. Max regained his senses rapidly and said, "Wow! You must be Shania. The other guys said you were good looking, but they were wrong. You are gorgeous!"

Shania laughed, "Thank-you, Max. Are we leaving or are you just going to stand there with your mouth open?"

"Uh, let's get out of here." Max reached for the door and it popped open. He swung it back and let Shania walk into the hallway. He had a terrific urge to put his arm around Shania's waist, but refrained. He had to think about not tripping over his feet as the couple moved down the hall. Hoping he wouldn't put anything in his mouth but breakfast, he tried to think of what to say to the doctor. What would they talk about?

When they were seated in the restaurant, Max relaxed and his humor returned. What was he afraid of? Shania was not intimidating, but very attractive. He was focusing on her sparkling blue eyes. She started the conversation after they had ordered.

"How did you get into police work?"

They discussed each other's professions for about a half-hour before Hugh and Sunul joined them. Max and Shania had eaten slowly because of all their conversation. Sunul and Hugh were surprised by Shania's lack of disguise but agreed with her that it wasn't necessary any longer. If Evan and Art had talked to their superiors, any trackers knew who she was. When breakfast was over, the quartet returned to the airport terminal to find a flight to the Falklands.

Sunul could see the British Airways Southern Flight counter when they entered the small two-story concrete building. He pointed and began moving toward the Flight Announcement Panel hanging from the ceiling above an agent standing at the glass desk. The brunette, about five-foot-nine, wore a pair of oversized glasses, but they added to her charm.

"May I help you, sir?" She directed her question to Max.

Max was surprised and indicated she should talk with Sunul. Shania poked Max and winked at him.

Sunul stepped up to the desk and asked, "The four of us would like to go to Stanley. When is the next flight?"

"We have a flight scheduled for 1:00 pm, but I'm afraid it will have to be cancelled. The pilot became sick last evening and has not reported ready for duty. I think he had some bad food or maybe he has the flu. Unfortunately, we're short of pilots. Two of our regular captains are in Antarctica right now."

"I'm a pilot. I could take the flight to Stanley and keep your service flowing normally."

The young lady smiled, "We have to have certified pilots, sir."

Hugh spoke up, "Miss, he can fly anything you have in your fleet. Have you a connection to the International Space Agency?"

"Well, yes. Some of our regular passengers work at the pole and need to contact the agency occasionally. Who is the subject of the inquiry?"

"Sunul Burke."

The clerk tossed her head back and exclaimed, "You're Mr. Burke?"

Hugh pointed at Sunul and answered, "No, he is."

"Oh, gosh! I know that name!" She looked at Sunul and said, "I've always wanted to meet you, but I never thought it would happen. I read about your landing on Mars. It was wonderful!" She extended her hand and Sunul politely shook it. While holding her hand with both of his, he asked, "Do you think I could make your scheduled flight?"

"I hate to ask you this, but I would have to verify your identity. Can I send a retinal scan to England for verification? Would that be agreeable?"

"No problem. Where's your scanner?"

She lifted the scanner from beneath the counter and placed it on the surface with the eyepiece facing Sunul. "Just look into the eyepiece as if it were a microscope. It will just take a second."

Although Sunul had submitted to retinal scans many times, he made no comment, bent over and placed his right eye over the lens. A red-orange wide-beam of light moved from top to bottom of his eye in two seconds. Irene sent off the scan and said, "It should only take a few seconds. The recognition software is very good."

Sunul was curious, "You don't have a British accent."

"I'm Canadian—from Churchill, western Hudson Bay. Used to the cold. You're all from the US?"

Sunul nodded and heard a bird sound from the desk display.

Irene looked at Sunul, grinned, and announced, "You *are* Sunul Burke. Our head office says you can fly any of our planes without restriction. You will be compensated at our regular pilot's rate." She looked up from the display and said, "I'm impressed! I've never met anyone as accomplished as you, Mr. Burke; it's a real pleasure."

"What's your last name, Irene?"

"I doubt if you've ever heard it before; it's Ashoona. It's an Inuit name."

"That's true, but I'll remember you. You've been very helpful." Sunul drifted over to a window and looked outside. "Is that the plane we'll be taking?"

"Yes sir. It's an older petroleum-engine two-motor, but very dependable. Cruising speed is 265 miles per hour. Time to Stanley is two-hours fifteen-minutes as the crow flies, but our pilots usually take a little longer; maybe ten minutes or so. East winds you know."

"Is it ready to fly?"

"It will be a few minutes. I'll have to check the tanks. Let me call maintenance."

A half-hour later, the group was in the air headed for Stanley, Falkland Islands. Hugh was a little nervous when he thought about being over the water for two hours, but after Sunul took the plane to 12,000 feet, Hugh relaxed, closed his eyes and listened to the hum of the engines. He suddenly jerked and looked out the window to see land. The noise of the landing gear dropping and locking into place had awaken him. He wiped a thin rivulet of drool from his mouth and looked at the others to see if they had noticed. Shania and Max were talking. Max was pointing at a picture in a magazine Shania was looking through.

"We'll be on the ground in a couple of minutes. You've been a great crew!" Sunul's voice over the intercom caused his three companions to laugh.

Chapter 28

Sunul followed directions from the terminal tower and parked the plane about twenty yards to the west of the two-story building. He shut down the engines and joined his friends. "That wasn't so bad—better than riding in a truck."

The others laughed, as if they could have driven across 595 miles of ocean.

"I'm hungry. Let's get something to eat." Max picked up his gym bag, opened the door behind the wing and dropped to the ground. "Anybody coming with me?"

Hugh helped Shania with her luggage, tossing her suitcase to Max, then he helped her to sit on the floor with her legs out the door. Max picked her up, carried her about twenty feet from the plane, and set her down next to her suitcase. Sunul and Hugh joined them and they walked to the terminal.

Shania had refused Max's offer to carry her. Although she enjoyed having Max's strong arms wrapped around her, she knew her fractured leg was about healed and she had to begin rebuilding the atrophied muscles; she didn't want to draw attention to herself for any length of time because of an obvious limp.

As they entered the terminal, a short, nearly bald man with wire-rim bifocals approached holding a flight display panel. "Which of you blokes is the captain?" He suddenly saw Shania and said, "Beg your pardon miss."

The man turned toward Max, expecting him to be in charge. Shania pointed at Sunul and answered, "He is. Sunul Burke."

"Ah, Mr. Burke. Happy to meet you, sir. Have you the log?"

"It's on the plane, Mr.—."

"Strathmore, James Strathmore, sir; agent in charge. I'll need the log. Which of you gentlemen is the doctor?" He scanned Hugh and Max and they simultaneously answered and pointed, "She is."

"Pardon me, Madam, but I expected a man; an older man. You look too young to be a person of the caliber we requested. We requested an Englishman, not an American."

Sunul had had enough. "Don't get your nose out of joint, Starthmore. She's a better physician than most any bloke from the United Kingdom."

"Strathmore, sir. I just mean we expected an experienced English gentleman, a W. C. Wilcox."

"Your W. C. Wilcox is unfortunately under the weather. He is recovering on the continent."

"Is his malady contagious?"

"We don't know, but he was prevented from coming to the islands. We thought it was due to his feeling of malaise. He was coming down with something and was advised by the airlines to not visit the islands."

"Yes, we can't afford to have disease injected into the population. Besides, the Antarctic settlement won't allow sickness of any sort. He would have had to return to Argentina."

"Mr. Wilcox was slated to travel to the Antarctic?"

"That is correct. He missed the two earlier flights to the Rothera Research Station. They are awaiting him. He is to take Mr. Simms's vacancy. Mr. Simms returned to London two weeks ago and the learned Mr. Wilcox is his replacement."

"Well, Doctor Shania Winslow is staying with our group. Where she goes, we all go."

Strathmore was frozen in place, he couldn't speak, not knowing how to contend with the words from Sunul. Sunul recognized his uncomfortable nature and changed the subject.

"We are looking for two young people, a young Caucasian woman and her companion, an Afro-American male of the same age. Could you please see if you have ever seen them?" Sunul motioned to Hugh and Hugh showed Strathmore Miranda's picture.

"I think so, but the woman is much older than in that picture. I expect she is as old as or older than you folks. There was a black male traveling with her, but they aren't on the islands."

"What?" Hugh couldn't believe what he heard. "Where are they then, back on the continent?"

"Oh, they're on a continent all right; south of us—Antarctica."

"Hmm. We hadn't planned on that. How long ago were they here?" Sunul was already planning on flying to Antarctica as a passenger with three companions.

"Let me think." Strathmore removed his glasses, held his eyes shut, and cleaned the lenses. When he put his glasses back in his volley-ball head, he said, "I believe they were here about six weeks ago. Yes, I recall now. They had a long discussion with one of the biologists—duration of several hours as I recall." Strathmore adjusted his glasses and continued, "They left on one of the new experimental planes. It was going to the South Pole."

Shania had been listening intently. "I think I know why, Sunul."

Everyone's eyes shifted to Shania. "They want to slow down the ageing process with the help of a physiologist and the severe cold weather. I'll bet they promised the researcher he or she would get a few publications from the work."

Strathmore volunteered, "The biologist is Sir George Dean Dalwitt, and you are correct; he is a physiologist at the Rothera station. He is a rather brilliant young scientist—only in his twenties. He is a descendent of Captain Robert Falcon Scott, the famous explorer that died during a polar expedition in 1912."

"You mentioned experimental planes? What type of plane are you talking about?" Sunul was unaware of any experimental planes on flights to the short airfields in the Antarctic.

"Boeing Aircraft, working with a new group of Canadian de Havilland Dash 7 engineers, has developed a more sophisticated replacement for the Dash 7 aeroplanes which are getting very old. Apparently the Dash 7 machines have reached the end of their service life. Metal fatigue is becoming a major problem."

Sunul was getting more curious by the second. "Can you tell me what the new aircraft is called? How many of them exist and where are they located?"

"Ah, yes." Strathmore's face lit up. "They are BdeH Dash 720X models. One is expected tomorrow and will go to the southern continent after tea. It will be carrying a large amount of cargo in preparation for the extensive amount of research during summer months. It may have a few passengers also." He looked at Sunul to see if he had answered all of the questions, then remembered, "Oh, there are five of the aircraft; two are on Antarctica presently. I am not aware of the other locations."

Sunul was a little apprehensive about flying an experimental aircraft, unaware of any of the peculiarities it might have in windy and extremely cold weather. For his introductory flight in the cockpit of the new plane, he thought it would be best for him to ride as copilot. Having never flown with a British captain, it could be interesting. He hoped the pilot possessed a good sense of humor.

The remainder of the day was spent finding clothes for the Antarctic expedition. The foursome taxied the two miles to Port Stanley to visit shops for the proper gear for the spring weather in the northernmost portion of the iciest continent on Earth. Satisfied with their purchases, they rented rooms for the night and went to dinner together at eight o'clock in the evening.

The next morning, the team met for breakfast, packed their belongings and boarded a taxi to the airfield, arriving at 9:30 a.m. Sunul sought out Strathmore, but he had been released for the day and replaced by a tall thin man with a moustache and a full head of gray hair. Mr. Steedham, a man of quite different character than Mr. Strathmore, pleased Sunul immeasurably.

Steedham introduced Sunul to the pilot, Captain Charles Dowding, chosen to fly the advanced design plane going to the Antarctic. The captain insisted Sunul call him Chuck. He was a little shorter and slightly younger than Sunul and the others, and was a member of the Royal Navy. He carried himself as a military man and had wavy black hair, but a scruffy beard, which seemed a bit incongruous. His heavy gray sweater and insulated work pants were a good disguise of his military background. Sunul noted Dowding's shiny black boots were the only thing the Navy man wore that looked to be military issue.

Steedham agreed to introduce Sunul to the plane, so the two men climbed into the cockpit. Chuck gave Sunul the once-over and was surprised Sunul had so few questions. The only new addition for Sunul was the wing extensions.

"Do the augmentations occur automatically, or does the pilot direct the change?"

"It's all computer controlled—but the pilot can override the automatic function, but I've never done it. When we reach altitude, the wings extend and the outboard engines shut down. At that point, we become a powered glider. Actually, climbing to 30,000 feet uses half our fuel, but the two functioning engines only consume around twenty percent of our remaining petrol."

Sunul had one last question, "What is the range of the plane with only two engines?"

"Loaded to capacity, 940 miles, but I think that is a bit conservative. I believe 985 miles is more like it."

"I'm looking forward to this trip. When do we head out?"

"I suspect we'll leave the islands right after luncheon and builder's tea. To you yanks, that's one o'clock. I've got plenty of questions for you during the flight. I hope I don't put you through the ringer."

"Don't worry, I haven't ever talked with a British pilot. I doubt if I'll be bored. Would it be appropriate for me to ride as copilot?"

"I assumed you would. My copilot, Miss Archer, won't mind. I believe she wants to converse with your doctor. She wants to know all about Mars."

"You know about us?"

"Yes, sir. It's my duty to be knowledgeable about all my passengers. I'm impressed with your little group."

Lunch was more like a feast for the crew and the Americans. Shania recommended that everyone should eat as much cheese and carbohydrates as possible. The calories would be useful at lower temperatures. Max watched what Shania ate and was surprised. He began to think she had been on a fast to be so slim, but he followed her suggestions. When the builder's tea arrived, strong tea with milk and sugar added, he felt his stomach might overflow at an inopportune moment.

The plane's mechanic suddenly appeared at the table. "Captain Dowding, we have a problem. I cannot find the correct spanner for the pressure sensor on the wing extension device. What should I do?"

Hugh stood up from the bench and said, "Show me what you need to be adjusted. I believe I can take care of the problem." He looked and Sunul, wiggled his artificial fingers and smiled.

Sunul commented, "I think Mr. Patel can help you. Show him the assembly."

The mechanic, the third member of the flight crew, Geordie, said, "Please follow me, sir."

Ten minutes later, Hugh rejoined the luncheon group, just in time to hear from the pilot, "Please get your things on board, we'll be in the air in—." He looked at his watch, "twelve minutes."

True to his word, the four engines were humming and the plane was accelerating down the runway and in the air after a relatively short takeoff distance. Nine minutes later, the plane was at 30,000 feet. Sunul had been observing the rate of climb and was impressed that the fully loaded craft handled so easily. When the wing extensions occurred, he was amazed that the complete transformation was accomplished so quickly and smoothly. He watched the right outboard engine's prop as it slowed and then quit rotating.

Chuck moved his fingers across the pilot's display and leaned back, smiling, "Now, if you don't mind, I've got a ton of questions for you."

After Chuck's first question, Sunul decided to tell him the entire story, starting with the journey to the Kuiper Belt and the return, which so many people had heard about because of the crash landing of the unconventional spacecraft on Mars. It took nearly an hour, being interrupted several times by new questions, for Sunul's account to converge with the present day events.

"Jesus, Sunul, I thought I had an exciting life. My life experiences have been trivial compared to yours— and you and your friends are still taking part in the adventure. I sincerely hope you can get your sister's cancer in remission, or eliminated altogether."

"Thanks, Chuck. My sister and I are the only Burke's left from our family. I'd like her to be around for a long time. How long will the plane be on the ground at Rothera?"

"It will take a day to unload the cargo. Much of it is packaged to go to other locations.
As soon as it is delivered and any materials addressed to the northern continents are loaded, we'll be on our way back to Port Stanley. I expect we'll be here about three days."

"When do we touch down?" Sunul wanted to find Miranda and Licon as quickly as possible, verify their well-being, and obtain some blood samples. He wanted to get back to Priscilla with the blood without wasting any time. Hugh needed to see Miranda and give her some things he and Triel had prepared for her last two birthdays.

Chapter 29

Landing on the crushed rock runway was a simple task for Captain Dowding. The breaks, reverse thrust, and the wing extensions combined to slow the plane after touchdown on the relatively short landing strip. The weather was nice for a spring day; the vestiges of winter had decided to present the Rothera Research Station with sunny weather for a third successive day.

Chuck cut the inboard engines and about a dozen men and women swarmed around the aircraft doors, waiting to pick up their overdue packages of research materials and letters from home, which were more satisfying than radio transmissions. More intimate thoughts could be expressed with written words, no matter the language.

One man, tall and thin, wearing a heavy parka in spite of the warmer weather, waited until the hubbub ceased and then approached the passenger door. He called into the plane, "Is there a medical doctor on board today?"

Captain Dowding hadn't heard the exact words and inquired, "What was that, sir?"

"I'm Ervin Edwards, Professor Dalwitt's assistant. He would like to talk with Mr. Wilcox, immediately."

"Mr. Wilcox remains in Argentina. We have an American doctor, Dr. Shania Estwick with us. She is eminently qualified." Dowding's announcement was received by Edwards with a raised left eyebrow.

"Oh, dear. The professor is going to be very disappointed. He specifically instructed that I should return with Mr. Wilcox." Edwards began pulling at his full beard and looking at the crushed rock at his feet. "What can I tell him?"

"Tell him the truth. I'd like you to meet Mr. Wilcox's temporary fill-in, Dr. Estwick."

Shania had been standing next to Chuck during his conversation with Mr. Edwards. She leaned down and extended her arm. "Please help me down, Mr. Edwards. I've got a bum leg."

Edwards looked up. His face turned from chagrin to near elation. He climbed to the plane, put both hands up, and helped Shania descend the three steps to the runway. "Have you any luggage, Miss?"

"Just one large suitcase. Mr. Webster will carry it; it's fairly heavy."

Max descended the portable steps to the ground with Shania's and his suitcases. He stood watching the assistant and Shania walk away and brought up the rear. The threesome travelled nearly fifty yards to one of the large research buildings, climbed an elevated wooden porch, and entered through an extra-wide door at least six inches thick. It was warm inside, probably in excess of seventy degrees, but seemed even warmer after being outside where it was forty degrees cooler.

Shania was escorted past three offices, occupied by bewhiskered middle-aged men and one younger woman, apparently their secretary; she was sitting in a stall at a centrally located computer and looked as if she was wearing at least three sweaters. She looked up and smiled as Max walked by. Edwards stopped at a door and knocked, then opened the door and entered. Shania followed and held the door for Max and the luggage.

"Please be seated, the professor will be right with you." Edwards did an about face, entered through the next door, and shut it behind him. Shania and Max could hear voices from behind the closed door but the words were unintelligible. They sat in silence for about fifteen seconds. Shania heard footsteps, the door opened, and a tall clean-shaven young man appeared dressed in a heavy sweater and jeans.

"Miss Estwick, please come in. We need to talk. Your assistant may join us."

Max said, "I'll wait out here and guard our luggage, Shania. I won't understand what you're talking about anyway. Give me a yell if you need anything."

Shania smiled and replied, "Thanks, Max. Don't let anybody carry off the bigger suitcase." She entered the professor's office and closed the door.

The young professor began by saying, "This case may be the first of its kind. My discussion with the two patients indicates their rapid ageing has been normal in every way, but the process is unparalleled in medical history. One patient is a female Caucasian and other is a male Afro-American. They are approximately nine human years of age and were born on a space craft."

Dalwitt sat back waiting for a response of amusement from Shania. However, her response was a great surprise to him.

"Yes, professor, I know both subjects of your investigation. I met them on Mars about eight years ago when they were still children. Their blood cured my cancer. I was not aware of their rapid ageing until about a week ago. But after thinking about it, I should have expected the accelerated ageing process."

"I don't want to waste time with my questions about life on Mars right now, I want to know if you have any ideas about treating my patients. Let me review the measures I have already pursued—by the way, without positive results."

The professor outlined the various attempts he had taken to prevent or retard the rapid ageing of his patients. Shania and the professor spent a little more than a-half-hour parsing the research notes that had accumulated on his com device. Shania was amazed at the number of chemical substances that had been administered parenterally.

"I noticed iron and platinum salts created some problems. What was the difficulty?"

"Compounds containing iron and platinum created lesions and mental difficulties, even at extremely low dosages. It was not in their best interest to follow those exposures. When those substances were tried, I discovered the patients possessed twenty-five pairs of chromosomes. I was shocked at their normal appearance."

Shania racked her brain trying to come up with a new substance or procedure, but couldn't think of anything the professor hadn't already tried. "Could I please observe the patients without them seeing me? I'd rather have them see me when they see Sunul and Hugh. Hugh is the father of Miranda."

"Miranda? Is that the female's given name?"

"Yes, it's Miranda Patel, and the male's is Licon Mason."

The professor smiled, "They said their names were Adam and Eve. I thought it was a little strange."

"When they read the Bible, and they realized they were the first of their kind, they chose Adam and Eve for their names. The alpha group went along with it—actually, the parents had no choice; the children didn't consult with their parents, they left the group and were never seen again, until now. If you don't mind, I'd really like to see the children now."

"All right, but you are in for a surprise. They're in the lab, two doors away. I'll let you observe them through a one-way mirror."

Shania followed the professor through a door and stopped in the small room adjacent to the lab. There was a two-by-three foot observation window for monitoring the behavior of patients without them knowing. Professor Dalwitt stepped aside and motioned for Shania to move closer to the observation pane.

Shania looked into the laboratory for a moment and then stepped back with her hand covering her mouth to keep from crying out. She turned away and looked at the professor. "I think we all need to meet them as a group. It might not be so emotional for Hugh that way. He will be shocked. There will be tears."

She retraced her path through the office and found Max sitting, reading a two-month-old International Astronomical journal. When she came through the door, he dropped the magazine on the small coffee table and stood, "Have you found them?"

Shania nodded and asked, "Could you please find Hugh and Sunul? We need to see Adam and Eve as a group. Hugh, especially, is going to need support."

"Okay. I'll be right back with them. Should I say anything?"

Shania paused and then said, "No. I'll talk with them before we go into the lab." She watched Max hurriedly walk down the hallway and out the insulated door. Her thoughts were terribly jumbled; but most importantly, she worried about Hugh. However, she couldn't stop thinking of the two children either. How were they going to react?

Max stood on the porch and looked for signs of Sunul and Hugh; their luggage was at the bottom of the steps leading to the entrance platform, but where were they? He scanned over to the plane. The rear of the fuselage had been folded down to unload large containers and he saw Sunul giving hand signals to the driver of a forklift. The driver was Hugh. Max watched as Hugh drove a large box to a truck and transferred the load.

Captain Dowding appeared from the back ramp of the plane, walked over to Sunul, and shook his hand, then shook hands with Hugh. Max assumed he was thanking them for helping unload the aircraft, but he couldn't hear what was being said. Sunul and Hugh turned toward the research building and saw Max. They waved and began jogging with their hands in their pockets. They had been working without gloves.

When the men got within a couple of yards, Max said, "Shania wants to see you inside. I'll follow with your luggage. Go straight in and down the hallway to the right. She'll be waiting for you."

Hugh and Sunul unzipped their parkas and stomped their feet to remove ice and snow before entering the building. As they moved down the hall toward the professor's office and lab they saw Shania standing outside an office door. Hugh was closest and Shania said, "I've seen them, Hugh. They don't look good."

Hugh almost pushed Shania out of his way, but Sunul grabbed his arm and said, "Slow down, Hugh, they're not going anywhere. Listen to Shania."

Hugh leaned back against the wall and asked, "Is Miranda disfigured?"

"No, but she looks very old. Don't be surprised when you see her."

"Okay. Take me to her. Is Licon with her?"

"Yes. They're sitting together in the laboratory. I'll take you in."

Sunul and Hugh followed Shania into the professor's laboratory. Shania approached the couple and said, "Hello there. Do you remember me?" Shania was blocking Hugh's and Sunul's view of the children. As Hugh got closer, he heard Miranda's voice.

"Oh, yes. I remember you. You are the doctor on Mars that had cancer. That was a long time ago, wasn't it, Adam?"

"Sure. I remember, too. We gave you a small sample of our blood. How are you?"

Shania smiled, "I'm just fine, thanks to you two donors. Someone is here to see you."
Shania stepped out of the way so Hugh and Sunul could see Adam and Eve in person for the first time since the children had left the group in the mountains.

Hugh was shocked when he saw his beloved daughter, she looked to be at least eighty years old and was very frail. But when Miranda saw Hugh, she recognized him immediately. "Daddy! You've come to see us."

Eve tried to stand, supporting herself with a cane, and lurched forward, dropping the cane and extending her arms. Tears were running down her cheeks. Adam tried to support her, but he was too frail and too slow to help. Hugh rushed forward and hugged Miranda, preventing her from falling to the floor.

Miranda's hair was gray, very thin, and her eyes were sunken. She didn't try to wipe away her tears, she just let them flow. Hugh's tears were freely flowing and he couldn't speak, his throat tight with emotion.

Sunul stepped forward and hugged Licon when he saw that Licon was concerned, or perhaps a little frightened, by Hugh's and Eve's emotional outburst.

The white-haired, hunchbacked Licon tried to stand erect, but he couldn't straighten his spine to stand tall. "How are you, Mr. Burke? It is nice to see you. How are my parents? Did they come, too?" Sunul grasped Licon's hand and shook it delicately. Sunul was taking care to avoid injuring the emaciated man barely able to stand before him. Like Hugh had reacted, Sunul's eyes began to water, but he was able to say, "I have a letter from your parents. It's in my pocket. Let me give it to you." Sunul guided Licon back to his chair and pulled the letter from his shirt pocket. It was sealed in plastic and Sunul opened the enclosure, handed the message to Licon, and stepped back.

Licon fumbled but opened the folded paper and tried to read, but couldn't focus on the handwriting. He asked, "Does someone have a reading glass?"

Sunul saw a large magnifying glass on the lab bench and handed it to Licon. After reading the letter, Licon refolded it and placed it in the original envelope.

"They want us to come back to Florida with you, but we can't do that. Eve and I only have, at most, a few weeks left. We want to stay here and have our ashes spread on the ice near the pole." He looked at Sunul as if it was a request that Sunul could grant. Then he asked, "Is there anything we can do for you in these last days? That is, we can still donate blood if it is needed. If that is the case, Eve and I will donate equal amounts." He smiled, "We don't want more from one than the other. You know, we still compete."

Eve was listening now and said, "That is true Mr. Burke. We will give equal amounts. Maybe Mrs. Burke will be able to determine how our blood defeats cancer. It would please us to contribute—you know, leave something behind besides our ashes."

Shania was touched by the generosity exhibited by Adam and Eve in the face of death in but a few weeks. She turned toward Max and buried her face against his chest. She began to cry and whispered, "Take me out of here, Max."

Max was touched by what he was hearing, too. He had wanted to leave the laboratory anyway, he had never experienced a living funeral. The air was thick with emotion. He put his arm around Shania and they left the room to escape the teary atmosphere.

Shania sat down in the professor's office and wiped her tears away with her hands. Max held out a handkerchief and she wiped her eyes once more and handed it back. He wadded it and wiped his own eyes.

"Pretty powerful feelings in there. I never thought it would bother me, but those old people are mentally so strong and yet so young in years. I hope I can be that way when I'm an old man."

"They have made getting blood samples an easy task. I almost hate to take some of their blood, but I want to save Priscilla."

"Why don't you get the specimen storage containers and collect the samples right now? Get it over with. You might be helping Hugh and Sunul by relieving the stress of the situation. Adam and Eve seem to have accepted their fate quite well."

"Thanks, Max. That's a good idea." Shania zipped up her parka and then remembered the containers were in her suitcase outside the professor's office; she didn't have to leave the warmth of the building. Max had anticipated her need for her luggage and reached in front of her to open the door. She swatted his hand and smiled, "I'll get it." Max sat back down, watched Shania drag her suitcase into the office, and pop the lock. She retrieved two small cylinders about the size of Max's thumb, a syringe, two cotton swabs, and stepped in front of Max. "Unzip me, please." She looked directly in Max's eyes, smiled, and said, "Don't get any ideas. I need some flexibility to take blood."

Max did what she asked and sat down. "I'll wait for you."

Shania disappeared into the lab and a couple of minutes later, she reappeared with Sunul, Hugh, and the professor.

Professor Dalwitt glanced at Max and announced, "That's all we can do today. Adam and Eve can only take so much before they suffer fatigue. I don't want to put them in hospital."

Hugh asked, "When can we see them again? I think we all have some questions for them." He surveyed the others and they were nodding their heads.

"They'll be fine tomorrow after a good night's rest. Let's meet in the faculty lounge, it's not far for them to walk. It's in the adjacent building, but we don't have to go outside. We can transport them in wheelchairs, although they don't like to give up their freedom."

Chapter 30

The three men slept in the guest bunkhouse with three visiting scientists from Ireland, Bermuda, and Sri Lanka, three countries that didn't have their own research facilities in Antarctica. All three researchers were studying deep water ocean currents. Hugh and Sunul were bombarded with questions about travelling to the Kuiper Belt. A few rounds of drinks and they were all sound asleep, contented with their day's activities and looking forward to the next work period.

Shania bunked with the group's secretary, the woman Max had observed earlier in the day. Wanda Cheshire was forty years of age and was taking two years off from working in the Smithsonian. Actually, the Smithsonian was paying most of her salary, for she was recording a journal for the magazine. Wanda inquired about Max, but Shania did not volunteer much information except to say he was very efficient with a handgun.

When Wanda discovered that, she lost interest and the conversation changed to a discussion about summer clothing in the US and new regulations for the US-Canada border crossings. She had heard there was now a fee involved. Shania assured her that what she had heard was correct, but the fee at the southern border had tripled in the last year. It was essentially a tax to support upkeep of the wall. Migratory workers had dwindled to such an extent because of robot pickers, fees had to be raised to pay border guards adequate wages.

At 1:00 p.m. the visitors met with the professor. He escorted them to the lounge where Adam and Eve had enjoyed their lunch. The patients were sitting in recliners anticipating the arrival of the travelers. The professor and the four American visitors were placed in a semicircle in front of Adam and Eve. Professor Dalwitt sat in a fold-up chair next to Eve.

Dalwitt started things off, "I don't think we should take more than thirty minutes for the questions. Who wants to start with a question?"

Max raised his hand and said, "I have one. When did you decide to come to Antarctica?"

Eve looked at Adam and answered, "It wasn't our first choice, but we couldn't figure out a way to get back home."

Hugh was surprised. "You mean on the space ship that brought us back from the Kuiper Belt?"

"No, Daddy. The moon where we lived until we became the babies."

Shania suddenly realized Adam and Eve were really not human at all but a hybrid of two different beings. "I don't understand why you wanted to go back there. There is nothing but frozen gases and rock out there so far from the sun."

Adam spoke, "Our creator put us there and we wanted to return."

Hugh frowned, "You mean God?"

"Not your God, Daddy—our god."

"Who is he, Eve?"

Eve laughed, "Our god is not a he. Our god is neither male nor female. Our god is everywhere; I guess like your God, but different. It is difficult to explain to you. Your brains don't work like our assemblages."

Sunul was trying to absorb what he had just heard. "So you decided to go to Antarctica because it is so cold there?"

Adam answered, "We studied chemistry after we realized we were getting old so fast. We thought we could slow down the reactions in our bodies if we moved to a cold place. Most of the temperatures on the planet are very high compared to where we came from. But, we didn't realize the human body is regulated to be at 98 degrees. Human DNA upset our way of thinking. We deceived ourselves. We met with the professor in Argentina and he offered to try to help slow down our ageing processes, but it hasn't worked. We appreciate all the effort he expended." Eve nodded when Adam waved to Dalwitt and said, "Thank-you, professor."

Dalwitt cleared his throat, "I'm sorry I couldn't help you, but your DNA has determined your time on Earth. I think I can speak for everyone; we have been honored to have you with us, even if the time has been short."

"I have one last question." Hugh hesitated for a moment and then said, "Do you communicate with your god?" He was addressing Adam.

"Not the way we are talking, but not from faith, either. We seem to know our god's wishes, but not by sounds. It's another form of perception, almost like a mother with her child. When we were in the ice far from here, we knew we were going on a long journey, but Eve and I didn't know where we were going, or how. We were supposed to enjoy the ride. It was wonderful. We learned so many amazing things."

Eve leaned forward, smiled, clapped her delicate hands, and said, "We have made our god very happy. There will be other journeys for us. Adam and I are looking forward to travelling again. We hope to remember you."

Adam looked at each of the visitors as if he were burning their images into his brain to keep forever. "Professor Dalwitt told me you will be returning to the United States soon. Eve and I wish you a safe and speedy trip. We know your homes are far away. Good luck and goodbye."

All of the visitors said goodbye to Adam and Eve individually and tears streamed again, especially from Shania and Hugh. Hugh knew it was the last he would see of his daughter. He didn't want to record her image for Triel to see to avert his wife's emotional trauma. He wanted Triel to remember Miranda as a vivacious young woman.

That evening, Captain Dowding joined the foursome in the visitor's lounge and made an announcement. "We are ahead of schedule for our return trip to Stanley. The plane is loaded and ready for takeoff. Can you leave in the morning?"

Sunul looked at the others and saw no objection. "We'll be ready by 0800."

"Right. We'll be in the air at 0815. Have a good night's rest. See you in the a.m." Dowding saluted and left the lounge.

"Well, I think I'll get some beauty sleep." Shania stood and said, "Goodnight, gentlemen." She left the lounge with a chorus of "Goodnight's" following her.

Max said, "I'm going to hit the sack, too. Breakfast at 0700?"

Sunul nodded, "Sounds good to me."

"Me, too. Shania doesn't need any beauty sleep, but Max could use some."

Max turned around at the door and said, "I heard that, Hugh." Fortunately, he was smiling.

All of the travelers were up at 0600 and taking showers. They met for breakfast, but had little to talk about. Meeting and then leaving Adam and Eve had been haunting them for the last day and a half, but there was nothing they could do to resolve the problem. Shania had the blood specimens and they all had memories, some happy from previous years and some fresh, but sad ones.

As the plane shot into the air and began climbing, they all looked back at the ice-covered continent, but none of them waved goodbye. It was time to let the plane lift their bodies and spirits. The next stop was the Falklands and after that, they weren't sure how the rest of the roughly 6,000 mile trip would unfold.

During the three hour return flight, Sunul spent most of the time trying to think of an expedient means to get back to the USA from British territory. He couldn't escape the foreboding of being attacked for the blood samples secreted in Shania's luggage. He decided to have Shania give one of the refrigerated ampules to Hugh. Chances would be slim that both suitcases would be lost or stolen. When they reached altitude he would talk with Shania and Hugh. He was positive they would agree to the plan.

With one of the blood samples moved to Hugh's luggage, Sunul felt some relief. Only a catastrophic accident would cause the loss of the samples. But as they neared Stanley, he still hadn't come up with a plan for quick return to Florida. He began to pray that the tiny refrigeration units would hold out long enough to ensure viability of the specimens. He couldn't imagine Priscilla not being able to raise her daughter, or even have another child. She was still a talented young woman artist with great potential.

When the plane taxied to the edge of the tarmac, two fuel trucks appeared from behind the terminal and began pumping fuel after the engines shut down. Sunul grabbed his luggage and met with the pilot as the passenger door swung open.

"What is our cargo? I don't see any unloading equipment."

"Garbage. Nothing but garbage. Thirty tons of it—a full load, including body waste."

"Where is it going, to Argentina for processing?"

"Nope. They won't have anything to do with it. They're still sore about the war in 1982—over a century ago. We have to fly it to Canada—about 7,000 miles. Strange things come about when a treaty is signed. No garbage can be left on the Antarctic continent." Dowding shook his head, disgusted with the waste of money and resources. "By the way, how would you feel about flying another load of garbage to the states? We've got two other loads, but only one pilot available. The home office wants us to get this crap out of here ASAP."

"What about a copilot? Will I have one? It would be advisable."

"You're right, but I doubt if I can find anyone as good as you are, even with you only having three hours of flying time, but I'll see what I can do."

"Why don't you loan me yours and you fly alone? That would be better if you can't find me another junior officer."

"That will do. I won't bother to look; you've got Archer assigned to you. She'll spell you on the first couple of legs. After you've flown a few stops, you can fly solo or start giving instructions to Mr. Webster. He looks like he might make a good pilot. I'll bet Miss Archer would enjoy his company, too. She can take over from you and he can copilot."

"That might sound good to you, but I don't need a war to start between two women."

Dowding grinned, "Oh, I didn't know he fancied Miss Estwick, but I should have. She's quite a looker."

Sunul had to laugh. "Chuck, you haven't seen her when she's cleaned up. Max won't have a chance if she is really interested in him."

Sunul and Archer traded off flying and early the next morning the plane was in a powered glide to the runway in Miami. The plane was ushered to a parallel runway and diverted to a parking location near a large rectangular concrete structure. Sunul was directed to shut down the engines and as soon as the props stopped rotating, a parade of four large trucks, led by a loader, approached the rear of the fuselage. Four men, one from each truck, climbed into the cargo bay as soon as Sunul dropped the rear ramp. That's when the noise began.

The travelers didn't stay for the garbage extraction procedure, they were met by a rep from the airline that owned the plane and debriefed in a limousine as it ferried them to the main terminal. Ten minutes later, Sunul and Hugh were on their com units talking to their wives.

"Gina, I'm in Miami and hope to be home by early afternoon. Shania and I are bringing the blood samples. Shania is excited about working with you to rid Priscilla of her cancer. By the way, how is Cilla doing?"

"It's great to hear your voice. You sound very close, not like those transmissions from the south. We're all excited to have you back home. Priscilla looks good and she is anticipating the treatment. I know you saw Licon and Miranda. You'll have to tell me about them when you get here."

"Yeah, we'll talk in private. I don't want the kids to know about them."

"Sunul—." Gina stopped abruptly, forewarned by Sunul's last words. She knew to leave the matter alone for now. "Hurry home, dear."

"Okay. I'll call from the airport when we touch down. Bye for now, babe."

A representative of the manufacturers of the experimental plane, Boeing and de Havilland, provided tickets on the bullet train to Orlando and the quartet made the 200 mile trip in just over an hour. Sunul rented a small plane and they were at the cape forty-five minutes later. He dropped Hugh off and then went home with Max and Shania. Max didn't have anywhere to stay the night so Sunul invited him to stay at the Burke residence. Shania seemed pleased that Max agreed to stay over.

Sunul recovered the blood sample from his luggage. It was the one Hugh had been transporting. He presented it to Gina and after all the kisses and hugs were completed, Shania and Gina began working on the samples, preparing an injection for Priscilla. They went over their notes from Shania's cure and decided on a trial dosage.

One milliliter was administered intravenously and Priscilla asked, "How long will it take before we'll know if it's working?" She looked at the two doctors expectantly.

Chapter 31

Shania was quick to respond, "In my case it was almost immediate. The cancer cells just started disintegrating, but since the donors have aged, the reaction time might be slower. We'll have to monitor your blood for immobilized cancer cells or metabolic products. We don't have imaging equipment here to watch the cell destruction. Let's wait about an hour and see what happens."

"Should I just lay down and wait?"

Gina replied, "That's not necessary, dear. Just carry out your normal activities—just like you had an influenza shot."

Priscilla stood up and said, "Well, I'm going to the park with Gisele. Would Libby like to come with us?"

"Why don't we all go? Shania?"

"Good idea. I'll ask Max if he wants to tag along. She blushed a little and added, "For our protection, of course."

Gina winked at Priscilla. Priscilla nodded and grinned. Shania got to her feet and started toward her bedroom, "I'll get my jacket and ask Max to come along."

When they were assembled on the front porch wearing their insulated jackets, the five ladies set off walking to the park no more than 100 yards away. They had gone about twenty yards, when Max came out of the house and yelled, "Hey, wait for me!"

Shania waited patiently as the mothers and children moved on. When Max caught up, Shania walked beside him for a few steps and then clutched his hand. Max looked down and smiled, "Are we an item?"

A few steps in silence were followed with, "Yes," then a lyrical laugh.

Following dinner and some limited conversation, Priscilla submitted to a blood test and urinalysis. Both were negative. The three women sat together at the kitchen table and discussed their course of action.

Priscilla asked, "Whose blood did you use? Would it make a difference?"

"We used Miranda's. Gina and I anticipated there might a difference between male and female, but we pretty much discounted the possibility after thinking more thoroughly. I asked Miranda and Licon if they had ever been sick. They acted like they didn't know what I was talking about. We explained what sickness was and they just shook their heads."

Gina commented, "Let's double the dosage this time and see what results in the morning. If we see no effect, we'll try Licon's blood."

"Checkmate!"

Max tipped his king over and said, "I think I need some chess lessons, Sunul. You are too good for me. Maybe I should play against your son?"

"Be careful, Max, he's number one on the school team."

"Okay. How about your daughter? Is Libby any good?"

"She hasn't shown any interest in games. She takes after her mom and is interested in biology and medicine. She's been asking a lot of questions about chemistry lately. She's working on memorizing the periodic table."

"Geez, Sunul. How about wrestling?"

"I wouldn't even try that with you. I'd get flattened. Say, how are you and Shania getting along? Gina says you two are awfully friendly."

Max smiled and sat back in his chair. "That relationship is getting better all the time. I think I have a winner. She is really something. That might be the reason I lost to you in chess; I think about her all the time."

Sunul grinned, "Max, you lost because you can't play very well. That has nothing to do with Shania, but it's a damn good excuse. We'll play again after you two are married."

Max laughed. "I doubt if that will make any difference. I'll still be thinking about her all the time. I'll have the same excuse if I lose."

"You mean when you lose."

After breakfast the next day, Shania introduced a double dose of blood into the vein in Priscilla's left arm. She held an alcohol moistened cotton pad over the puncture wound for a minute, checked for leakage, and applied a small bandage over the injection site. She patted Priscilla on the shoulder and said, "We'll wait a couple of hours and then run some tests. Hopefully, we'll see something this time."

Priscilla checked her watch and replied, "At eleven o'clock, we'll check. By noon, we'll know the results, right?"

"That's right. I bet we'll see something this time." Shania gave Priscilla a thumbs up.

Unfortunately, the tests were negative. The blood apparently had not been effective in destroying the cancer. Gina went to see Priscilla in her bedroom where she was reading a children's story to Gisele in

French. Gina waited until Priscilla looked up from the book.

"The tests were negative, Priscilla, but don't give up; we've just begun the procedure. Shania and I are going to review our procedure and see if we have somehow neglected something. And remember, we've still got Licon's specimen which we haven't tried yet."

Priscilla was sitting on the bed beside Gisele. She had closed her eyes and hung her head. She looked up, "So you still think there's hope?" She was twisting the hair from her wig around her fingers and looking at Gina with a vacant stare.

Gina sat beside Priscilla and put her arm around her sister-in-law's shoulders. "Sure. If I didn't, I would tell you right away. We'll try Licon's blood tomorrow. Keep your chin up. We'll figure this out. Shania and I are going to review our notes again. We might have overlooked something that happened on Mars. We're the only people that have experienced this before. Maybe our memories are a bit foggy, it's been several years."

The same routine was carried out using blood donated from Licon with the same unfavorable results. The doctors had tried two infusions in one day, using a total of three milliliters of blood. Though there were no indications that the cancer cells were being destroyed, there were no adverse effects. The blood infusions were being tolerated.

Late that evening, after Priscilla and Gisele had retired, as well as miles and Libby, Sunul and Max joined Gina and Shania at the dining room table to discuss the situation.

Shania and Gina were obviously frustrated and their disappointment was apparent.

"What are we missing?" Gina asked. She was bouncing her leg nervously, and Shania was pressing her hands against her temples.

"I don't know, but we must be doing something wrong. I don't think it's the blood. It should be just as effective now as it was years ago." She looked at Max and Sunul, "Can you think of anything we might have missed."

Max replied, "Well, I wasn't on Mars at the time. Go through the procedure with us. If we can get the whole picture, maybe we can make some suggestions."

Sunul added, "And I didn't go into the dome back then, so I didn't see the treatment take place. Tell us everything you remember—don't leave anything out."

Shania surveyed the group and said, "I was the patient, so maybe I should relate what I remember." She started at the very beginning, with the arrival of the children and their mothers from the stricken crude space ship.

"Aunt Gina, I'm all wet." It was Gisele's little voice. She was coming down the steps from the second floor bedrooms.

Gina rushed to Gisele and saw that the five-year-old's pajama pants were soaked. Gina stripped off the wet bottoms, picked up Gisele, and carried her to the downstairs bathroom.

Meanwhile, Shania had halted her recollections and refilled all the coffee cups. She stuck her head in the bathroom and asked, "Can I help?"

"In the blue dresser in Miles's room, grab a clean pair of underpants. I've got a diaper in here."

A few minutes later, Gisele was asleep on the sofa, and Shania resumed her narration. Gina and

Shania took about ten minutes to recall everything that had taken place in the Martian medical facility.

Sunul seemed to be stumped. He shook his head, "Sorry, I don't have anything."

All faces turned to Max and he said, "I just might have something." He smiled and scanned the expectant faces. "It's the noises the kids were making. What did you think they were doing?"

Gina replied, "We thought they were talking to each other—kind of synchronizing their thoughts."

Max had an intent look, "I don't think so, Gina. I think they were hypnotizing Shania."

Shania frowned, "Really? I don't remember being hypnotized."

Max grinned, "You wouldn't. Do you remember Gina poking you with the needles?"

"No."

"I close my case. You, my dear, were hypnotized—very thoroughly hypnotized."

Gina gasped and put her hand over her mouth. "When a person is hypnotized, all their inhibitions collapse and a drug acts at full potency."

Shania pushed away from the table, moved quickly to Max, threw her arms around his neck, and kissed him. "I think that's the answer! Max, I love you!"

Max looked out from Shania's arms and said, "I'll help you like this any time. I like the rewards." He made room on his lap for Shania and held her closely, then kissed her again.

Sunul and Gina were laughing. Sunul was more cautious with his response, "We won't know if that's the answer until we try it—correct? We need to find a hypnotist."

"I can do it." Max held up his hand with his index finger extended.

Shania reacted, "What? You can hypnotize people?"

"Sure, how do you think I got you to kiss me?"

"You had nothing to do with that, buster." She gave him a peck on the cheek.

Sunul stood and said, "It's getting late. I'm going to bed. We can begin the new procedure in the morning. Let's pray that it works."

Gina was the first up in the morning and went to the kitchen to start coffee.

"Aunt Gina?"

"Yes, Gisele. Are you dry?"

"Yes, but I don't need a diaper anymore. I'm too big." Gisele joined Gina in the kitchen and sat on one of the bar stools. She rubbed her eyes and said, "Mama was crying last night. She was so sad. Does she miss Daddy?"

"Probably, but the medicine we have isn't working. Maybe she was upset about that. Would you like some juice?"

Gisele nodded.

About ten minutes later, Priscilla came in the kitchen and saw Gisele wearing a diaper and boy's undershorts. "Sorry, Gina. I'll do the laundry today. We'll need some clean sheets. I didn't hear her get up; I must have been sleeping very soundly."

Gina told Priscilla what the group discussed the night before. "Have you ever been hypnotized?"

"Not that I know of. Would I remember?"

"Not unless someone told you about it. Max said he can hypnotize you and that might make the blood treatment successful. Max is pretty confident hypnosis will solve our problems. He thinks Licon and Miranda used hypnosis to prepare Shania for optimum functioning of the blood."

"Let's do it!" Priscilla's mood had made a complete reversal. The signs of depression were completely gone, and she wanted to get on with it.

"As soon as everyone has eaten, we'll try the hypnosis and give you another infusion of blood. I think we've figured it out."

It was 9:30 when Max started the hypnosis and at 9:45 Priscilla received one milliliter of Miranda's blood. Shania and Gina waited until 11:00 before they ran the chemical tests which were positive for the remnants of cancer tissue. Gina called Priscilla into the home laboratory and gave her the good news.

"Priscilla, we think we got it! But, we have to confirm the absence of the cancer by X-ray analysis. I've called the base and they're sending over a portable computerized tomography unit and someone to interpret the results, Dr. Jolene Madsen."

It took half-an-hour before the van containing the portable CT unit appeared in the driveway. Priscilla was escorted into the van and ten minutes later, the cancer treatment was pronounced 100% successful. Priscilla was overjoyed and darted from person to person thanking and kissing. She gave Max an especially long and tight hug and kissed him on both cheeks.

When she got to Sunul, she said, "I love you, dear Sunul. You went eighty million miles for me."

"You're my only sister, Cilla. I would have done anything for you. Actually, I travelled over 100 million miles." They hugged and everyone laughed.